ISLAND JUMPER

AN ARCHIPELAGO SERIES

M. H. RYAN

CHAPTER 1

THE WORLD MOVED, time continued. Things would change, even if I wanted to slow or stop in a moment.

This was our fifth day on a chain of islands we named Pela—a shortened version of archipelago.

I had awakened on a tiny island, alone and confused. Then Benji appeared, dressed in her yellow Sponge Bob bikini, filled with enthusiasm and good humor. She was my breathless wonder, both beautiful and sweet. She was also a master with the bow and arrow, mangos, and movie quotes.

Neither of us knew how we arrived on the island. The last thing we remembered was the *Veronica* and Captain Rebecca Brown sailing us into a storm wall. A lightning bolt hit the deck of the boat and then I woke with white sands, sunshine, and an angry sea pig.

Benji and I found Aubrey the next day on an island we dubbed Food Island. Aubrey played tough, and she was. She also had a strong desire to be rescued. She was loyal and one of the sexiest people I'd ever seen, with an all-around track star body. She wore frayed, booty jean shorts with a red bikini top, and when she smiled, it lit up my world. She understood more about plants than the rest of us, and was well versed in spears and sarcasm.

On the same day, the three of us rescued Sherri from a water boar attack. Sherri filled out her patriotic red, white, and blue bikini with incredible assets. She, like Aubrey, was a track star. A jumper, as she called herself. Her big, blonde hair still seemed perfect, even now. She had become Pela's first patriot, as she loved every moment of it out there. She was a true adventurer at heart, and I wondered if this was her calling. She knew about the ocean and tried to enlighten us on the bizarre animals that seemed to want to kill us at every turn.

A day after we found Sherri, we rescued Kara. I hadn't spent much time with her yet, and the fact that she didn't talk a lot didn't help me get to know her. When we found her on Yin Island, she seemed broken but a couple of days on Yang Island have helped her. She had moments of almost happiness brightening that cute face. Her pale skin had many tattoos that I spent some time looking at, and knew what many were. The tattoos let me knew we shared a passion, but they seemed deeply personal, so I didn't bring them up with her. I planned on working on a connection with her, though. We got caught staring at each other more than once since she arrived. Each time, I drowned in the ocean of her grayish-blue eyes. She had this intensity in her, as if something wanted to get loose but was being held back.

The four women were incredible in their own ways, and we even had a cat we rescued from the tar pits on Tar

Island. Or was it Goo island? We hadn't voted on that one yet. Well, she was close to a cat. Much like the sharks were close to sharks but with more teeth and aquatic adaptations. Moshe had big feet that allowed her to swim down and attack whales. She was small and brave, and she had saved my life.

Now we were all on our home island, called Yang Island. As in Yin and Yang. Now, every Yang had to have a Yin, and that is where we found Kara. Kara's island was a nightmare of a burned forest. I wanted to give up everything in the small time we spent there. Kara said she spent one night there and the island talked to her, sort of. That's why we named this Yang Island. This island made us feel good, as opposed to Yin Island, that made us hopeless and angry.

The idea that these islands could influence the way I felt seemed crazy, but many things seemed crazy since we arrived. Did I mention I could feel the emotions of animals?

I glanced at the ocean as Sherri spoke about another idea on the modifications on the raft. Ever since I woke up to take the morning shift, I felt something different out there and couldn't shake the feeling we were being watched.

"What do you think, Jack?" Sherri asked.

I looked at the sand and what Sherri had drawn. It had a larger raft in the middle, supported by three large logs underneath it, with outriggers on each side.

"Looks good but heavy," I said and used a stick to draw in the center of the raft. "With this design, we can install a center mast and attach a sail. I think if we double up on the emergency blankets, we might capture a good amount of wind power."

"Yeah, that's not a bad idea," Sherri said.

"That's a great idea!" Benji added.

"But it's still going to be too heavy. We have to be able to carry this thing up on to the sand," I said. "Any material ideas, Aubrey?"

Aubrey looked up from the design in the sand. "Yes, I think we have a perfect tree for this. Let me show it to you just down the beach."

We followed Aubrey down the beach on the dry side of the island. Moshe, the sea cat we rescued, ran between my legs and then ran into the forest, playing in the foliage and pouncing on the ferns. Its large paws, wide mouth, and slick fur distinguished it from a house cat of similar size. We had a theory it was still a kitten though. I wondered how big it would get, and if it had friends out there. The last thing I wanted to fight would be sea cats the size of mountain lions.

She stopped in front of a stand of dead trees. They were tall, maybe forty feet up and straight, with leafless branches starting way up high.

Aubrey went up to the tree, feeling around the trunk and knocking on it like a door.

"I'm pretty sure this is a balsa tree," Aubrey said. "And it's been dead long enough that I bet the top half is dried out. These trees are light and buoyant."

"Sure, I know balsa wood. I used to make model airplanes out of it," I said.

"Right, and it's the lightest option we have," Aubrey said.

"Awesome," Benji said.

"I think we can cut into the bottom of the tree with your knife and then use fire," Sherri said. "We can burn the base until it falls."

"Sure, but let's make sure we don't burn the forest down," I said, half joking. "How long do you think it will take?"

"I don't know," Sherri said.

"It will depend on how dry the tree is," Aubrey said. "Could go quick or take forever."

"You two want to work on this?" I motioned to Aubrey and Sherri.

"Sure," Aubrey said. "We'll grab embers from the fire back at camp and start burning the base of the tree."

"Good, we might need two or three of them for the new shelter as well."

"We'll see how it goes," Aubrey said, not sounding very confident.

"Just keep an eye on the ocean and the sky," I said. "If you need help, just scream. I should be able to hear you from most of the island."

"I definitely heard some screaming yesterday," Kara said.

"Kara!" Benji said, appearing shocked.

"I can get rather loud when things get intense," Aubrey said, eyeing me.

"I like intense," Kara said, staring at me with raised brows.

"Yes, well…" I said, clearing my throat.

"I can make an ax," Benji said. "If I can find the right

type of rocks. There's a pile of rocks down the beach, not far from here."

"Yeah, if you get an ax made, bring it over," Sherri said, looking up at the tall tree. "We'll start working on this in the meantime."

I didn't like leaving them alone, but I had confidence they would be able to take care of themselves. Plus, I wouldn't be too far away. The benefits of a small island.

Benji and Kara followed me down the beach. The gentle waves rolled in about halfway up the white, sandy bank, leading to a pile of smooth rocks. I stared out into the water, feeling the many creatures dwelling in it. Together they formed a noise that I referred to as the static of the ocean. On the horizon, I could see Yin Island. A small trail of smoke led up from it, and if any rescue ship was within a hundred miles, they should spot it. Planes too, but we had yet to see a single plane in the sky, not even a jet trail.

"Do you know what to look for?" I asked, turning my attention to the pile of rounded rocks.

Benji walked over the rocks, and they clattered like a bag of marbles. She touched one and moved on, picking up a few more before setting them back down. Most of them looked the same to me, with varying colors of gray and black. Then she picked up a black rock, studied it, and grabbed a second rock from the pile. She hammered one against the other, making a loud clacking sound. A chunk broke off from one, and she smiled, picking up the small piece that had broken off.

"I can make arrowheads and spear tips with this kind

of rock," Benji said. "My arrows will be twice as deadly, and I bet our spears will go right into a croc as well."

"You can make all that from a broken rock?" Kara asked.

"See, look at this," Benji said, holding up the small piece of rock.

I took it and turned it over in my hand. It had a razor-sharp edge on one side. We could use these for knives and just about a million other things.

"Benji, how did you know this rock would break like this?" I asked.

A bit of color hit her cheeks. She did that a lot and it was adorable. It made me want to hug her and tell her she had nothing to ever be embarrassed about. She was amazing in so many ways.

"It just stood out from among the rest for me. I don't know how to explain it, but I just felt it. There are others in this pile. A lot of them."

"Can we make an ax out of that?"

She sighed. "No, not really. It will break or dull too quickly," she said and picked up a flat rock. "But this rock is really dense and is already kind of shaped like one."

She held the flat, dark gray rock in her hand, rotating it and looking at the narrow edge on one side then the thicker edge on the other.

"Do you break that one down?"

"No," she said. "This was an endurance kind of thing in summer camp. This type of stone, we'll have to grind down by hand on another rock."

"Grind down a stone? By hand?" I asked.

She handed Kara the rock and then started pulling at other rocks.

"Jack, help me grab this," Benji said.

I pulled off a few more rocks and then helped Benji lift a larger rock out from under the other rocks. The large rock was about fifteen inches around and flat, like the ax rock.

"We can use this stone to grind down the ax head."

"I got it," I said, taking the full weight of the rock that weighed about fifty pounds.

"Thanks," Benji said, and gathered up a few more rocks in her hands. "We should take it to the stream. Water and sand help the process go faster."

Kara and I followed Benji to the stream leading out from the geyser pond. It carved through the forest, leaving a trail of white sand on either side of it and eventually out to the ocean. The waterfall gave a continuous but pleasant noise.

"Put the stone on the shore here," Benji said, pointing to the big rock I carried.

I sat the stone down next to the water. Benji knelt next to the water and set her rocks down. She motioned for the stone from Kara.

"Okay, this is the sucky part," Benji said as she wet the large stone and then rubbed sand over it. "We have to take this stone and sharpen this end." She pointed to the narrow part. "It may seem like it's never going to happen, but it does and will."

With both hands on the stone, Benji slid it against the wet rock, moving it back and forth. The muscles in her back and arms flexed.

"Just add water and sand as needed," Benji said and got up handing the stone to Kara.

"Okay," Kara said. "I've been pushing stones for most of my life so this should be easy." She smiled, kneeling down.

"Yeah, those curling arms," Benji said, flexing.

The amount I knew about curling was about equal to stone ax making. I watched Kara for a minute, wanting to take over or expecting her to quit but she smiled and appeared to enjoy the task. She might have been tougher than I thought.

"How thin do I make the edge?" Kara said.

"The thinner the better. And really push into it. It takes a lot of force to grind it down," Benji said. "I'm going to start breaking down these other rocks and see if I can make some knives and arrowheads."

"You two are amazing," I said. "That looks grueling, Kara. You doing okay?"

"I'm pretty good at grinding hard," Kara said, looking back at me, pushing the stone done hard. Was she trying to look sexy? Then she jerked back her hand and cried out in pain.

I knelt next to her, taking her hand in mine. The tip of her ring finger looked red and sore.

"Does it hurt?" I asked, blowing on it to dry the water off.

She smiled as I held her hand, hoping she hadn't broken anything. "You just gave me the chills," Kara said, staring at me.

I got lost in those eyes. It reminded me of a storm in the ocean, and each time she blessed me with eye contact, my heart raced, and I had trouble breaking off my gaze from her. Something else had fired up in her eyes this time, a heat that pulsed from her. It made my stomach feel warm, and I watched as her mouth parted. Those red lips were striking against her pale skin. I rubbed the back of her hand and moved up to her soft arm, feeling the goosebumps she mentioned. She had a few tattoos on her arm that looked like tree branches with small flowering buds.

"Do you want me to get the first aid kit?" Benji asked.

Kara took her hand back from me and looked at the stone. "No, I'm fine."

"I'm happy to have you here, Kara," I said.

"No one is happier to be here than me," Kara said.

"I know, and I'm sorry we didn't get to you sooner. I don't know how you handled being on that island for so long."

She looked solemn, feeling her wrist. "I wasn't in a happy place, even back home, and that island showed me how horrible things could get. Now, for the first time in a long time, I feel something other than emptiness. Maybe it's happiness, but it's been a stranger for so long I'm not sure what it feels like."

"Whoa, that's deep," I said.

She smiled, looking up at the trees above us. "I doubt anyone could feel bad living here. Plus, we have each other."

"I'm so happy to hear that. I was afraid Yin Island broke you."

"No, and have I thanked you for saving me from that terrible place?" Kara asked.

"Yes, several times."

"It will never be enough," Kara said.

I touched her shoulder, and she put her hand over mine. "I'm thrilled you're here with us, and I hope happiness becomes a friend you know well."

"Thanks," Kara said, giving me one more look that made me suck in a breath before she went back to grinding the stone down.

Benji had picked up the rocks she gathered and sat down on a fallen tree. She took one rock in her hand and hit it with another rock, breaking pieces off of it. She inspected the broken pieces and set them on the tree and then broke off another piece.

"Okay, you two going to be all right here?" I asked.

"Yeah, this is going to take hours," Benji said.

Kara seemed lost in her task.

"Keep an eye on her," I said, motioning to Kara. "And you're close to the geyser. Not sure if it will burn you from here, but if you hear it bubbling like a witch's cauldron, you two come hauling ass back to camp, okay?"

"No problem," Benji said.

With the ladies set up and doing awesome, I headed back to camp. There were many things that I needed to do in preparation for the expansion of the camp. If we were going to lose the emergency blankets to the boat, we'd need another way to waterproof the shelter.

Since the bird attack on our camp, we hadn't had time to rebuild a proper shelter. Now with another member in our camp, I wanted to make it even larger, with room for expansion to accommodate future members, which was our ultimate goal. There were more of them out there, I just knew it, and as soon as we could, we'd be back on the sea, searching for them.

Our current shelter sat on the ground, a haphazard build late in the night. It had served us for a couple of nights, but it was risky. A half-dozen boars had been on this island, and a greater number of crocs. In fact, this island was a hatchery for crocodiles. Their eggs were stuffed into the sand. They were probably drawn by the warm water deluge from the geyser. That was part of the reason the birds were on this island, digging up and eating those baby crocs like snack cakes.

The first thing I wanted to do was to prepare for the larger logs that would make for the base of the platform. I needed to cut into the current array of trees we had used for the support of the main beams. With four beams, we'd have a large base for a massive shelter, and it would be strong enough to build walls and hold a roof.

I set to marking out the trees and started notching them by hitting the back of my knife with a decent-sized stick. It was slow and tedious, but it felt good to be working toward a better home for the women. They tried to hide it, but I could see living outdoors and in fear was wearing on them. Hell, it was wearing on me as well. You didn't realize how fantastic things like electricity, plumbing and toilets were until you didn't have them. Here, such luxuries would be something akin to magic. While indoor plumbing and Netflix might be a ways down the road, I wanted to set up some of the most basic comforts.

After a couple of hours, I had the four trees notched and ready for the larger beams. They seemed level to my eye, and I figured we could always cut some shims and prop up the low sides. We'd be sleeping on the platform, and there was something about lying down on a surface that made you acutely aware of its levelness.

A rustle of plants and bushes drew my attention to the forest. Benji and Kara were jogging through the forest, heading toward camp, right when the geyser blew.

They laughed, and I realized that I hadn't heard Kara laugh before. As the warm water rained down over the forest, they walked up to me, arms full of their stone weapons.

"We ran fast," Kara said, smiling.

"I thought it was going to blow all over my back," Benji said.

Kara laughed hard at this.

The forest rustled with more sounds, and right then, Sherri and Aubrey jogged up to camp.

"Fire's pretty much a bust," Aubrey said. "We've gotten maybe an inch or two into it. It just heats up, charcoals, and stops. What I need is a goddamn chainsaw." Aubrey looked frustrated and tired. She had black marks from the charcoal on her arms and hands.

"Yeah, or an ax," Sherri said, eyeing Benji.

"Kara was making an ax," I said.

"You hear that?" Aubrey asked, holding up a hand and looking back into the forest.

"It's just the bigger drops of water hitting the ground," Sherri said.

I took a few steps toward the forest, hearing it as well. The forest floor sounded like it stirred with movement, with leaves and twigs getting pushed around.

"Get your weapons," I said, grabbing a spear and checking the knife at my hip.

The girls hopped into motion, grabbing the spears we made that night. We all heard the noise in the forest now. There was no mistaking it—there was something there, and from the sound of it, a herd of somethings, all coming straight for us.

I raised my spear as a rustle of leaves caught my eye at the forest floor. Then a tiny croc emerged from the leaves and stepped onto the sand, heading straight for us.

"Aw," Benji said, kneeling down toward the croc.

It ran under her and headed for the waves. Soon a few more came from the forest and ran through the camp toward the water.

"There could be hundreds of them coming," Sherri said. "They'll usually all birth around the same time. Safety in numbers."

Another group of baby crocs came out of the forest, maybe a dozen of them. One ran straight for me, and I bent down to pet it. The thing stopped and bit my finger with its little mouth. I felt the tiny sharp teeth and pulled my hand back, pulling it free of the thing's mouth. I checked my hand to make sure it hadn't broken the skin. It hadn't.

Moshe let out a meow and pounced on one of the crocs, biting the back of the things neck, killing it. It tore into the thing, eating it.

"Gross, Moshe," Benji said.

"Cool," Kara said, watching the cat. "Should we let these things live?"

"Yeah, we might have to face them again at some point but it isn't really fair to kill them like this."

"Most will die in the first week anyway," Sherri said.

"We're not going to be here long enough for these things to get big," Aubrey said, wiping some of the charcoal marks off her arm.

Kara picked one up and petted it. The croc didn't move to bite her, and they appeared to stare at each other, like the owner of a pet. Then she set it back on the sand, ushering it toward the shore.

"We'll kill you when you're big enough, little guy," Kara said.

I didn't feel any hate from the croc babies, but there was this urgency, as if getting to the water meant everything to them. The feeling of them fascinated me, as if I had a tiny connection to this new life form.

"This is amazing!" Sherri said, as a whole group of them went between her feet, some running over her toes.

Aubrey kicked one off her foot in disgust.

Then a ship's horn blew in the distance, and we went still.

CHAPTER 2

Benji opened her mouth, but Sherri raised one finger, silencing her.

The rustle of the leaves and the rumble of the waves became deafening noises that I tried to silence. Then the horn blasted again. This time, we all turned to the forest, the direction the sound came from. It sounded distant but real.

We didn't say anything as we all ran into the forest. The baby crocs had thinned out, but I still had to jump over many and even dodge a few holes they came from. The heat from the geyser made me instantly sweat, and everything in the forest seemed to drip with the warm water. The after-geyser fog started building around the island as well, keeping low near the forest floor, which made it even harder to go as fast as we wanted to.

When we reached the pool below the geyser, it steamed with hot water, hiding much of its surface. The steaming waterfall cascaded over the rocks and splashed over the pond, sending small waves against its sandy shores.

I ran past the watery edges and up the rocky hill, to the highest point on the island. Once I reached the top, I felt the hot rocks under my feet. Not hot enough to blister, but bad enough to make a person prance over it like hot sand on the beach. I stood still, both feet planted, and stared toward Yin Island.

The first thing I noticed was the smoke from the island leading into the sky. The island wasn't more than a speck on the horizon, but when part of it moved. It wasn't the island but something parked just offshore. I made out some of the shapes and knew that was the *Veronica*.

"Here," Benji said, handing me the telescope.

Through it, I confirmed my first thought and lowered the scope.

"It's the *Veronica*. We need to make a fire on the shore facing Yin Island. That ship should be able to spot it."

"You heard him, let's get the fire going!" Sherri said, clapping her hands.

Aubrey squealed in delight as she ran down the rocky hill.

"The ship is near Yin?" Kara asked, staying at the bottom of the hill the whole time.

"Yeah," I said, hopping off a rock and landing next to her. "Don't worry, we don't have to go there. It will come to us."

"No," she said, running with me. "That island… something is wrong with it."

"I know. It must have seen the smoke and fire from that island. It's probably checking it out, looking for us."

"Maybe," Kara said as we ran together toward the camp. "But it feels off to me. I don't like this, Jack."

"I won't let anything bad happen to you," I said, but she didn't look convinced.

The other girls were cheering in excitement. After the feeling we may never get off the islands, the idea that a ship could be here shortly and bring us back to civilization was enough to get my heart racing. It wasn't that I wanted to leave the islands as much as I wanted to get these fantastic women home and back to safety.

We converged on the fire pit and they grabbed as much dried wood as they could carry while I grabbed a couple logs that were partially on fire. The cat hissed at our activity, feasting on what looked like its third croc.

With wood and fire, we jogged along the sandy shore for a minute until we were facing Yin Island.

"Okay, right here should work," I said, pointing to a spot near the edge of the forest but close enough for them to see the smoke unless they were blind.

"You think the other girls are on the ship?" Benji asked, excited.

"That would be incredible," Sherri said. "Who knows, maybe there could be another whole adventure waiting for us after this."

"This is like TV interview kind of stuff," Aubrey said with excitement. "I hope they have hamburgers on the ship." The girls set down their wood and went right into building a pyramid of kindling.

"They do," I said, and then thought of where the chef currently resided—it wasn't on the ship. We found Frank dead on Tar Island, an apparent suicide.

With the dried wood placed, I set the fire inside the wood pyramid. The girls were damned good fire builders by then. Soon the flames were reaching up and setting the wood on fire. The fire grew, as well as the smoke.

The girls went to the water's edge, jumping and yelling at the ship.

Kara stayed back with me.

"I don't like this, Jack," Kara said.

"You've said that twice now, why?" I asked, smiling as I watched the girls dancing near the water's edge.

"You're going to think I'm crazy." Her voice cracked.

I stopped smiling and faced her. She had tears in her eyes, and I gave her my complete attention.

"What is it?"

"The island, it spoke to me. Mostly I thought it was just in my head, but it showed me things, as well, and that ship is one of the things it used to mock me."

"Probably just a memory from before the storm," I said.

"No, it wasn't that. It was partially burned, and there wasn't anyone on it, and it was just different…but it was more than that, it was the emotion that the island fed me with that image. It taunted me with it. Like showing me something that was coming. Something horrible."

I looked back to the ocean and then used my telescope. How did Kara know about the partially burned section of the ship? After hearing her words, I had second thoughts about the ship, but I dismissed them. Islands didn't talk to people and perhaps Kara had lasted longer on the ship before getting tossed off. Maybe she had some memory of it on fire, and she had to abandon ship.

"I hope you're wrong," I said.

"I do, too, but we should have our weapons, just in case that ship isn't what we think it is."

The ship hadn't moved yet, and after a few minutes, our beach fire beacon dwindled to a small wisp of smoke. The girls ran back to the fire, but none of them had any more fuel for it, and the forest around us would be soaked from the recent geyser burst.

After a quick conference, they agreed to run back to camp where we stored more wood. I jogged with them, Kara at my side. We made it back to the camp in a minute.

While the girls gathered wood, I snatched up a few spears and Benji's bow and arrows.

"What's with the weapons?" Aubrey asked. "We need more wood."

I took in a deep breath and looked at what was in my hands. She was right. Nothing was more important than getting these girls back to safety, and if the next bundle of wood I carried made the fire big enough to demand the attention of the *Veronica*, then that's what I'd have to do.

I set the weapons down and grabbed as much wood as I could carry. Kara, on the other hand, picked up the weapons and headed out with me.

We jogged back down to the beach, and as we neared the place where the fire had been going, I noticed the smoke was gone. I slowed and flung my wood on the sand when I spotted a canoe, pulled up on the sands.

A woman stood near the fire, pouring water over the embers from a leather bag. She then stomped on the ashes with her bare feet, extinguishing the last signs of fire.

"Who are you?" Benji asked, reaching for her bow that wasn't there.

"She's not a sister?" I asked.

"No, she's not with us," Sherri said.

The woman was about our age but not as athletic of a body as Sherris, Aubrey and Benji. She had a thin body, similar to Kara, but with a deeper tan. Her odd clothes covered more of her tan body and were made out of what looked like patchy animal hides. Her light brown hair was long but messy, as if she hadn't washed it properly in ages. She was small, like Kara, and pretty in a more tomboy kind of way, with larger facial features and broad shoulders that were at odds with her diminutive size. All of it created an appealing look, like a hot, small, female Indiana Jones.

At her side swayed a large knife that looked as if it was made from stone. It slapped her firm thighs as she took a step back. She turned to each of us with an expression of pure bewilderment.

"You don't have shore fires," the young woman said, pointing at the extinguished fire. "Especially not here."

"Do you realize what you've done?" Aubrey said, moving closer to the shoreline. "Help, we're over here!"

"Who are you?" Benji asked again.

"My name is Eliza," she said as if it sounded foreign to her.

"Eliza," Benji said. "We're going to start this fire again and get our rescue ship here."

"Rescue?" Eliza said.

"Yes, that is the *Veronica*, we are from that ship,"

Aubrey said. "And you're ruining our best chance of getting out of here."

Eliza took a step back, dropping her water bag, her mouth hanging open in shock. "You all cannot be from that ship."

"Why?" I asked.

"Only death comes from that ship," Eliza said.

"Death," Kara echoed. "That is what the island showed me."

Eliza took a few steps toward her canoe. All of us running up on her hadn't scared her, but the idea that we came from that ship seemed to terrify her.

"We won't hurt you," I said.

"I think the ship is turning!" Aubrey said, jumping up and down, waving her arms.

Through the telescope, the ship had indeed turned either toward us or away from us. I couldn't see the details enough to know for sure. In a few minutes, it would be obvious.

Sherri hugged Aubrey.

"It's still coming," Aubrey said.

"I can't stay here," Eliza said. "And if I were you, I would hide from that ship. Just don't let it find you."

She took a few steps toward the canoe when a massive shark with an arrow stuck in its back clamped down on the back of the canoe. The wood cracked and broke apart under the pressure of the shark's jaws. The shark pulled the canoe into the water. The girls screamed and backed away from the water as the shark took another bite and yanked the canoe further into the sea.

Eliza screamed, jumping into the shallow waters and

grabbing the front of the canoe. The shark yanked the canoe from her, sending her forward and falling into the water. Eliza, quick on her feet, jumped up and grabbed a bag from the canoe just as the shark pulled it under the water. Bits of wood and what looked like rope floated away from the island and got lost in the small waves.

Eliza, on her knees at the water's edge, stared at the space where her canoe had been. She slapped the water and screamed in rage and then hugged the bag against her chest.

Benji had her bow and arrows from Kara and pointed one at Eliza.

"Benji," I said, gesturing for her to lower her bow.

Eliza stopped screaming and looked back at us. "Do you have any idea how long it took to make that?"

"I'm sorry, that sucks. We've lost things as well," I said.

"If that ship is coming here, I'm finding a way off this island," Eliza said, getting out of the water as a shark fin rose from the surface.

"Why? We can all get on the ship," Aubrey said.

"I'm not getting on that ship and you can't make me," Eliza said, touching the stone knife on her hip.

"Eliza, do you aim to do us harm?" I asked, holding out my hand.

"No, I wouldn't hurt you people unless forced to. You're the first people I've seen in…a long time. You're a man, right?" She let go of her knife.

I chuckled, "Yeah, I'm a man."

"I thought so. You look different than them and me." She motioned to the girls.

"Okay," I said, bemused by the bizarre exchange.

"I spent many months, maybe longer, making that boat," she said in agony, looking at her hands.

Through the telescope, I could see the ship was indeed heading in our direction.

"It's still heading for us," I said.

Aubrey cheered and hugged Sherri again.

"Please, we have to hide," Eliza said. "We can't be here. You have to believe me."

"I believe her," Kara said.

"Yes," Eliza pointed at Kara. "See, she knows. If that ship finds us here, we all die."

"Why?" Benji asked.

"My mom called it the devil's ship. One day, we woke with it on our shore. My mom hid me well, but I was small then, easy to hide. She was big like I am now." Her voice cracked. "She was too big. It found her. It took her."

"What found her?" Sherri asked.

"I don't know. I only caught a glimpse of it. It was all black like the night sky. My mother screamed, and I wanted to leave my hiding spot. I wanted to help her, but she made me promise…she made me promise on my life that I would not leave that hiding spot. So I stayed hidden like a good girl, and when I heard its horn, I came out, but my mother was gone."

"Wow," Benji said. "I'm so sorry."

I stepped closer to her, squinting and looking at the familiar features on her face.

"Who is your mother?" I asked.

"My mom?" Eliza asked. "Her name was Rebecca, Rebecca Brown."

I fell back, hitting the sand with my ass. "I see her in you."

"You knew her?" Eliza asked, rushing toward me. She stopped when Benji had an arrow pointed at her.

"Yes, she was the captain of the ship you're warning us about; *Captain* Rebecca Brown is on that ship. She's the one that brought us here."

"My mom brought you here?" Eliza seemed dumbfounded. "That's impossible."

"Wait, what?" Aubrey asked.

The ship blew its horn, making Eliza jump back from it.

"It doesn't matter. All we need to understand is that we need to hide, right now, before it's too late," Eliza said.

"Behind the waterfall," Benji said.

"No," Aubrey said. "You can't be buying the shit Little Miss Tarzan here is selling."

"She's not wrong," Kara said.

"Jack?" Aubrey said.

"If there is a chance that ship can do us harm, we should at least hide and see what comes out of it."

"Oh my God," Aubrey said. "This is our rescue. This is what we've been waiting for, and we're going to hide from it? Your mother is on that ship, you know?"

"My mother is not on that ship," Eliza said firmly.

"I'm with Jack," Sherri said, walking to the forest edge next to me. "From what we've seen out here, I say we play it safe."

"Aubrey, please come with us. If it looks safe, we'll come out and get on that ship," I said.

"This is crazy," Aubrey said, but walked into the forest, heading for the pool.

Before I left, I took one last look at the ship through the scope. The burn marks on the ship obscured some of the ship and ran up to the bridge windows. It might have been caused by the lightning on the deck. On the deck, I thought I spotted something moving, but as soon as I thought I had it, it was gone.

More than that, I felt something from whatever was on the ship. It was angry, like the whale, but there was this hunger, an extreme hunger that made my own stomach growl. It felt cold, and a chill ran over my whole body. I knew one thing— whatever was on that ship, it wasn't human. I couldn't feel humans, only the animals.

"We need to go," I said.

CHAPTER 3

THE FIVE OF us and Moshe stuffed ourselves into the small cave, or what was more aptly described as a cleft between two rocks, behind the waterfall. The hot water splashed and sent steam over much of the area. It gave us a nice concealment, and the pounding sound of water would mask any errant noises that came from us.

"This is stupid," Aubrey said, standing behind me and trying to get a good view of what she was sure was an imminent rescue.

No one else spoke, but Eliza glared at Aubrey. Eliza was the shortest of the group but had this fire in her that the other women didn't seem to want to tempt.

After a while, the ship's horn blew out a long, deep note, and sounded as if it was right on the shoreline. The girls tensed, and I felt a few hands grabbing ahold of me.

The waterfall, while loud and wide, didn't cover the entire opening. To the right, an opening about six inches wide gave me a clear view of the forest and the edge of the pool.

Another few minutes passed, and I heard a snap of a branch and leaves falling as several big birds flew to the forest floor. They quickly started snatching up the baby crocs that were still wandering the forest, either lost or late to hatch.

I had hoped to see Rebecca Brown in her khakis, there to save the day, not these colorful and dangerous birds we'd already fought off yesterday. What if the rescue team encountered these winged beasts and was overwhelmed? I tensed again and took a step toward the opening.

Eliza gripped my arm like an iron vice and pulled me back an inch. The girls wrestled her off me, but she kept her eyes on me, wide and terrified, begging with everything but words for me not to leave the cave. She pointed out the opening, shaking her head.

I felt it before I saw it—the *hunger*…the *desire*.

Something moved in the shadows near the birds, almost like a shadow itself, but the movement seemed more liquid, as if the waterfall's mist played with my view. It moved behind foliage and trees in smooth, quiet movements.

My breath felt cold, and I shivered even as the hot steam from the water saturated my clothes. The thing, while looking like a shadow, appeared to have a head and two arms coming from its humanoid body. It turned and faced us with a featureless black face, as if it was wrapped in fabric. I froze, afraid that any movement, even breathing, might alert the thing to our presence.

Every part of me was screaming that this creature of the shadows was dangerous. I felt its hunger; it was starved, but it wasn't a food kind of desire but a need for something different. It had disgust for something, almost everything, as if the island itself repelled it. It also had a mission, a determination that helped it plow through the hunger and distaste. I'd never felt such complex emotions before. The sharks had a few, but this thing had many threads of bad intentions that weaved a dark tapestry.

Moshe let out a deep, guttural growl, and Benji quickly picked her up. The cat looked as rigid as steel, the fur on its back and tail puffed out. The cat's fear radiated off it and gave me a sour flavor in my mouth. I motioned for Benji to take the cat to the back. She did, petting the cat and whispering in its ear. It seemed to work, and the cat settled down.

When I turned back to the thing, it still faced us. It seemed to tilt its head up, and where a nose and face would have been was just an undulating blackness. It took one step toward us when a screech from above drew its attention. A few more birds landed. The birds pecked at the ground and seemed oblivious to the shadow creature near them.

I risked a breath of air. Most of my thoughts focused on keeping the girls safe. I didn't know who or what it was, but I *felt* it. As human as this thing looked, I knew I couldn't feel humans, and from what I felt, it had no intentions of rescuing us. Eliza had been right—if we had greeted the docking ship with a ticker tape parade, as planned, I don't think any of us would have lived through it.

The birds feasted, apparently unaware of the dangerous thing near them. Shadow man or not, if we had been down there, we might have had a lot of trouble with our feathered enemies. If they killed each other, leaving nothing alive in the fight, that would be fine by me. A killing-two-birds-with-one-stone kind of thing.

The shadowy figure moved in a swift motion toward a bird. That's when I spotted the blade. The shadow slid past the bird, swiping through its neck. The bird's head fell to the ground while its body moved around, apparently unaware that the plug for its computing power had just been yanked from the wall.

In a few more movements, the thing went through several more birds, similarly slicing them. The few birds left took flight in a flurry of screeches. Feathers and leaves fell to the forest floor, raining over the shadow.

It kneeled next to one of the birds who was bleeding badly from a cut along its neck. The shadow lowered down against the bird, mostly blocking my view from behind a series of bushes, but I heard it—a sucking sound, followed by a slurp much like my Aunt Meredith would do when she drank straight from the soup bowl.

A hand touched the back of my arm, startling me from my trance-like state. Aubrey gave me a terrified look, as did the rest of the girls behind her. They couldn't feel the creature in the same way I could, and I was glad for that. As it went from one dead bird to the next, I felt a different feeling building from the creature. The deep hunger was still there, but some of it had been quenched.

It moved out of my view and for a few minutes, I waited, staying as still as I could. Then the coldness left me and the strange feeling of hunger dissipated into the nothing.

With a feeling of warmth, I turned back to the girls.

"I think it's gone," I whispered.

They all, but Eliza, rushed around me, hugging me in silence. I felt Kara shaking against me.

"What was it?" Aubrey whispered.

I was still processing what I had seen and felt. With a dry swallow, I tried to find the words. That's when the ship's horn blew. It sounded close but not *as* close, as if it had left our shores, perhaps to haunt another island and suck the life from it. Then it struck me—the horn call itself. Not a short toot but a drawn-out blow, which in the boating world was a warning.

"What was it?" Benji repeated Aubrey's words.

Then it hit me, and I said, "It was death."

CHAPTER 4

I REGRETTED my words and tried to explain that I didn't mean death itself but more of an abstract way of what death was but the name stuck and the girls were upset thinking the grim reaper was out there.

They even insisted on waiting a few more minutes before creeping out from the waterfall and climbing up the rocky hill. A way out, I spotted the ship, sailing away from us. Eliza stayed below, staring at the dead birds.

We all walked back to camp, spending a few seconds to look over the corpses of the birds. They were a mess of feathers and meat, and Benji nearly hurled at the sight of it.

The camp looked normal, and even the campfire had a few red embers still glowing. Our partial shelter looked untouched. I didn't think that shadow thing ever made it far enough in the island to have seen it.

"You knew," Aubrey said, pointing at Eliza.

Eliza's eyes went wide and then they narrowed, glaring at Aubrey.

"Yeah, I knew about the ship. It took my—"

Aubrey took Eliza by the shoulders, and I saw the muscles on both women flexing as they pushed against each other. Aubrey, larger and more muscular, should have handled Eliza with ease, but the little woman held her own as the two tangled.

"Tell me now how to get out of here. Where do we go?" Aubrey demanded.

Eliza, probably deciding she was not going to match up in pure strength, slid back and tried to elude Aubrey. Aubrey adjusted, but the momentum pushed Eliza backward, and she stumbled on a block of wood Sherri had used as a stool and they slammed against the white sands together.

"Get off me!" Eliza said, struggling to get out from under Aubrey.

"You know how to get out of here. You had a boat," Aubrey said, some spittle spraying Eliza's face.

Sherri and Benji were close, waiting for the second their friend might need help, even if it appeared Aubrey had things handled. Eliza glanced at the girls and stopped struggling, letting out a long breath.

"I don't know what you mean. Out of where?" Eliza pleaded, gripping the bag she took from her canoe.

"And what's in the bag?" Aubrey said, pulling at it.

"No!" Eliza yanked it back and hugged it tightly. "It's private."

"You have to know how to leave here," Aubrey said, some of the fire leaving her voice.

"I just saved you. Is this how you treat people?" Eliza

struggled to get the words out, tears building in her eyes as she gripped her bag against her chest.

Aubrey growled, gave her one last push, and got off of Eliza. She stomped away from her, but Eliza stayed on the sand, looking at each of us, terrified. I knew it wasn't just Eliza Aubrey was pissed at. She had pinned her hopes and dreams of getting rescued by that ship out there, and Eliza was the easier outlet for her disappointment and grief. Aubrey's energy had spread to the other woman as well, and even Kara was eyeing the new woman in our camp with contempt. Moshe paced near the fire pit, the fur on her back standing up as she stared at the newcomer.

"Aubrey, please," I said.

She let out a huff and folded her arms.

I reached down and offered a hand to help Eliza get back to her feet. She stared at my hand, confused. Then she looked over me from head to toe. She didn't take my hand and got to her feet on her own, while keeping an eye on my hand and me.

"It's okay," I said. "We're just a little confused, and we don't know you, but we don't want to hurt you."

Eliza took a step back, eyeing the women. She wiped her nose and said, "That's a strange way of showing it."

"I think we all need to sit down and have some—"

"Mangos!" Benji said, shouldering her bow and bouncing over to the food bag. "I wish I had more ingredients. I have the perfect sweet mango chutney recipe for moments just like this, but I'll see what I can make."

Benji studied Eliza for a moment as a painter might eye their subject, weighing and trying to see through the layers and barriers. Benji had expressed that the proper mango recipe could solve almost any problem and also match the person's needs. I had yet to see her try it on me, but I have seen her assessing me as she was Eliza. In time, I suspected she would present me with my mango recipe.

"What's a mango?" Eliza asked.

Benji gasped and worked quicker, muttering that this changed everything.

"Eliza," I said. "Is that ship coming back here?"

"I don't know. It might pass by my island twice a year, I think."

"Do you know what that was in the forest? The thing from the ship?"

"I don't know." A heavy tear fell from her eyes and streamed down her face. "This was only the second time I'd ever seen it."

"Do you know a way back to the mainland?" I asked.

"What do you mean?" Eliza asked, wiping the tears from her face.

"You know, civilization?" Aubrey asked. "Where all the people live?"

Eliza shook her head. "You're the first people I've seen since my mother left."

"Do you know how you got here?" I asked, starting to feel like an interrogator, but we needed fast information here before we made any assumptions with Eliza.

Eliza shook her head. "My mom said that she and my dad were on his boat when a strange storm hit them. They awoke on the island I lived on for my whole life, and my father tried to explore, but he was killed just offshore by what my mom called a sea monster. I've never seen one, though. I made her describe it to me." She ground her teeth and touched the stone knife at her hip.

"A sea monster?" Sherri asked with wide eyes. "Sorry about your dad."

The idea of a monster sent chills down to my toes.

"I never got to see him. My mom said she didn't even know she was pregnant at the time."

"You were born here?" Kara asked.

"Yes."

Aubrey sat down on a stump and buried her face in her hands. I didn't need my extra sense to know she had just lost some hope.

"How old were you when your mom…was taken?" I asked.

"I was thirteen," Eliza said. "Or that was my mom's best guess."

"How old are you now?" Sherri asked.

"I had my nineteenth birthday three months ago; it was the same time I…"

"Same time you what?" Kara asked in almost a whisper.

"I get these feelings that I should do something, or something was going to happen. And then a few months ago, I had a strong urge to build a boat. It was an obsession. I carved that canoe out with a few axes and rocks, burning it in the middle of the night when I could hide the smoke, but I knew I had to get it done. I knew I had to leave that island soon."

"An intuition?" Kara asked, rubbing her feet along the sand.

"Yeah, my mom said I had the intuition of a seasoned hooker," Eliza said and then smiled. "She said she would tell me what a hooker was when I was old enough."

"It's a person—" Aubrey began to say.

"That helps others," I interrupted.

"With hand jobs," Aubrey muttered.

"What's a hand job?" Eliza asked.

Benji cut the mangos on the cutting board as her face turned red.

"It's just someone that fixes other's nails," Sherri said and then winked at me.

Aubrey groaned.

Eliza looked at her nails, probably puzzling why her mother would tell her that she had the intuition of a seasoned professional manicurist that gave *hand jobs*.

"How does this intuition work?" I asked.

"I don't know; it's just a feeling I get. It led me here, to you all…I think to save you from that ship."

"Your hooker's intuition led you to us?" Aubrey asked, looking up from her hands.

"Yes, and it knew months ago. It's why I built the boat."

Aubrey groaned with disapproval.

"A feeling," I said. "I know about those."

"I feel the islands. I started off alone on a terrible island that almost killed me," Kara whispered. "I like this island though. This is a good place."

"I feel the rocks. It's like they speak to me," Benji said, popping a cube of mango in her mouth.

"I hear the animals, or sense their emotions," I said.

She looked to Sherri and Aubrey but neither said anything.

"Do all people have these abilities where you come from?" Eliza asked.

"No, and we didn't either until we arrived on these islands," I said.

"All I've ever known is my island," Eliza said. "This is the first time I've left."

"You've been alone on your island for the last six years?" Sherri asked.

Eliza nodded her head.

"Oh no, sweetie, you must have been so alone," Sherri said.

"I got by," she said, holding her bag tightly against her body. "My mom showed me how to survive on that island."

Sherri walked over to Eliza and hugged her. Eliza's face got buried in her bosom. Most of the tension of us versus her, melted away at that moment.

"We got you now," Sherri said, patting her head.

Aubrey huffed, but that was as much protest as she was going to put up.

My heart went out to Eliza. I couldn't imagine what she had been through, living there on her own for so long. I would have lost my mind. Being alone, I would have risked too much to get off the islands, as her dad probably did. I wouldn't have waited for the urge to build a boat and leave—I would have swum into the waters to try to escape and to find others. Every second I got to spend with these women around me was a gift.

"Eliza, you're welcome to stay with us," I said.

Sherri let her go, and Eliza seemed confused. "You want me to stay with you?"

"Sure," Kara said. "This is the best island I've felt. It makes you happy."

Eliza glanced at me with a hint of red hitting her cheeks. "I do have strange feelings here." Her hands went to her navel as she kept her gaze on me, moving up and down my body.

Aubrey and Sherri laughed, covering their mouths.

"What?" Eliza asked.

"You've never seen a man, right?" Aubrey asked.

Her face went redder, and she looked to the ground.

"Sweetie, no," Sherri said. "We're not laughing at you, it's just that you end up on this island and Jack is the first man you've seen…"

"And you're lucky to see him," Benji said. "He's far more handsome than most men and so kind and smart and strong."

"And big and good in bed," Aubrey said.

"I don't know what you mean," Eliza said. "I just have this… *feeling* in my gut and… I've never really felt this way. Is it the island?"

"Sweetie, did your mom never talk to you about… you know, sex stuff?"

"No," she said. "What's *sex* stuff?"

"Oh my," Sherri said. "We're going to have to have *the* talk."

I cleared my throat and then said, "You're welcome to stay here with us, Eliza, but we do work hard here, so I hope you're up to it."

She looked confused but sniffled, wiped her eye, then smiled. "I guess. I mean, I was meant to be here, I think."

"Well, since we're stuck on these islands for now, we could use another set of hands," Aubrey said.

"And I'm really helpful," Eliza said with bright eyes. "I can trap. I can cook. I can cut wood and make fires."

"And you can make a canoe," Sherri said.

"Yeah, that one takes a while, but yeah, I can make one again," Eliza said.

"We're on a mission here as well, Eliza," I said. "We believe there are more of us out there. They could be alone as well. They might need our help. We plan to find them."

"If we can help others, we must." Eliza's gaze moved side to side as if she was performing complex math in her head. "I feel it," she said, breathlessly.

"Feel what?" Aubrey asked.

"My intuition," she said, eyes wide and looking out into the ocean. "We need to go soon. I feel like someone needs us out there."

"Mango's ready," Benji announced, carrying a flat piece of wood with the food on it.

A rumble shook the trees, a noise that I would have mistaken for thunder, but the whole island shook. I spread my hands out, keeping balance, and then the shaking stopped.

"What the hell was that?" Aubrey asked.

"That was an earthquake," Kara said. Kneeling down, she put her hands into the sand.

"Dammit," Benji said. "Stupid earthquake." She'd dropped the tray and now knelt, picking up the sand-covered bits of mango.

"I'll have to make more now," Benji said, looking as pissed off as I'd ever seen her.

The island rumbled again, softer this time, but I felt the movement against my bare feet. I glanced at Kara, who still had her hands on the sand.

"This isn't good," Kara said.

CHAPTER 5

OVER THE NEXT day and into the next morning, the island shook two more times, but that wasn't the strangest thing: it'd been well over twenty-four hours since the geyser blew. Some of us hypothesized that the shaking had knocked something loose and now it no longer built up pressure but instead just went to the surface with continuous bubbles. The other theory was that the force was now locked and building, with nowhere to escape, and that was causing the earthquakes. Kara subscribed to the latter, saying she could feel the pressure like tension in her chest. None of us really knew what it meant, so we kept working.

Working took my mind off things. An idle mind would be allowed to wonder and daydream about the possibilities and unknowns. Plus, the work gave us a chance to see Eliza in action.

Eliza proved to be a useful addition to the group, not only with her hands, but with her enthusiasm. The girls took a lot of pleasure whispering to her and then eyeing me. I didn't want to imagine what they were talking about. They shared quiet laughter and inside jokes, all of it was in good humor, and made the hard work more tolerable, if not actually fun.

We abandoned the idea of burning through the trees and found the stone axes performed well, allowing us to cut down two of the dead trees. With one of them, we expanded the shelter platform by almost double before last night. Benji called it "the stage." We made it large enough to sleep us all, with some room to spare. Nothing a hotel could brag about, but sleeping under the stars with soft waves rolling in and out, a gentle breeze pushing around the palms and trees, it felt special to me. Not to mention the gorgeous women I got to share it with.

We spent some time last night talking about Eliza's mom and everything we'd been through in the previous five days. She soaked it up like a dry sponge, asking a million questions for all of us. What was it like out there—the cities, the cars, the planes, and the people? When we found out she had never heard music—which didn't surprise me, her mom hated music—we sang a few songs for her, like an attempt at "Bohemian Rhapsody" by Queen that had us Scaramouche-ing in laughter.

Eliza cried as we sang "Country Road" by John Denver and asked if any of us had been on this country road in West Virginia. We hadn't. Benji said she wanted to reenact various movies, as it was mandatory that she understood some of the classics. Kara and Benji gathered plans to put on a show at some point.

It had become everyone's favorite thing to pour as

much of our culture into Eliza as she could handle and that seemed to be bottomless.

Unfortunately, Eliza didn't have much information to share with us about the islands, as she'd stayed on hers the whole time. After her mother was gone, she wasn't sure if she could do it alone, and at times, she thought of just going into the sea and let the monsters take her, or setting the island on fire and letting the ship come get her, much like it had for her mom. The one thing that she kept relying on was a feeling that she needed to stay alive. She needed to live and thrive, and when the time came, she would know. She believed that we were the thing she had been waiting for and was so happy that she didn't give in to the empty feeling of being alone.

Surviving on her island hadn't been too difficult, as she said it not only had a hot spring with fresh water but it also had chickens and a mixture of fruit trees, and a couple of nut trees. Before she left, she said the island had been shaking, just like this one, and that many of the trees were dying. The ground had formed cracks in it, with steam rising up.

It was an unsettling thought, but one we didn't dwell on. There wasn't much we could do about earthquakes.

In tight sleeping quarters last night, I heard the noises of the restless. Kara and Eliza both struggled through the night, while Aubrey, Benji, and Sherri nestled up against me. I once awoke to soft whispers and found Eliza talking to the inside of her bag, or more like arguing. I think she heard my movement and pretended to go back to sleep. I heard her though, whispering until I fell back asleep myself.

Through the morning, we'd finished the modifications to the raft.

We all stood next to the raft, admiring what we had built. The soft waves rolled over the white sand, hitting the three large logs we'd attached the bottom. The outriggers floated up and down as the water rolled in and out. The platform was about a foot off the sand now, and the deck would accommodate probably seven of us and of course, one kitty.

At the center of the raft, a mast rose up fifteen feet. Sherri spent several hours getting the hole through the center log and then pinned the pole to the bottom with a wooden pin. The light breeze pushed against the square sail, sending ripples down the shiny, emergency blanket. It fluttered and then stiffened as the breeze increased. The mast had a few notches that we could slide the sail up and down with or close it off entirely.

Unfortunately, it took the last of our rope and most of our duct tape. With the mast and sail up, it limited some of the movement around the raft. We spent a while practicing drills for shark attacks and other foreseeable obstacles we could come across. I knew there would be confusion out there but if we had some drills to fall back on, we'd be far better off.

Eliza stood back, staring at it in wonder.

"I hope it floats," Kara said.

"It will," Aubrey said. "I just wonder how much that sail's going to work."

"The sail!" Benji said, looking at it with admiration. "You're so smart, Jack, to think of that."

"Well," I said. "It was a group effort."

And it was. Each of us worked hard to get these modifications completed and we weren't done yet. This was just the start if we wanted to make this place comfortable and safe to live on.

"Okay, the new raft looks awesome, but where are we taking it?" Aubrey said.

"That way," Eliza pointed to the north, an area we'd never been. The sack she brought with her was now slung across her back like a backpack.

"Why there?" Aubrey asked. "And if you tell me about your hooker's intuition…"

Eliza's lips thinned as she looked at the horizon. Aubrey had been skeptical of our extra senses and rightfully so. I wasn't exactly a hundred percent with even mine, but I was getting used to it, because it felt as real as the air we breathed and it seemed to be getting stronger.

"I think it's as good of a direction as any other," I said. "We'll go north. We haven't been that way, so it's probably safe to say we'll find a new island."

"Or just endless seas with currents strong enough to strand us worse than we are," Aubrey said.

The island rumbled again, sounding like thunder. The trees shook and the leaves fell. The sand around the beach smoothed out, and I sunk several inches into it. The shallow water rippled and bounced near the shore. I took a step toward the raft, and then it all stopped.

"That was a big one," I said with a chuckle.

"It's getting worse," Kara said, with her hand crossed over her chest.

"On my island, it started a few months ago, right when I started building the canoe," Eliza said.

"There's nothing we can do about it but we *can* find another person out there. So, let's put this raft in the water," I said.

"We sure?" Aubrey said, looking at the clear, blue sky. "Why?"

"I don't know. Could be a storm coming," she said, shaking her head. "It's nothing, let's just go."

I stood at the rear of the raft and the ladies stood at the sides, making sure they didn't get their hands on the black tar coating much of it. I didn't like the idea of going back to Tar Island, but I knew we'd have to make another trip to get more of the shark repellent. Another day perhaps, but right then, we needed to get this monster-sized raft on the water.

"Okay, on three," I said. "One, two, three."

We lifted the raft, and I was actually pleasantly surprised at how light it was with all hands on deck. We carried and then slid it into the shallow waters. The hefty-looking logs dipped a few inches in the water before floating off the surface. We guided it a few more feet into the water, nearly knee deep for me before Kara hopped on board first.

"Everyone get on," I said.

They got onto the raft, some helping others, and I was the last one on.

Among raft modifications, we also made more paddles and spears. Eliza hadn't used a spear before, but she took to it with ease.

"It works!" Sherri said, rushing to me with a big hug.

"Of course it does," Aubrey said.

"I just want to let you guys know," Sherri said with an

arm around me still, "That this is the greatest adventure I could have ever asked for, and I love you all."

Eliza beamed with a bright smile. Aubrey rolled her eyes as she faced the bow.

"Benji, you want the honors of opening the sail?" I asked.

"Yes!"

She rushed to the mast and raised the two long branches holding the sail up to the lower notch. She secured the bottom branch on the lower notch and then slid the upper branch to the higher groove. The sail fluttered and then stiffened against the wind. The raft pulled hard enough that we all had to do a balance check.

"Wow," Benji said.

I used the back paddle to steer us into the small waves and in a northerly direction.

The girls cheered at the speed, and I smiled. It felt good to have a win. I studied the design, thinking of further modification we could make to capture more wind. We'd just need some kind of fabric or something to catch the wind.

Kara went to the front of the boat. "The logs are cutting through the water."

She had spent hours cutting the front of the boat. She gazed back at me with those ocean eyes, and a big smile. She was so stunning, with the dark tattoos contrasting to her pale skin, and ever since getting her off that island, she seemed happier by the hour. She held my gaze, her mouth parting as her smile faded. She blinked, looked away, letting out a long breath.

A dorsal fin popped up near Kara and she staggered back, landing on her butt.

"Jesus," Kara said.

"Shark," Benji said.

"Another one on this side," Aubrey announced.

I reached out, feeling the sharks. They weren't pissed, but nervous feeling. Beyond just the two, wait, three sharks, I felt that unfamiliar presence again. The unwelcome member to the party that I suspected the sharks knew of as well. I wondered if they were nervous about this other presence or the tar we'd smeared over the ship. I hoped it was the tar, because I didn't want to see what made these sharks nervous.

"That way," Eliza said, pointing out to the horizon.

I used a paddle as a rudder and steered the raft a few degrees in that direction. With the wind at our backs, the raft pushed along the water, gaining as much speed as we could have mustered with paddles alone.

"Save your energy, girls," I said, watching them paddle.

Aubrey and Sherri pulled up their paddles.

"Good, now I can just work on my tan," Aubrey said.

"This is so cool," Sherri said. "I mean, we built this!"

"We should name her," Kara said.

One of the sharks slapped its tail on the water before diving below. A mist of ocean water sprayed over us.

"Why don't you name her, Eliza?" I asked.

"Me?" she said, looking surprised and then touched the bag on her back. "I think we should name her Luna."

"Oh," Benji said. "Like Luna Lovegood from Harry Potter? I loved that name, and if you ask me, she would have been a good partner choice for Harry, perhaps better even than Hermione."

"I don't know this Harry Potter, but it's another name for the moon," Eliza said. "I've always loved the moon and its many faces."

"Don't know about Harry Potter?" Benji muttered, talking about adding it to the list of plays we'd need to be performing for Eliza.

Aubrey gazed at the sky, looking around it all, and then she shivered, as if she got the chills.

"It's a good name," I said.

Over the next thirty minutes, I kept an eye on the horizon, looking for the next island and through the telescope, I finally spotted it, like a green smudge on the horizon. Too far to make out the details, but it was an island for sure. Small, but a tall one.

"I see it," I said. "Straight ahead."

I handed the scope to Aubrey. She eyed it and then it rotated between the girls, all wanting to take a look.

"There's something in the water," Sherri said, pointing off the bow with scope in hand.

I looked ahead and saw nothing but one shark fin and open ocean.

Sherri put her hand to her stomach and looked pale. "We should adjust our course. How do you not see it?"

I took the scope and looked and then without it. All of us were gathering near the front of the raft that I felt it dipping a few inches forward.

"I don't see anything," Aubrey said.

The shark in front of us dipped under the water with a dramatic flair of tail whipping and water splashing. Then the two behind us did the same. It wasn't precisely fear that I felt from the sharks but there was a trepidation there laced with curiosity.

"We should turn the boat," I said, rushing to the back of the raft and grabbing the rudder.

"Go left!" Sherri said.

I still didn't see what we were avoiding, but if it spooked Sherri and the sharks, that was enough for me.

That's when I felt the boat speeding up, as if we were being pulled along.

"What's that?" Kara said, pointing ahead.

About a hundred yards ahead, I spotted what Sherri had a while ago. The water frothed and swirled in an area as big as a tennis court, and at the center, the ocean plunged down into the whirlpool as if someone had pulled the plug below.

"Whirlpool?" Aubrey said. "A fucking whirlpool!"

The raft sped up more, and I turned as hard as I could but it was still pulling us in.

"Paddle!" I said.

The girls jumped to their stations and started paddling hard.

The raft tilted, and we all leaned to the left and got a horrific view of the maelstrom. The water swirled around the center, where it plunged into the depths like a black hole. If we didn't get out right then, we would reach this whirlpool's event horizon and never be able to escape.

CHAPTER 6

I'D SEEN WHIRLPOOLS, mostly in my bathtub as a child, watching the water go down the hole. In my child mind, I thought there was a risk of me being sucked into the drain, and then I'd be trapped in the pipes like that kid that fell into the well all those years ago. I understood how they worked, and I suspected that it was a tidal thing, which was pulling water down through something I couldn't see below. All of this adult knowledge didn't help me from the terrifying sight of the watery, black hole right in front of us.

The other thing was the sound of it—the slurping and the churning sound of water as it spun around the center. That was something I'd never expected, the whirlpool to make a noise like it was trying to lap us up into its belly. The edge of Luna dipped into the swirling edge of the water, and it didn't seem as there was anything we could do to stop it. The raft tilted and went faster it got sucked into the circular current.

"Paddle you bitches!" Aubrey screamed as she paddled as hard as I'd ever seen her.

The women responded, taking action and paddling as I steered us. Moshe's claws dug into the bamboo as the sea kitty held on for dear life. Our once mighty raft, now named after the moon, was seemingly along for the ride as we orbited the center for one full rotation.

The paddling helped keep us from falling any closer to the center but we weren't moving up and out either. The women were tough, but they weren't immune to fatigue. They were going to wear out quickly as this level of effort. I had to come up with something, or we were going down to wherever the black hole led.

Benji cried out, paddling hard, as a shark fin skimmed the inside wall of the whirlpool. So the stupid sharks naturally possessed the power to escape the grip of the vortex. And I thought we might have a chance of swimming down and away from it, but that would leave us looking like silver platers for the sharks, ripe for a quick bite. Plus, Benji wasn't much of a swimmer, and I had a suspicion Eliza might not be either. Something about your dad being killed by sea monsters might make a mother keep the waters off limits.

After a few more rotations, the girl's frantic pace slowed a tad, and we dipped down a couple feet toward the center. The raft tilted at an angle, and we all leaned to our left as we spun clockwise around the funnel.

Through the white foam and blue water, I could see a dark shadow of something large. It was calculated and angry at the same time, a dangerous mix that I hadn't really felt from a shark before. I wondered what it was trying to figure out.

This was turning into an aquatic merry-go-around of nightmares. The wall of water held the shadows of a massive shark with a plan forming and below led to certain death for at least some of us. Neither was an option I was willing to accept. There had to be something we could do.

Then I felt a change in the shark, as if it had come to some conclusion. I watched the dark shadow in the water disappear, but it wasn't gone for more than a couple seconds before swimming straight at us from the other side of the whirlpool.

The shark breached the side wall of the whirlpool, leading with its wide-open mouth, full of seawater foam. It flew out, and I thought it was going to smack right into our raft, but the shark must not have counted on our forward momentum. The shark, realizing it had miscalculated, turned its head toward me, trying to bite me mid-air. An arrow struck it in the mouth just as it crashed into the other side of the whirlpool. It clipped the back of Luna with its tail fin. The impact was strong enough to send me to my knees.

The impact sent a splash of water over us before the quick spin of the water erased any evidence of the fantastic thing we all just witnessed.

"What the…" Aubrey said.

"Flying sharks?" Eliza asked, looking terrified.

"Keep paddling," I yelled.

Then I saw the shadow again and felt the shark boiling with anger below. Strategizing wasn't in its head anymore, just a desire to put us in its mouth and squeeze.

"Is this normal?" Eliza screamed over the sound of the swirling water.

"This is not normal," Aubrey said.

In the shark-launching-distraction, we had dipped a few more feet toward the center, even as the women paddled. We spun around the center faster with each rotation. This was a losing fight, and we needed to think of something drastic. If we all swam for it, maybe I could distract the shark long enough for the whirlpool to suck up and inevitably spit the raft back out of its funnel. It would hopefully float up, and they could get back aboard. We risked more than losing our supplies; we risked losing people.

From the other side of the whirlpool, I noticed the shark's shadow deepen, and I watched as the mouth of the shark emerged once again from the wall. Now, the idea of getting sucked into the black hole below us, and most likely drowning us, wasn't nearly as horrible as this shark jumping from the whirlpool, straight for us. It wouldn't need to put its mouth on us, it would just need to use its immense body to slam into us. The impact would damage the raft and most likely send us all into the swirling water of death.

Thankfully, once again the shark hadn't taken into account our rapid speed around the whirlpool and launched straight for us. By the time it cleared the distance, we had moved a good ten feet. It got so close to me that I punched it in the gut. The physical contact with the shark sent me to my ass as it slammed back into the water right behind us, sending another splash of water over us.

Now the shark had become pure rage and I felt it more intensely than before.

The shark was a heat wave of anger moving around the whirlpool, and I didn't need to sense the women to know they were terrified and losing hope. This wasn't the first time we'd faced a dire situation, but this one felt perilous.

Then a crazy idea hit me.

"We need rope," I yelled over the swirling roar.

"We used it all on the raft," Sherri yelled back.

"Eliza has rope in her bag," Kara said.

"You looked in my bag?"

"Sorry, I had to make sure it wasn't something that could hurt the people I care about," Kara eyed me.

"Give me the rope!" I said, reaching toward her.

She stopped paddling and reluctantly pulled out a nice bundle of rope. I grabbed it, feeling the weight and the intricate weaving of what felt like nylon. Eliza looked at the rope as if she was passing me her child, tears brimming in her eyes.

"Aubrey, I need you," I said.

Aubrey set her paddle down.

"Grab a spear, the biggest one with the notch," I said.

Aubrey grabbed it and brought it to me. I unspooled the rope onto the raft and hoped it was strong enough and long enough. I tied my best cinching knot onto the back of the spear, pulling it as hard as I could. Then I found the other end of the rope and started tying it off to the bottom of the mast.

The shark's shadow moved at the opposite side, and I felt the rage still building in it. It wasn't going to leave us alone, and now I was counting on it.

With the rope secured on both ends, I handed the spear to Aubrey.

"We need a gold medal throw here, all the way into its mouth," I said, with water misting our faces and dripping down into the whirlpool below. We had a minute at most before we went into the drink.

Aubrey didn't say anything but nodded, probably realizing what I planned and the chances of it working.

"Everyone to the back of the raft," I said, holding onto the rudder.

They all stopped paddling and stood next to me. The weight of us lifted the front of the raft off the water, and I took a deep breath, searching for the shark out there.

"It's coming," I said.

I concentrated and sent an urge to the shark to launch at a certain point in front of us. I had no idea if I had any effect, but I kept the thought, sending it as hard as I could to the shark.

Then I heard shark breach the water right at the point I was thinking. Its open mouth flew out first from the water, pulling a hundred gallons of the sea with it as it took flight once again. Its blinding rage radiated out from it. It had no other thought but to kill us and rip our flesh, gorge on us until the blood would draw its friends. They would eat until we were a brief red stain on the sea.

Aubrey yelled, all the muscles in her champion body flexing, and sent the spear straight at the shark's open mouth. The rope line trailed with the spear like a party streamer, and everything seemed to slow as we all watched the thick, wooden spear enter the shark's mouth and into the tiny black hole at the back of its throat. The spear went in and kept going, until just a foot of the spear stuck out from its mouth.

The shark gagged on the intrusion, and I felt the shock and pain radiate from it. It tried to turn mid-air, but it belly flopped, sending a wave of water over us.

"Hold on!" I said, grabbing Sherri and Benji as they knelt down, gripping the ropes we'd tied around the bamboo.

"This is insane," Sherri said, screaming as the rope zipped out from the raft.

I sent another thought out, concentrating as hard as I could on one idea, pull. The rope line ran out and the tension set in against the line. The mast the rope had been tied to creaked, and I braced myself behind the girls.

The jolt forward nearly knocked us all off the raft. Kara rolled back toward us, and I held her, pinning her to the raft floor. She gazed up at me as I kept her under me. In that second, I got lost in her eyes, as I had so many times. Her straight, black hair had gotten wet, and some strands clung to her face. She didn't look scared as she held my gaze and pulled me against her. It felt longer, but it all had happened in less than a second.

Pinned against Kara, I held onto a loose rope, keeping us both on the raft. The shark was scared and wanted to get away from us at all costs. I felt the same kind of urgency from the baby crocs. To the shark, it was get away from us or die and I kept feeding that thought down its throat. It kept pushing harder, using what energy it had left to flee.

The line creaked under strain and the raft turned up the whirlpool wall. With us in the back, it kept the front of the raft lifted up as we moved toward the top.

"Paddle," I said.

The girls jumped into action, and started paddling hard. Behind us, the whirlpool slurped and sloshed as if it had no intention of letting us go. The mast groaned and bent.

"Hold on, Luna," I said.

The front of the raft dipped into the water as it neared the top.

"We're going under," I yelled. "Hold on."

The girls dropped down to the deck of the raft and grabbed hold of it. The shark, in all its pain and fury, pulled at us harder. I screamed at it to pull. The front of the raft dipped under the crest of the whirlpool, and emerged on the other side. It pulled us out of the funnel and onto the flat water beyond. Looking around, I confirmed all the girls were still aboard.

"Paddle!" I yelled, and they got back to their stations.

I got off of Kara and jumped to the side, right behind Sherri, and started paddling.

The shark pulled on the line, but the urgency had lessened. The fight was leaving the shark the fear and rage dwindling toward a resignation. It knew it was going to die. It turned, swimming in a loop, heading us back toward the maelstrom.

The front of the raft turned as the line went from tight and straight out front to bending to the right. It wouldn't be long until it pulled us right back into the black hole.

I rushed to the front of the boat with my knife and reached out, trying to keep as much of the rope possible, and then cut the line. The raft jolted back from the release of tension.

The girls kept paddling, concentrating briefly on one

side to straighten us, and then we were clear from the whirlpool. Looking back, it took a second to find the circular dip in the water. The whole thing blended into the ocean, but Sherri had seen it way before any of us. If not for her, we could have sailed right down the middle of it, where it would have swallowed us up.

"That was the coolest thing I've ever seen in my life," Sherri said with a shaky laugh, and then she screamed at the sky with excitement, holding her paddle over her head.

Her statement broke the tension, and the other girls cheered with her. They stood, holding their paddles high. Kara ran to me and jumped into my arms, wrapping her legs around my waist and her arms around my neck.

"You saved me, again," Kara said.

Now, I've held Sherri, Benji, and Aubrey, but there was a different energy that came from Kara. Her small frame and weight barely pulled at me but she gripped me tight with her legs, and I felt her pressing hard against me. She squeezed me once more and then got off, letting her hands slide off my shoulder and down my chest with a long sigh.

"Sherri, you're right," Kara said. "Thinking you're going to die in one minute makes you appreciate every minute after."

CHAPTER 7

THE WATERS WERE CALM, but as a precaution, I put Sherri at the front of the raft, keeping an eye on the water. She seemed to have a good feeling for the water and spotted that last whirlpool far ahead of the rest of us.

Eliza gave us the direction, but we had the island in sight now.

The shark that saved us was gone. I wasn't sure if it had died and sunk to the bottom, becoming nothing more than a feeding frenzy from the static of the ocean, or if it had somehow lived and swum to safer waters. The creatures around these islands did seem resilient, so I didn't rule out the possibility of that shark returning.

Thankfully, the mast had survived the pull of the shark, but now it bent forward and had the tendency to move with the wind more. A decent breeze pushed us along at a good pace.

Benji held her bow, constantly rotating in anticipation of more attacks. I could tell her I didn't feel any danger, but this gave her something to do, and after what we just went through, we all needed tasks to keep us busy.

Aubrey paddled, not saying anything, but she kept looking at the cloudy sky as if sharks were going to fall from it.

"Can I have my rope back?" Eliza asked.

"Oh, yeah, sure," I said, kneeling down and untying the knot.

It had cinched so tightly at the bottom, I had to take my knife out and cut a small section off. Eliza let out a gasp as I sliced through it.

"Mr. Rope," Eliza said as I handed her the piece of rope.

Eliza coiled the rope up and placed it in her bag, patting the bag and looking upset. I guessed if I spent the amount of time it would take to make a rope like that by hand, I would have given it a name and sentimental value.

We spent the next thirty minutes sailing and getting closer to the island. I looked through the scope at it. The island was small and didn't have a single tree on it. The green grass seemed to cover most of the island but for the gray rocks that peppered the shore and poked through the large hill rising up from the island.

The hill might have been fifty feet tall and seemed to be the whole island, as if some great mountain was below and all that showed was the peak. The shoreline held some flat ground but most of it was jagged, black rocks, wet from the ocean spray and waves. The waves were larger there as well, curling up one or two feet tall before hitting the rocks in white foam.

"Not much of an island," Aubrey said.

"That's not the island," Eliza said. "It's past it."

"What?" I asked.

"It's in line with the other one," Eliza said. "So I didn't know it was the wrong one until we got closer. It's definitely the wrong one; we should keep going."

"We're going to check that island out before moving on. Every island we've been on has held a person. We can't assume this one is any different," I said, and no one disagreed, although Eliza fidgeted with her bag and looked scared.

I studied the small island, hoping to see evidence of another soul on it—I had good reason. Each island we found had held a person on it. Now, on one island that person was already dead, Chef Frank, but the rest had one of their friends.

The waves rolled under the raft as we neared the shoreline. I had the girls bring down the sail and move to their paddling positions.

"Let's round the island and see if we can find a safe place to land."

They paddled and I steered, and as we rounded a section of rocks, we saw something incredible.

On the back side of the island there was a plane, mostly submerged in water, lying near a sandy shore. Large rocks stuffed along the shoreline obscured portions of the plane.

"Wow," Sherri said. "Is that some kind of fighter jet?"

"Looks like a World War II jet," Kara said.

Most of the metal framework around the plane had fallen off, but some of the paneling remained, and a red, white, and blue star emblem was still faintly visible on the belly of the aircraft. The tail had broken off, and one wing sat halfway in and out of the water with waves rolling between the open frameworks. The front propeller appeared to be intact and stuck up from the sea. At the front of the craft, a shadow of what looked like a painted shark's mouth still remained.

The sight of this plane answered questions and brought up more. Somebody and some things that had not originated on our ship had come here as well. From the look of the shell of a plane, it had been there for a long time. Had it crashed? It must have. There wasn't really a chance of the thing washing up on the shore. It might have even gone through a mysterious storm wall, as we had.

"There's a good landing spot," I said, pointing to the shoreline near the plane.

"Okay," Sherri said, paddling toward the sandy beach I pointed out. "This plane here is crazy."

We were staring at it like it was an alien ship, and for Eliza, it probably was.

The bigger waves rolled under the raft, tilting us forward and back. We paddled, pushing hard into the next wave. Luna rode the wave, and drove us hard onto the sandy beach that was only about ten feet deep before meeting a wall of broken rocks about five feet high. The tides were mild on our home island, but I suspected the tides here reached all the way to the rocks.

I jumped off the front of the raft with a knife in hand, first looking for anything that might want to kill us, but the island seemed void of any animals. I motioned it clear for them and they jumped off the raft as well.

The sand here felt coarse and large. It almost hurt to

walk on, versus the soft, velvet-like sand of Yang Island. All of us but Kara pulled the raft onto the sand. She walked to the black rocks, touching them, and then knelt down and rubbed the sand between her fingers. The white sands mixed with some of the black sand, giving the beach a salt-and-pepper look.

"It's not a bad island," she said, getting back to her feet and wiping the sand from her hands.

"What kind of island is it?" Benji asked.

"I'm not sure; it just is what it is, if that makes sense," Kara said.

"No, not really," Aubrey said. "And are we expecting something different here? It's not like islands have feelings."

Aubrey looked to the sky and crossed her arms. The cloud cover had thickened and the wind had picked up a tad.

Kara smiled and replied, "I said it's not a bad island, but there is something here. Almost like contempt, as if staying here and just existing might be enough."

"So, contempt island," Aubrey said, shaking her head. "I'm not sure why we can't find cheeseburger island or pizza island."

"You can make fun of me," Kara said. "But after the crap island I was on, I'll take contempt any day of the week. And don't act like you don't feel anything. You can't stop looking at the sky. What's the deal?"

Aubrey looked down from the sky. "Shut up. It doesn't take some ethereal talent to see that there is a storm coming." She folded her arms and glanced at the sky. "A bad storm."

"We should make this quick then," I said, looking at the sky.

"Whatever, I'm checking out this plane," Sherri said, crossing the sand toward the plane. "I mean, how many places in the world can you see something like this?"

"Be careful," Benji said. "There could be a dead body in there."

"If there is," Kara said, "It's nothing but skeleton by now."

"Why?" Eliza asked as she held onto Moshe.

"That plane is old," Aubrey said. "Like more than half a century old."

"I've never seen a plane," Eliza said, looking at the metal.

"It's something we use to fly in," I said, catching up to Sherri.

"I know. My mom told me about them, but I always kind of thought she was just telling me stories."

"Sherri, let me check it out first," I said.

There could be a dozen different things that had taken up home in the partially submerged plane, and all of them would want to kill us. With my knife out, I stepped into the water and got to the plane first.

The glass dome that had once covered the cockpit was gone, leaving the insides open to the elements. A few of the dials and gauges were smashed in, maybe from the impact of the crash or the pilot impacting it after the crash. Ocean water flowed in and out from the bottom of the aircraft when the seat and pedals would have been. It appeared that anything that didn't rust or degrade was gone. Nothing but an empty shell of a plane now. I inspected some of the metal and thought it would be a good idea to see if we could salvage some of it. I doubted we'd ever run into sheets of aluminum again. Might even be able to harvest enough of it off this plane to fashion a roof on the shelter back home.

I ran my hand along the metal, feeling the smoothness of it and touched some of the rivets still in place. Halfway through the plane, the metal frame twisted, from what I assumed was the crash landing. Had the pilot survived the impact? It seemed unlikely, considering the wreck, and I wasn't sure if they had ejection seats in this kind of plane. If he had ejected and landed in the water, then he would have most likely ended up in the belly of some shark.

If he had landed the plane, ending up right where it currently sat, then he might have had a chance. The shallow waters where the plane landed wouldn't allow for the larger sharks to enter, and the sharp rocks would keep many predators at bay. If the pilot landed on this island and survived the crash, then there was a chance he could've survived.

"I'm going to search the rest of the island. Need to make sure someone isn't on the other side, and maybe we can find some supplies here," I said, backing away from the plane. "Just keep an eye on the water."

"And the sky," Aubrey said, and then looked at us with narrowed eyes. "What? There's a storm coming. It doesn't mean I feel it. It's just...look at the clouds."

"We didn't say you did," I said, not really wanting to push Aubrey into admitting she felt the coming storm, but it seemed to be worrying her, and I imagined that meant a bad one was coming. All the more reason to explore the island while we could.

"Can I come with you, Jack?" Kara asked.

"Sure, I could use your extra sense. Just tell me if you feel anything… strange on the island," I said.

"Um, sure, I can do that."

"The rest of you, see if you can salvage anything from the plane. Those panels and other things on this could be useful."

"Aye, aye, captain," Benji said with a salute.

"Yeah, have fun, Kara," Sherri said and then gave her a big wink.

"Uh huh, don't forget to tell Jack if you feel anything strange," Aubrey said with a smirk.

I didn't understand much of the interaction between the girls, but I had an island to explore and hopefully a person to find. If we were fast enough, maybe we could get ahead of this impending storm Aubrey kept advertising.

CHAPTER 8

PAST THE PLANE, and near the next edge of the island, I climbed over some black, porous-looking rocks, maybe old volcanic rocks. Once at the top, I reached back and helped Kara onto the pile and then onto the slope of the grassy hill that covered the rest of the island.

Ahead of us stood the hill, bigger than I initially thought, maybe closer to eighty feet up. The short grass moved in the wind and covered almost everything on the hill but the protruding rock outcroppings that scattered over it. At the top, we could have a fantastic, panoramic view, but I wanted to walk the perimeter, to see if this island offered anything else that we could use.

"The grass feels nice, like a bed," Kara said, brushing her feet on the grass and then looking up at me. "We've never been alone before, Jack."

"Oh yeah," I said absently, scanning the grassy hill, looking for the best route to take to avoid the various rock outcroppings.

Had we never been alone? I guess with as many people

as we had now on the home island, alone time wasn't something that happened unless planned. I looked back to her, and she gazed up at me with those ocean eyes. They seemed more prominent than average eyes, as if she had more to see and maybe more to give. When we first found Kara on that terrible island, those eyes were so sad, and all I wanted to do was hug her and tell her it was going to get better. And it did, for her. She loved the new island, and I think now I got to see the real Kara, with bright, beautiful eyes that matched her petite, perfect face. Her milky white skin gave the black hair and tattoos an alluring contrast.

"Yeah, Benji, Sherri, and Aubrey have a rotation of sorts on you," she said, getting closer to me.

"What?" I asked. A rotation? I hadn't even been with Benji in an intimate nature. Was her turn coming up? I wanted to laugh at the notion.

The wind whipped up Kara's hair, and she pulled it back behind one ear. Another gust undid her effort.

"I'm happy to spend some time with you," Kara said, with her head tilted down so she had to look up into my eyes.

"Well, me too," I said. "It seems like all we do out here is work. Not enough time to just hang out."

"Island and chill," Kara said with a smile.

I laughed. "Well, if Aubrey's right, we better get around this island before that storm hits."

"Okay," she said, looking at little disappointed.

I walked the path with Kara at my side. I kept her to my right, on the higher side of the hill, so the height difference wasn't as dramatic between us. Less than a minute into our walk, she stumbled over a rock and fell into me.

"Sorry," she said, not letting go of me.

"Here," I said, getting her back to her feet. "Just hold onto my hand."

"I'm not some kid," she said testily.

"I know. It's for safety." Though, truthfully, it wasn't just safety. I wanted to have some contact with her.

She grasped my hand, and I was surprised at the strength I felt in them and the roughness of her hands. I rubbed my thumb over the back of her hand and touched her smooth skin. She looked up to me, smiling.

"This is nice," Kara said. "Did I thank you for saving me from that terrible island and on that raft?" she asked.

"Yeah, a few times, and we're the lucky ones, to have found you. You are an awesome addition to the team out here."

"Thanks, but I wasn't much help when you first found me. I'm sorry about that."

"Never apologize for being a human. You went through a lot on that island. Just being there for an hour, I wanted to kill myself," I said, with a laugh. "The fact that you can smile is a miracle."

"It's not hard to smile when I'm next to you," Kara said.

We continued down the path, with me leading the way. The island seemed to be nothing but rocks and grass, and my hopes of finding something useful diminished.

"A place like that gives you an appreciation for the places and times that aren't bad," Kara said. "Even in that whirlpool, pretty confident that I was going to die, wasn't as bad as spending the night on that island."

I sighed, hating that she had suffered as much as she did. It made me want to double our efforts to find the others. We weren't going to stop until we found them all.

"What do you think made that island the way it is?" I asked.

She frowned, and I felt her grip tighten as we walked around a large rock outcropping, forcing us to go higher on the hill.

"I didn't really believe in true evil," Kara said. "I mean, that I didn't think things were just wrong because they were born that way or created to be evil."

"Like a gun isn't evil but the person behind it could be?"

"Yes, like the gun but before, I didn't really think the person behind the gun was born evil. I mean, how can a baby be evil? At some point, the mind is corrupted."

"Corrupted?"

"Abused, or broken, or even some imbalance in their head that makes them the way they are. What I'm trying to say is that before that island, I didn't think things could be just evil. But on that island, I felt it. It didn't have a face or a name, but it was there, as real as you are next to me, and it felt ancient and powerful, as if I was nothing but smoke in the wind in. It didn't feel as if it had ever been anything other than what it was. It just was, always had been, and always will be…evil."

"Like it was born that way."

"Or created that way," Kara said, and stopped to face me. "Jack, I think there is something out there that doesn't like that we are here, and it, or part of it, was on that island. It wanted more than just my last breath—it wanted my spirit. It wanted everything. It had this hunger in it." Tears welled in her eyes, and I could see her holding back a blink to keep them from falling.

I had felt a hunger in something else that seemed evil as well. The shadowy figure.

"You're gone from that place now, okay? I won't let anything happen to you."

"You promise?" she said, blinking and sending those big tears down her face.

I moved closer and wiped them from her cheeks with my thumbs while I gripped the back of her neck with both hands.

"I promise."

She hugged me, putting her face into my chest. I kissed the top of her head and held her.

"I'm so happy we found each other," Kara said.

"Me too," I said.

"I feel safe with you. As if that island isn't going to get me with you around."

"I'll never leave you then." I wanted her to feel safe and heal more than anything.

She let go of me and then looked up as I looked down to her. She moved her face against mine, and I felt her tears, still wet on her face. She slid her cheek against mine and then against the edge of my mouth where her mouth met mine. She kissed me. A gentle kiss, with a hint of her tongue against my top lip. Brief but firm, as if she had held back.

Taking a step back, she opened her eyes, meeting my gaze.

"That was nice as well," she said.

"It was," I said, and started to feel as if I had fewer words for her than I should. "I think you—"

"I like you," Kara said.

"I like you as well."

"At first I thought it might have been because of that Yang Island. That island is sort of like pouring gas on the sex flames, so I wanted to wait until we were somewhere…not there…and see how I felt, to make sure that I felt the same way still."

"To be honest, I didn't think you were that into me," I said.

She rolled her eyes and bit her lip, then laughed. "Come on. I see the way you look at me, at all of us—even Eliza, God help her—but you have to see the way we look at you."

"I don't know. I've just been trying to make sure we have a safe place to live, and then we keep needing to go on these missions."

"Adventures," Kara said with air quotes. "Isn't what Sherri would call them?"

"Adventures," I said. "That does sound more fun than missions."

"Yeah, Sherri loves this shit. I'm not even sure she wants to be rescued."

"Let's see where this *adventure* takes us," I said and offered my hand to her. "Maybe you can tell me more about this curling?"

We continued our path along the bottom of the hill,

climbing over or working our way through the obstacle of rocks. Kara told me about her sport. She had been a state champion, and even competed well against the Canadians. I loved just watching her talk, and hearing such happiness in her voice. The Kara that had curled up on the raft and cried was gone. This new Kara loved life and was genuinely happy. She had a brother named Carl that she adored and a family dog she named Alfred. Even as happy as she was, I knew from the tattoos that there was a history of sadness in her life. I had wanted to ask her about them since I noticed what they were, and what they were hiding, but hadn't had the right moment.

The wind picked up a little bit, and the sun had darkened as the clouds thickened above. Aubrey had been right—a storm was coming.

I suspected we were getting close to doing a full circle around the island when we climbed over another rock pile, and I spotted a cave near the shoreline. I wasn't sure why, but I ducked down, expecting the crashed pilot to appear and be pissed off.

"What?" Kara asked.

"A cave," I whispered, starting to feel foolish of my apprehension.

We were about twenty feet above the opening at the shoreline. The salt-and-pepper sand ran right into the opening, which wasn't more than four feet around. After a few minutes, I climbed down some rocks and dropped onto the sand. Kara landed right behind me, and we walked to the cave.

"Hello?" I called, leaning in and hearing my voice echo around inside.

If one of the girls had ended up here, she would have gone into this cave.

The wind blew harder, creating almost a whistle sound near the entrance to the cave. Mixed with the ever-increasing waves crashing on the shore, it was impossible to hear if anyone responded.

"We should check it out," Kara said.

"Okay, just stay behind me." Ignoring my gut telling me to leave it alone, I took my knife out and headed into the cave.

CHAPTER 9

WE CROUCHED DOWN as we entered the cave. The entrance had a musty smell, like wet dirt, and I ran my hand along the smooth walls. At first, it ramped down for about ten feet, getting narrow enough that we had to crouch low before it started ramping back up and getting much darker as we lost sight of the entry. Ahead had a glow to it, as if there was another opening. After a dozen feet in, the cave widened and expanded into a cavernous room. We both stopped, staring up to an incredible spectacle above us.

"Whoa," Kara said, reaching for and grasping my hand.

Whoa was right. The cave should have been dark, with only a faint light coming from the tunnel, but this more extensive part of the cave, as big as a house, had a soft bluish glow to it. On the ceiling were hundreds, if not thousands, of small, sparkly sources of light, almost as if there were glowing diamonds on the ceiling. They twinkled, and if I concentrated on one, it went out, replaced with one right next to it. I used my extra sense and felt into the cave. There was a static, much like the ocean, and I assumed that was what was giving off the glow, but I didn't feel the heat or colors of emotions. They just existed.

"Hello," I called out.

My voice echoed across the cave, and the twinkling lights seemed to go out as the sound wave rolled around the room, dimming the light considerably. As soon as the sound stopped, they went back to fully luminous.

"What the…" Kara said, softly, but still dimming a section of nearby ceiling.

"They react to sound," I said, and each word sent of dimming pulse. "Hello!"

My yell sent the whole room into a momentary state of darkness. My voice echoed around the room, and soon, the lights rolled back on like a wave across the room. I gazed down at Kara, mouth open and eyes wide. It defied words.

"This is so beautiful," Kara said, walking into the larger part of the cave, pulling me along.

Her voice had a similar effect, sending ripples of darkness across the ceiling.

"What do you think they are?" Kara asked, looking at the ceiling as it moved again to her voice.

"I don't know. I've heard of glow worms in caves, but nothing like this."

"You think they're safe?"

"Not sure."

I wasn't confident in the safety of this place, but we still had to make sure it didn't hold a person or body in it.

Letting go of Kara, I moved forward with a knife in hand. The floor had gradually been getting harder since we entered the larger part of the cave, and now, five feet into it, it felt as hard as concrete yet had a sandpaper-like texture on the surface.

It also continued to go up at a good angle for about fifteen feet, until we reached a plateau. The top flattened out to about the size of our platform back on our island. The floor on the plateau felt just as hard as the hill leading up to it. On the back side, it descended into a dark area I couldn't see. I squinted, trying to peer into it, when Kara took my hand tight and pulled me closer to her. She took both my hands in hers.

I turned her hands over and rubbed my thumb over the tattoos on her wrists, a familiar circle with a few lines inside the circle.

"Twenty One Pilots," I said.

She gave me a wry smile. "You knew?"

"I knew."

"You part of the clique?"

"Let's just say I'm an honorary member."

I'd studied her body art when I could, and the more I did, the more I realized how much of it was from Twenty One Pilots. On both of her wrists were the band's main symbols, with circles and lines in the middle. Their position led me to think she was hiding something under the symbols.

I let go of her hand and touched the side of her stomach, above her hip, gliding my hand over the words inked into her.

"Truce."

She looked at me with the same kind of wonder as she had the ceiling when we first saw it. I didn't get a *whoa* but an open-mouth stare.

"Holy shit, why didn't you say something before now?" Kara asked.

"I wasn't sure if you wanted to talk about it. That song, these tattoos, felt as if you might have gone through a tough spot at some point."

Our words played with the lights, sending shadows over her beautiful face.

"I did, and I thought it was behind me, until I woke on that hell island. I think these," she moved her hand over her tattoos, sliding her hand up her stomach and to the bottom of her left breast, contained in her thin black bikini, "saved my life out there. They were my armor against the evil."

"'Truce' is one of my favorite songs from them," I said.

"Are you even a real person?" she whispered, moving close to me and pulling my hands around her waist. She pressed her head against my chest, and I held her under the soft glow.

"Truce" was a song by Twenty One Pilots, talking about death and living your life, just staying alive for another day. I always took it as an agreement with the listener to not kill yourself. If she had these tattoos, I suspected the bumpy line I felt on her wrist wasn't a result of the tattoo but rather the reason for the tattoo. She had covered her past.

"We're alone in here," Kara said against my chest.

"Yeah, this is nice," I said, my fingers combed through her hair.

"Do you want to fuck me?" Kara said.

I stumbled back half a step, and the lights danced strangely, as if they too shared my shock.

"Yes."

Her hands went to my chest and started working the buttons down. Unbuttoned, she yanked my shirt off me and lay it on the ground behind her.

Now, up to this point, I'd seen Kara as a demure type, with an overall temperament of a quiet introvert and soft eyes that you could drown in and be happy because of it. The Kara ripping my clothes off had—and I don't know how it was possible— larger eyes. As if she could devour me with them. The soft light of the cave was enough to see the desire on her face. She wanted me, and I wanted her as well.

"The other girls—" I managed.

"What about them?" Kara said, reaching to my shorts and finding the button holding them together.

"I've had sex with Sherri and Aubrey."

"I know. It's okay, Jack. They let this happen." She reached into my shorts and under my underwear, grabbing me. "They weren't lying." She moaned out as she squeezed me.

"This is fast," I said, trying to catch up to where she was. It didn't take long, running my hand over her soft skin, touching the various tattoos along her stomach and cupping her breasts.

I grabbed her by the face and kissed her as she kept her hand on me. I could feel myself growing against her grip, and she moaned as I kissed her. The vibrations and sound of her pleasure sent me to another world.

Her bikini was a maze of strings wrapping around her body, and my searching hand couldn't find a clasp, so I grabbed from the top of it and just slid the black bikini down to her waist, exposing her breasts to me. They were B-cup perfections, and her nipples were a deep red that came to a point, giving me another color along her monochromatic skin and hair.

My shorts fell to my ankles, and I kicked them back. My boxer briefs were still on, and her hand was still inside them, gliding up and down my shaft as we kissed.

Breathing hard, she went to my neck, kissing and then biting some of my skin as she moved to my chest, coming back to my mouth with an aggression I wasn't expecting but welcomed. She grabbed the back of my head as she kissed me, massaging and pulling at my hair. Her strength came as a welcome surprise.

"Lay down with me," I said, freeing her hand from my boxers.

"You first," she said.

I lay down on my shirt. She kneeled between my legs, bent down as she ran her hands up my legs and over my erection. Her black hair fell over her face as she kissed my navel and went lower. Keeping my underwear on, she put her mouth over my shaft, and I could feel her hot breath through the fabric as she applied pressure and only a hint of teeth biting down on me. Her finger worked through the material of my underwear until I felt her bare fingers touching me. She had worked through the double flap thing most men's underwear had. With a few motions, she pulled me out from the flap and slid her fingertips along it.

She looked up, laughing, and had the cutest, most mischievous smile I'd ever seen. Her laugh sent waves over the lights of the cave, and she looked up at the display.

Crawling over me, she adjusted the bottom of her bikini to the side and straddled me. She slid her slick sex over mine and then put me inside her. Her face winced for a second before melting into a look of ecstasy.

She started with a slow movement, as if getting used to me but she quickly went to faster and her small body began to grind against mine. With each thrust she moaned louder.

Each sound sent waves over the cave lights, and as she kept crying out in pleasure, the whole cave dimmed to near blackness. My hands found her stomach and then her chest. I felt her as she pounded against me. If she kept this pace up, I wasn't going to last long.

I sat up, gripping her sides in an attempt to slow her down. She looked down at me, smiling and shaking her head. She wasn't going to slow down, and that turned me on even more. She sped up, and I felt her deep and wet.

"Do it…with me," Kara said in a panicked breath. "Now, now, now."

She cried out, and I obeyed her, finishing in her. I reeled forward, grabbing her in an embrace as I released. Her cry went into one heavy breath and then I fell backward, pulling her onto me.

We kissed as the lights of the tunnel returned. We didn't kiss long, and she rose up, keeping her face near mine. Some of her beautiful black hair clung to her face and she smiled.

"Thank you," she said, still puffing a bit.

"Well, normally I last a bit—"

"No, I needed it fast. Oh God, did I need you fast. That was so fucking perfect."

She rolled off of me and then slid against me, putting her head on my chest and her leg over my crotch. We lay there for a few minutes until we heard a roar of thunder outside. It sent a wave over the ceiling, dimming the cave for a moment.

The storm had arrived.

CHAPTER 10

WE RUSHED OUT of the cave just as a massive lightning bolt struck the ocean in the distance. It had to be many miles away, and I counted the seconds before the boom. It had to be a good thirty miles away. The wind had picked up considerably as well and blew at us with powerful gusts.

The waves, still large, were crashing at the shoreline more frequently, creating a continuous noise. The sky had darkened as well. I searched for the sun, but couldn't locate it through the cover.

"Come on," I said, running down the beach that I was pretty sure connected to the one we landed on.

We climbed over a finger of rocks pointing out to the sea and spotted the girls on the beach and next to the plane.

"Hey!" I yelled at them.

Kara and I ran through the shallow water and got to the beach before the plane. Sherri, Aubrey, Benji, and Eliza got to the sand at the same time. Eliza held onto Moshe that seemed perfectly content to being held. Dang cat was getting soft on me.

"This is bad," Aubrey said, looking to the sky.

"Did you guys find anything?" Sherri yelled out over the sound of the wind and waves.

"We found a cave, not far from here," I said.

"It's amazing," Kara said.

"Why are you so happy?" Eliza asked, petting Moshe's head, but no one answered.

The other girls smiled and nodded their head, as if they knew.

"What?" Eliza asked, getting annoyed. "She's all big smiles over there, and we are looking at one nasty storm here, people. Nothing to be happy about here. The storms can get bad out here and I don't think Moshe likes the thunder."

"My parent's dog hated thunder," Sherri said. "Poor pug would hide under the bed."

"Let's secure the raft up high on the bank and get to the cave before it starts pouring," I said.

That's when I noticed the girls had gotten off several panels from the plane. They sat on the shore, rocking in the wind.

"Nice work, ladies," I said, admiring the sheets of aluminum.

We pulled the raft high up the hill and onto the green grass and stuffed the aluminum panels under it. Thank goodness, Aubrey had found the balsa wood. If we had used palms or some other tree, there would have been no way we could have lifted it onto the bank. With the raft secured, we grabbed our supplies and made our way down the beach to the mouth of the cave.

The storm had worsened, and the gray clouds were now closer to a shade of black. The wind whipped across the beach, sending stinging grains of sand against us. The wind swept over the ocean, creating a constant mist in the air that seemed like rain. We were going to be soaked again if we didn't get in the cave.

Lightning struck closer and the some of the girls gasped, Moshe hissed at the noise.

The boom hit us, and it wasn't more than five miles away now.

I picked up the pace and led the way into the cave, with Benji taking up the rear. I had my knife out, and she had her bow. While Kara and I hadn't seen anything in the cave, that didn't mean it was empty. We didn't spend much time exploring it. Moshe ran up next to me, smelling the ground and pacing around my legs.

We stepped into the larger, glowing room, and I felt the same awe as I did the first time. It was just as fun to see everyone else's reaction to it.

"Holy shit!" Aubrey said, looking at the glowing ceiling.

"See, it's incredible!" Kara said.

"It's reacting to our sounds," Sherri said. "Usually things that glow are predators, though, so I wonder what they are scared of."

"This cave smells like sex," Aubrey said.

Kara laughed and leaned against me, wrapping her arms around me.

"You guys had sex in here?" Eliza asked, confused and

appearing to sniff the air for this smell Aubrey mentioned. "Are you trying to get pregnant?"

"What?" Kara asked. "No. We're all on the shot."

"Got a sorority discount on birth control. We're good for a few more months," Sherri said. "And sweetie, we're going to have to another talk soon."

"I know stuff," Eliza said, setting Moshe down on the sand. "But it's not like men were falling out of the trees while I was growing up. Jack is the first one I've seen, remember?"

"Well, maybe Jack here can help us with the lesson. Nothing like a visual representation," Sherri said, looking at me and winking.

"That would be really helpful, actually," Eliza said, and I wasn't sure if she was kidding or not.

"Umm, there's a place up at the top of the hill that flattens out. Perfect for setting up a camp while this storm clears," I said, thinking the girls seemed to get pleasure in making situations uncomfortable for me.

Most of the girls seemed amused by this, but Eliza seemed confused and looked at my crotch for a while before looking at the rest of my body. There was no way I was going to be some visual representation for Sherri. Eliza was a woman, just like the rest of them. If she wanted to see me and my…male parts, then that would be something that would have to come from her.

At the plateau, Sherri called out, "Is there anyone here?"

Her voice echoed around the cave, dimming it to near blackness for a moment.

"That echo is so cool," Aubrey said.

"I'm an idiot!" Benji yelled.

To which I replied, as her echo lessened, "You're an idiot!"

She laughed and rushed to me. "Yes. The Grinch. Such a classic. If we are here for Christmas, I'm reenacting the whole movie for Eliza."

On the plateau, we spread out one of the emergency blankets on the ground, and I took notice of the holes, tears, and ripped edges. It wouldn't be long before the whole thing ripped apart. Thankfully, whoever the ditch bag came from had put in a thick, high-quality blanket. That cheap, regular blanket wouldn't have lasted through the first night. Moshe paced around the edge of the plateau, looking down the sides before moving on and looking again. I reached out to her and knew she wasn't scared but rather curious, just like every other cat I'd known.

The cave opening brightened with a flash of light and then thunder rocked the cave, sending us into complete darkness. After a few seconds, the ceiling lit up again.

"That was close," Benji said.

"I hate these kinds of storms," Eliza said, holding her bag against her chest.

"How many types are there?" I asked.

"Most just rain, but these one's boom. I don't like the booming ones," Eliza said.

"Yeah, well, we should be okay in here," I said.

"Did you guy explore the cave?" Sherri asked, looking at the back end of the platform and into the darkness.

"I didn't feel anything back there," I said.

"I think we should check it out, all the same," Sherri said. "I think there is another room over here."

I followed Sherri down the back side of the plateau and to a dark space near a rock wall. As we got closer, I saw the shadow was actually a doorway into another room. The glow creatures weren't in this room, but their soft light illuminated the room enough to see the dead body inside.

CHAPTER 11

SHERRI'S SCREECH at the sight of the body had everyone at our side in seconds and briefly extinguished what little light we had. I walked into the dark room first, trying to use my senses for any creature that might be in the room, but it felt blank.

"This must be the pilot," I whispered, as if a loud sound might entice the spirit of the pilot to reanimate its long-dead corpse.

On the chest of the pilot's jumpsuit was a name: LT. Danforth. At least I had a name to the skeleton now. The suit sagged around the body that looked as if it had been dried to nothing but skin on bones. The skin stretched over the pilots face like some horrible surgery gone wrong, with his teeth exposed in some strange, open-mouth look of surprise. His eyes and nose were nothing more than dark holes in this dark room, and I imagined at some point the odor in this confined space would have been unbearable, but now, it smelled like the rest of the cave.

Next to the body was a small booklet and a backpack spread over what looked like a green blanket. Moshe went next to the body, smelling it before moving on. Apparently, a long-dead man didn't interest her as much as the corner of the room she was smelling.

"Is he dead?" Eliza asked.

"As a doornail," Benji said.

"What does that mean?" Eliza asked, clutching her bag.

"I actually don't know what that means," Benji said.

"It just means that a doornail has no life and neither does he. Might as well say dead as a rock," I said.

"Dead as a rock makes more sense," Eliza said.

"Good, now that we have that settled," Aubrey said, getting closer to me and looking down at the body.

"I've never seen a dead body," Eliza said, looking to us for some kind of acknowledgment that this was strange for us as well.

"You think something killed him in here?" Aubrey asked.

I wondered the same thing, but none of his clothes appeared to be marked with slashes or even blood. His face, while terrifying and looked more or less like a thin leather bag pulled over a skull, didn't appear to have any damage.

A pencil sat in his right hand with a booklet on the ground near his hand. I knelt and picked up the booklet. The hard leather binding over the hand-sized book had cracked, and I shook the dust off as I opened it.

At first, it was just numbers or calculations on what I thought was fuel. A few longitude and latitude numbers were spread over the book and I thumbed ahead, skimming the many pages of numbers. The numbers were written with hard straight lines and were clear to read. They kept in the lines and were evenly spaced. Most of it had been written in a black pen. A few ink blotches were the only fault I spotted. A flipped the pages until I spotted the lighter writings of a pencil about halfway through the book. In pencil, the letters were neat as well but I quickly realized that it was closer to a diary than some flight log.

11/28/1951

Bad storm last night and crashed on the shores of an island. Transponder and radio appear to be broken. Trying to make repairs.

I squinted, trying to read more, but the pencil was much lighter than the pen had been in this dark room. I closed the book and sighed.

"He has a journal," I said, tapping the small note pad on the palm of my hand.

"What's it say?" Benji asked.

"That he crashed back in '51 and his radio wouldn't work. Too dark to read much more than that." I said. "I think we should see what supplies he has."

"As much as I'd like a full set of clothes," Aubrey said, "I'm not wearing some dead, mummy guy's jumpsuit."

"Jumpsuit," Kara said absently and eyed me.

"Me either, but maybe that blanket?" Sherri said. "I

mean, it's been there for decades, right. What could be on it?"

"They used to throw blankets covered in smallpox to the Native Americans, you know," Aubrey said.

"I don't want smallpox," Benji said, backing up.

"They'd gotten rid of smallpox by the fifties," I said, and was pretty confident in that, no need for a Google search here.

I went to the pilot's backpack and quickly realized it wasn't a backpack but a parachute. The straps and everything on it looked as good as new.

"It's a parachute," I said. "This is a major find. I bet we could use that fabric and rope for all kinds of stuff."

"A bigger sail," Benji said.

"Exactly and the rope I bet is better than what we have now," I said.

"I don't know," Benji said. "Eliza's rope towed us right out of that whirlpool."

"Mr. Rope," Eliza said, holding onto her bag, the very place she stuffed what was left of Mr. Rope.

"Well, Mr. Rope saved our asses," Benji said, patting Eliza on the shoulder.

Eliza smiled and shifted her feet.

"And another pack wouldn't hurt either," Sherri said, gesturing the parachute I held. "Lieutenant Danforth, thank you, sir."

I took the pencil from his hand and slid it into the back of the small, leather-bound notebook.

"He had a fire in here," Eliza said. "And there are a few fish bones as well." She nudged the pile of ash with a toe.

I put my foot next to his and realized that Danforth had incredibly small feet. I wasn't too keen on taking those shoes off anyways, his whole leg might come off from the effort.

Aubrey knelt next his feet and grabbed his ankle, pulling the shoe off with a few snaps and stirred up some dust. She rushed to the second shoe and wasn't as gentle, pulling the whole foot off with it. A burst of dust kicked up and spread over the small room. I breathed it in and coughed. It seemed just like any dust I'd encountered, but it wasn't. This was dead guy dust.

"Oh my God," Sherri said, covering her mouth and rushing out of the room.

"What?" Aubrey said. "He's dead, it's not like he needs them."

I left the room as well with the rest of the girls. The dust didn't make it out of the room and we all climbed back up to the plateau. The glow of the room gave us plenty of light and we sat in a semi-circle on the blanket.

"We should bury him when the storm passes," I said.

"Okay," Benji said. "I think that's a good idea."

Aubrey kept her attention on the shoes, looking inside them and pulling things out.

"You're wearing those?" Benji asked, horrified.

"Uh, yeah, if they fit, and I can get them clean enough," Aubrey said, each word sending a dimming pulse over the cave.

A faint flash came from the opening, followed quickly by a thunderous boom. The ceiling light shuddered and fluttered as the sound bounced around. The lights came back on, and I heard the roar of crashing waves at the mouth of the cave.

Moshe had settled on Eliza's lap as she sat cross-legged facing me. The cat raised its sleepy face at the noise and lay back down.

"I thought this storm was going to be bad," Aubrey said as she inspected her new shoes. "Glad you two found this cave."

"Yeah, this is amazing," Sherri said. "I mean, this is like some next level shit in here. We'll have stories that no one will ever believe."

"Speaking of stories," Benji said, gesturing to the notebook in my hands.

I was reluctant to read it, but if it could provide some insight into this world, the smart thing would be to go through it, even if it chronicled a man's death.

"Oh yeah," Eliza said. "I never really thought there were other people trapped her but me and now…there are so many of you. I'd love to hear more about this guy."

"Yeah, read it, Jack," Sherri said.

I open up the small, black leather book and found the page I last left off on and started to read it out loud.

11/28/1951

Bad storm last night and crashed on the shores of an island. Transponder and radio appear to be broken. Trying to make repairs.

11/29

Tried fixing the radio but was not able to. Set up an SOS on the beach and I found a cave. A strange cave, that if I describe I fear I may go section 8. No signs of my squadron or any other aircraft in the sky, but I feel as if something is in the ocean. Searching for provisions.

11/30

No food. No water on this island. Praying for rain. I think there is something in the water watching me.

"Whoa, whoa, whoa," Aubrey said. "He feels the ocean… he can sense something in the water."

It was and wasn't a question, and I had the same thought as I reread the words. This man might have had the same gift I have, if he had the same feeling of being watched by the ocean. Even now, if I reached out to it, I could feel the presence of something just outside the cave, watching, wondering, with a wave of anger brewing down under it all. It didn't want me in there, and its emotions came at me in colors of purple.

"Just keep reading, Jack," Sherri encouraged. "This is the closest thing we've had to Netflix since arriving."

"Oh, well, who was too tired to play Jack Black in *Nacho Libre*?" Benji said.

"Hey, I wanted to play the sexy nun," Sherri said.

"Aubrey is obviously the sexy nun," Benji said.

"And I'm the fat guy in tights?" Sherri asked.

"And also the lead in the play," Benji said.

"Ladies," I said, holding up the booklet.

"Sorry, Jack," Benji said. "Please, continue."

I cleared my throat and got back to my place.

12/01

Prayers were answered and it rained last night. Got plenty of water now. Hard to sleep, though. The cave glows, and I can hear it, like static on a radio. I fished today and caught what I think is a sea bass, but it has teeth like a piranha. I used a rock to kill it. I don't know how, but I knew where it was going to be. This place is unlike anything I've experienced.

12/02

Keeping busy with trying to fix the radio. Still no signs of a search party. Starting to wonder where I am, and whatever is in the ocean, won't go away. I've got a plan forming though. Just need more time to think about it. I want to make sure they are real.

12/03

Plan didn't work. Sharks were in the waters. Found wood on the beach, though. Going to explore cave more. It seems to be much larger than I originally suspected.

12/04

The cave is much bigger than I thought, and I'm not the first man in it. There are drawings past the room I stay in—the devil's drawings of fantastic beasts. I'm starting to think something is wrong in this place. I can feel it below me.

12/05

Out of water again, and the fish seem to be aware of me now. Harder to kill.

12/06

They're watching me. Didn't leave the cave today.

12/07

My wife's birthday today. Made a sand castle. Did I die in that crash? Is this a punishment for what I did?

12/08

Can't stop the noise. It's watching me. Can it read my thoughts?

12/09

It rained. Thank God. I forgot to put out collectors, but got some by dumb luck. Went swimming today and a small shark attacked me. I killed it. At least I have something to eat now.

. . .

12/12

Last few days have been bad. REAL bad. I think I'll live, though. As soon as I'm strong enough, I'm going to kill it. I think it's scared of me. Good. It should be. I think I felt more out there today. Plan on swimming tomorrow.

12/13

Went into waters again. The fish are easy to kill now. I can draw them to me. The watchers are getting nervous. I can feel it. They all are. I try to control them, but they are strong. I need to get stronger.

12/14

More driftwood came to the shore, and I made another torch. I went deeper into cave. Wish I hadn't.

He drew a map of the cave, like a cut section. The beach and cave entrance were easily discernable, and I followed the various paths leading down several levels below us. There were small rooms off larger ones with dead ends. Then there was just a squiggly line on a larger room. I took that as far as he explored, but there was more that he hadn't gotten to. The girls all looked at the map as I passed it around.

"What do you think he saw down there?" Eliza asked.

"Nothing good, I imagine," Benji said. "This story is giving me the creeps." She pulled her knees against her chest and looked at the ceiling.

"You want me to stop reading it?" I asked.

"No, keep going," Sherri said, handing me the booklet back.

I wanted to continue it, as well, but I didn't like where it was going, and we all knew where it ended—in that room not far from us.

12/15

Is there a god present here? The evils of the mind are impossible to escape.

12/16

Watcher man has returned. He has friends. I can feel them out in the water. I can point to them. Thought I heard a ship's horn, but there was nothing there. I screamed at them until my throat hurt. I hate them, but I'm getting stronger, and they're getting more scared.

12/17

I can see another island!!! Maybe twenty miles. Making a raft from the parts in the plane.

12/20

Been busy building a raft. Haven't written in a few days. Out of water again. So thirsty.

. . .

12/21

I think the watchers are planning something. I can feel their thoughts. They don't like me here. I think they want to kill me. But I am nearly strong enough, and I think they know it.

12/22

Was going to leave today. Raft complete, but a terrible storm hit outside. The ceiling is dancing.

12/23

Very bad day. Raft is gone, carried away by the storm. I think the watchers took it. They don't want me to leave this island. My head hurts.

12/24

I have a plan. There are many of them now, and something is coming. I don't want to write too much as I think they can see it. I hope they can't hear my thoughts, but I am starting to hear theirs.

12/25

Merry Christmas. Where are you, Jesus? I need you. I'm building it.

12/26

Got more parts off the plane and have another makeshift raft, but I cut my hand badly. I'm leaving tomorrow, first light. I don't have a choice. God may laugh at my plan, but I am adrift out here and I fear no compass can help me now.

12/29

I tried. God, did I try. I was out there, with them all. So many noises. I failed, or maybe it was the watchers, not allowing me to leave again. What are they hiding from me? I have to kill them all. It's the only way. I think I'm strong enough now.

12/30

My thoughts are sharp, and I can swim in the dark. I caught one and killed it tonight. It wasn't as hard as I thought. They are scared now; I can feel it.

"Whoa," Benji said. "Do you think he went crazy? What are these watchers he's referring to, and what did he kill?"

I took in a breath, not wanting to tell the girls about some phantom thing I felt in the waters, but feeling obligated to explain now that I've read another person has felt them and apparently dealt with one as well. He even called them the same thing—watchers. That creeped me out more than the rest. We were generations apart, decades away and at two different times but we both came to the same name to describe the thing in the ocean.

"I've felt this watcher, as he called them, in the water as well," I said. "I didn't say anything because I wasn't sure what it was. It could have been a shy otter for all I knew. It didn't seem to be a threat."

"He's like you," Aubrey said. "He can feel them. Have you ever seen one of these watchers?"

I shook my head. "No, just a blind feeling."

"I don't like it," Benji said, looking at me with a concerned expression.

"I don't either, but I'm not going crazy like this guy. It's just a feeling of being watched by something. You know, like when you feel something and you turn around to find someone staring at your back," I said.

"Hey, I feel the islands," Kara said, laughing. "If anyone is crazy here, it's me."

"I feel rocks," Benji said, tilting her head to the side.

"I have a hooker's intuition," Eliza added, and the group laughed.

"There's more," I said, holding the booklet up. "Do we want to continue? We know how it ends." I gestured to the room still holding his body.

"It's freaking creepy, but we need to continue. Any information about these islands is invaluable," Aubrey said.

"Okay," I said and started reading again.

12/31

I killed again. I thought I might have been strong enough, but I only got a headache. I'm getting stronger though. They seem to be growing in numbers, like a cut-up starfish. But I can't stop. I'm not sleeping at night anymore. The end is getting closer. My maker hasn't abandoned me. I am the maker.

01/01/1952

Happy New Year, my love.

1/15

The date is a guess. I'm not sure what day it is anymore. It's been a while since I wrote in this. Maybe a week, or a month. Not sure it matters anymore. Time doesn't exist here. I can't get them out of my head. Found more wood today. I think if I go deep enough, I can escape them, get them out of my mind.

1/16

The cave is deeper than what is possible. I fear I may get lost. I feel something down there. I reached for it, and I think I woke it. Now I feel it, even at the top. It's slow though.

Another map showed an even larger cave than before, ending with a squiggly line again.

1/17

It's closer now. They all are. I have to escape. It's suffocating. My strength is my will, and I will it.

"You think something is in this cave?" Aubrey asked, looking into the darkness.

Kara placed hand her hand on the plateau and then Benji did the same. I didn't dare reach for what Danforth felt, but I knew all too well the feeling of what he called "the watchers." He said he killed them. Many of them, from the sound of it.

"This is not a bad place," Kara said.

"I think I can feel the hollow spaces below us," Benji said, shaking her head. "That's crazy, right?"

Another flash, and thunder boomed through the cave.

"No, it's not crazy," I said.

"It seems like this guy was going crazy, though. I couldn't imagine being stuck, alone, on an island like that," Sherri said.

"I can," Eliza said.

"Oh yeah. Sorry, sweetie," Sherri said.

"That's okay. I'm sort of still getting used to having people around me," she said. "At least I didn't lose it like this guy."

"I have to hear the rest," Benji said. "Even though I don't want to hear it."

"Me too," Sherri said. "Keep reading."

Moshe meowed. Apparently the kitty wanted me to continue as well.

. . .

1/18

I've decided to go low. There is more wood today. Cutting and prepping. If this is my last entry, tell my wife I love her, and to my daughter, I'm sorry.

1/21

Another guess on the date. I was down there for a long time, in the darkness. I reached the bottom, I think, if there is a bottom. I should be dead. This place isn't real. I'm not real. It's running now. Always running. I fear I may have started it. I need to leave here. I'm so tired though. If you read this, whoever you are, don't go down. DON'T DO IT.

He drew what looked like a gear with many spokes on it and inside, was a weaving of lines and more circles. It was a far better drawing than the maps, and I imagined he spent many hours on it. I didn't know what it meant, though.

I showed the girls, and they shrugged.

"This is fucking weird," Aubrey said.

I nodded in agreement and continued.

1/22

I'm trying again to make it to the other island. I can see it out there and know it has to be better than here. Anywhere is better than here. I'm strong enough now. They will listen. They will obey.

. . .

1/26

I was out there. I told them to leave me alone and they did. They listened even as I killed them. They kept making noises though. I couldn't stop them all! I was close this time, but I fell asleep. They took me back here, to this godforsaken island. The bastards. I'd rather be dead.

1/30

This is my last entry. I'm putting on my suit and trying again tomorrow. I hear all their thoughts now, and they are staying far away. But I am coming to them soon. They can't keep me here. I know what this place is now, and exactly how to stop them once and for all. Oceans will run red.

I flipped through the blank pages behind this last entry. I closed the notebook and looked back at the opening and the room that held the man behind these words.

"Jesus H. Christ," Aubrey said. "What the hell happened here?"

"He died here," Sherri said. "A man went crazy and died here. We shouldn't have even read that…thing." She couldn't even look at it.

"What do you think he found out about this place?" Eliza asked.

"I'm not sure, but it seemed a paranoia set in and he couldn't shake it," I said, thinking of my own feelings and the watchers. Was I going to go down a similar path as

Danforth? Would the noises get so loud in my head that they'll drive me crazy? Would I get stronger?

"Paranoia leads to conspiracy theories," Benji said. "I had an uncle like this. He won't even leave his house anymore."

"Oceans will run red?" Aubrey said. "This guy went a little deeper than some 9/11 conspiracy. He wanted to kill."

"He killed something," I said. "He mentioned killing them several times."

"Yeah, the watchers," Eliza said. "Should we see what's in this cave?"

"No," Benji, Aubrey, Kara and Sherri said at the same time.

I laughed. "I guess we aren't spelunking then."

"What's spelunking?" Eliza asked.

"Just a fancy word for cave exploring," Sherri said.

"What's your intuition telling you about exploring this cave?" I asked.

"I'm not sure, it's mixed. Like good and bad could come from it."

Thunder roared through the cave, giving Kara a jump.

"Well, I'm not one to shy from a little exploring," I said, turning the notebook to the page with the map on it.

"Yeah, me either," Sherri said, getting up. "It could be fun."

We went back into Danforth's room and found the small opening at the back. Moshe paced near it. She had been smelling the same spot earlier. She seemed nervous as I got down on my knees to the small opening. I crawled a few feet in before I felt a solid wall. As my eyes adjusted to the low light, I could make out the gray wall. It looked as if someone had poured concrete into the tunnel and smoothed it out.

"What's in there?" Benji asked.

"It's sealed off," I said, feeling the rough surface.

Etched in the concrete was a circle, with spokes on the inside and teeth on the outside, like a gear, same as the picture Danforth had drawn. I closed my eyes, feeling the symbol, and before I realized it, I had reached into the cave, deep, and there was a hint of something down there. Something like I've never felt. I jolted back and scurried out of the small tunnel, jumped to my feet and backed away from it.

The feeling was gone, but the memory of it lingered in my head.

"What?" Sherri said.

Kara knelt, touching the ground. "Something's changed," she said. "It's growing or moving."

"It's moving, and soon I think it will be running," I said, not knowing what that meant, but I felt it and so did Danforth.

"Are we in danger?" Eliza asked.

"No, not yet," I said. "It's slow, but we should leave this island as soon as we can."

"He told us not to go down here," Benji said. "We should have listened. Now this thing is coming. It probably killed Danforth."

"We're not dying in here," I said. "Let's get back to the plateau, and if I sense we're any closer to danger, we'll take our chances out in the storm."

We gathered back around the top and sat in silence as the storm raged outside. The thunder increased in frequency, and waves sounded as if they were hitting the mouth of the cave. During all this, I kept my extra sense open. I felt what Danforth called "the watchers" out there. They were curious and—something new—slightly afraid. Maybe for the storm, but I wondered if it was this island or us being in this cave.

The other thing I felt was below. Far below. I knew it was alive, since I could feel it, but it wasn't alive like me or the sharks out there. This thing felt connected to the island in some way. My head hurt, the more I thought of it, and I suppressed my extra sense and lessened the noise.

As the minutes and hours passed, the girls' mood lightened, and Benji started telling Eliza about movies and movie theaters. Eliza had many questions, but most of all, she wanted us to tell her about music and sing songs for her. This time when we sang "Sweet Caroline," she joined in for the chorus and held her hand over her mouth at the end, trying to stifle her tears.

I was never that good at memorizing music lyrics, but the girls were amazing. They had a competition well into the night about who knew more. They sang songs, laughed, and joked about what we'd been through so far. Their thoughts of what was below us had all but disappeared. Good, better for them to not dwell on what we couldn't change.

As we got tired, I assigned shifts for sleeping. I took the first shift and sat in the glow of the cave, listening to the storm outside and the creature or maybe creatures, steadily increasing speed below.

In the middle of the night, Eliza screamed and grabbed her bag tightly. She went back to sleep almost immediately, as if she had never awoken fully. The girls stirred, but they didn't comment and quickly went back to sleep.

Kara seemed as restless as she did the first night. I thought of waking her, comforting her, but it was better to let her rest. We had another big day tomorrow, and I couldn't wait to get away from this island.

CHAPTER 12

IN THE MORNING, we left the cave to a partially clouded beach. It felt good to have its rays on my skin. The light in the cave felt unnatural to me. A heatless light. I couldn't shake the feeling that I had done something wrong, something very wrong, on this island.

"The plane's gone," Benji said.

The space that it had been was now just waves and rocks. I looked around in the deeper water to see if it had been pulled further out, but it was just gone.

"Storm must have gotten rid of it," I said.

"After like seventy years, it leaves now?" Sherri said. "We could have salvaged more from it."

"There's another storm coming," Aubrey said, looking at the thin clouds.

"Great. When?" I asked.

"We got most of the day," Aubrey said. "But the next one might be even worse than this one."

We crossed the beach and breathed a collective sigh of relief when the raft sat just as we left it on the grassy hill.

We got it back down onto the beach, strapped our bags to it, and were able to secure the aluminum panels to the raft through some of the rivet holes. We also had a new backpack with a parachute inside, thanks to Danforth.

Aubrey, Sherri, and I went back into the cave and retrieved his body. There wasn't much weight to the man, and we carried him to a rock cliff edge, where we dug a shallow grave. Eliza seemed fascinated by the whole process and kept asking questions about burying the dead and why. She helped put a pile of rocks over the pilot's body, and in the end, Aubrey set his shoes on the rock pile. She had never even tried them on. No one else moved to claim them.

With the raft loaded and ready, we pushed it onto the water and raised the sail. The breeze pushed against it, and I steered to the island that had probably consumed Danforth until the very end. I just hoped we didn't have as much trouble as him.

Getting some distance from the island, I no longer felt the thing below, and I relaxed. We were away from it.

"Feels good to be off that island," Eliza said.

We all nodded in agreement, but didn't discuss it further. I felt the notebook in my pocket and patted it. If we found a way back to the mainland, I'd want something to give to his descendants. Maybe his wife was still alive. He mentioned a daughter as well. Danforth could have great grandchildren that would probably appreciate closure to the story.

"Yeah, it does," I said, glancing back at the grassy atoll.

"Snake," Benji said, pulling an arrow back in her bow.

"Snake?" Aubrey said, looking at where Benji was pointing. "Oh, hell no." She quickly moved to the center of the raft with a spear in hand.

I spotted it as well: a large, green snake, swimming on the surface of the water. I reached out to it and felt the wickedness in it, like a sour feeling in the back corner of my mouth. Every thought it had revolved around killing, eating, and reproducing. It bobbed up and down in the choppy water, about thirty feet from our raft. It raised its head, and its forked tongue slid out as it tasted the air. It liked what it tasted and moved toward us.

"Get ready," I said, grabbing a spear.

That's when a massive shark came from below and bit down on the snake, s. The shark's momentum launched it from the seas, with the snake twisting in its mouth. The shark jerked to the side, splitting the snake's body in half and then crashed against the water, sending a splash and wave in our direction.

The part of the snake with the head moved around on the surface of the water, and I felt the fear and anger in it as it tried to escape what was certain death. A dozen more feet and the thing stopped moving.

Almost instantly, a school of smaller fish created a boil around the dead body of the snake. The sound of splashes and sucking was revolting. In less than a minute, the boil of fish was gone, and there was no snake left behind, just a foaming patch on the ocean waters.

"Well, you don't see that every day," Aubrey said.

"Was that piranhas?" Benji asked.

"No," Sherri said. "They aren't in the ocean. Could be something like it, though. Not sure."

Over the next thirty minutes, the shark that ate the snake kept near our raft but didn't get too close, and I never felt the rage in it that made me think it was going to risk everything and attack us. The shark actually wasn't a bad companion, as we kept spotting snakes in the water, but they were leery of the shark patrolling us so they kept clear.

"That's the island we need to be on," Eliza said, pointing to the lush, green island ahead.

As we approached it, I felt the creatures on it as thick as I felt the creatures in the ocean. A static of hundreds or thousands of minds racing about their day, in search of basic necessities, like food, water, or a mate. For me, it was snow on a screen, but I felt hints of that sour snake wickedness.

The island itself wasn't much larger than Yang Island, but every inch of it was covered in jungle. The leaves were all massive and green. The trees had wide bases, covered in moss, and thinned out as they rose high into the sky like vines reaching for the sun. The canopy of the jungle spread over the whole island, giving deep shadows further into the jungle.

This would have been a tough place to start off at, and I wondered if we would be able to find a person in the thick foliage.

We searched the shoreline, but there didn't appear to be any beaches. The green growth reached right into the ocean, exposing green roots as the waves rolled against them.

"Jesus," Aubrey said. "It's a freaking jungle in there."

"This is awesome," Sherri said. "I've never been in a jungle."

"Yeah, but…" Aubrey said, taking a deep breath. "This shouldn't be here. At best, it should be like the other islands, because of temperature, rainfall and such. This is a completely different ecosystem in the same vicinity as others."

"Like these islands have anything consistent on them," Kara said. "I'm curious to get my hands on this one, see what it's like."

"There's tons of life on it," I said. "Look, there's a spot we can land."

A small section of beach appeared behind massive trees that looked to be made of a thousand roots running over the ground and toward the ocean. They were taller than the trees back on our island, reaching higher than the palms. The canopy seemed to intertwine with other trees as much as the trunks, sending a deep shadow over under them. Between the trees was thick foliage that didn't allow us to see deeper into the jungle.

A white beach stuck out from the greens and browns. It wasn't much larger than a few of our rafts and appeared to be the only beach that hadn't been overtaken with growth. We brought the raft up close to the beach and something moved in the nearby tree. I didn't see it, but the branches and leaves shook as it traveled deeper into the jungle. A bird perhaps, scurrying away from the people.

The raft slid up onto the beach, and I jumped off the front first, looking for anything that might attack us. I tried to feel for the creatures, but there were too many to make out any specific threat, and I could feel their overall temperament changing. They weren't welcoming us to their island, but they were curious and also nervous.

Moshe got low and growled at the jungle, as if there was something in it she didn't like. Kara patted the sea cat's stiff back.

Aubrey and Benji were next off the raft, flanking me to each side with their weapons. I laughed, thinking of us as an invading force, landing on some foreign land with weapons drawn. In a way, we were. This island may have never seen a human. They might not have a fear of us yet.

A green bird, about the size of a baseball, flew out from the forest and landed right on my shoulder. I reached for it when it bit me on the hand.

"Son of a…" I swatted at the bird.

Moshe hissed and jumped up to my shoulder, then launched off me after the bird, but the bird flew from its reach and into the jungle.

I checked my hand. The little bastard broke the skin, a dot of blood forming on the back of my hand.

"Stupid little bird," Benji said, drawing her bow back.

"Save it," I said. "Let's get the raft up on the sand."

We pulled the raft out of the water and then gathered some of the bags from it. I never wanted to leave all of our supplies in one place. We'd carry as much as we could on us. We left the plane parts, the parachute, and paddles on the raft. Then we tied it off to a nearby tree.

"Hello," I called out into the jungle. "Anyone there?"

I waited a few seconds, hoping any humans would just come on out. The idea of going into that jungle wasn't appealing. I'd seen too many jungle shows with spiders and creepy crawly type creatures in the jungle to not give it the respect it deserved. Plus, the snakes. I felt them in the jungle, and there were many of them. We'd seen plenty in the water, and I imagined this is where they all came from.

Damn snake-filled jungle. What kind of crap luck did we have?

Kara kneeled and touched the sand and then moved closer to the jungle before turning back to us.

"The island isn't bad, but it isn't good either. It's hard to describe, but it feels deceitful, like a lie," she said, and shook her head, as if not satisfied with the answer.

"Well, better than hell island," Aubrey said. "I can work with an island that's a liar."

"Maybe under all this jungle beauty is a hideous beast, waiting to entrap us," Benji said in a joking manner.

"No, it's like it's hiding something," Kara said.

"Well, hopefully it's hiding another person from the boat," I said. "Where do you think we should go, Eliza?"

"I think we should go that way," Eliza said and pointed straight ahead.

"I should have kept those shoes," Aubrey said with a sigh. "I got the right side."

"I'll watch the left side," Benji said.

"Eliza and I will take the front," I said, holding a spear, with a knife at my hip.

Eliza nodded and held onto her homemade knife.

"Kara and I will watch our backs," Sherri said. They both gripped their spears.

"You ladies are amazing," I said, shaking my head in wonder.

"This just better be worth it," Kara said. "Something

feels off with this place for me, and if a tiny bird can draw blood here, no telling what the hell else is holed up in this island."

"Snakes," Benji said and Aubrey grabbed her spear tighter.

"Freaking snakes," Aubrey said. "I hate them."

"I think they're constrictors, so just don't let them get around you," I said.

"Oh, that's real comforting," Aubrey said. "If one gets anywhere near me, I'm stabbing it to death."

"I'll be right there with you," I said. I didn't like snakes either.

Moshe meowed and walked near me in a circular path. She seemed on edge about something.

Eliza and I took the first steps into the jungle. It felt warmer under the canopy and wetter, as if it had just rained in there. We didn't get ten feet in before the wall of bushes, ferns, and leaves impeded our way.

"Benji, Kara," I said. "Can we get those axes?"

Kara and Benji handed us their homemade axes. Not much more than a stick with a rock tied to the end, but it should work for getting through some of this jungle.

I chopped at the foliage and smashed it with my ax like a hammer. Eliza did the same, and we moved forward into the jungle.

"We're not exactly dressed for jungle trekking," Aubrey said, snapping the front of her red bikini.

"Oh, come on," Sherri said. "Can you imagine how sweaty we'd be?"

"Yeah, it's not too bad for you guys," Benji said.

"Imagine if you wore something as a goof and were stuck with it?"

Sherri laughed. "I like your Sponge Bob bikini."

"Well you should, you're the one that bought it for me," Benji said.

"You look sexy in yellow," Sherri said.

Benji rolled her eyes and went back to scanning the jungle around us.

There were birds like the little bastard that nipped me on the beach, but I think they kept back because of Moshe. That cat prowled around us, hissing at the birds and jumping up anytime they got near us. There were a few butterflies as well, and what looked like a moth flew by. This island had what none of the other islands had—a large population of small animals.

The sounds of the jungle echoed around us, from birds chirping to other things making what sounded like a scratching sound. The elevation of the jungle continued to climb steeper as we got deeper in. In about ten minutes of chopping, hacking, and stomping through the jungle, I had a good layer of sweat building on my shirt.

Eliza looked as if she needed a break but she kept moving and didn't complain. She kept looking over to me and at my sweating body. I thought she might ask me something but then just went back to swinging the ax.

"How much further you think?" I asked.

"It's close," Eliza said, breathing hard.

We had climbed a good fifty feet in elevation, and when I looked back, through the thick canopy, the blue ocean revealed itself. Ahead, it seemed to be leveling off more.

Another few minutes and I pushed through a rather large bush with leaves half the size of my body and a clearing was revealed.

I shielded my eyes from the bright sun as my eyes adjusted from the dark jungle. The girls and cat walked into the clearing with me. Not much bigger than a forty-foot circle, but when you'd spent the good part of the last hour trekking through the thickest bush I'd ever seen, this clearing was stunning and a huge relief.

"What's up with this?" Aubrey said, seeming to not trust the clearing.

I walked out into the clearing with Benji, Eliza, and Aubrey at my side. That's when the floor of the jungle fell. I crashed down through broken roots, dirt, and sand. I hit the bottom first and reached out to try to soften Benji's fall while Aubrey and Eliza fell onto each other.

Gazing up from where we fell, I saw the bright sunlight and the edge of the jungle about twenty feet up through a tangle of roots. The ground had collapsed under our feet, and I wondered if we fell into some kind of sinkhole. Sherri's face appeared above, looking down at us in alarm.

"You okay down there?" Sherri yelled.

I wasn't sure. I rolled over to Benji, and she appeared to be okay, so I rushed to Aubrey and Eliza as they were getting back to their feet.

"You guys okay?" I asked.

"Yeah," Eliza said.

"Just got the wind knocked from me," Aubrey wheezed as she struggled to get up.

"We're okay down here," I yelled back up.

The wet dirt stuck to them in patches of brown over their skin. Aubrey's hair had what looked like a damp chunk of grass on it. I plucked it from her hair and tossed it to the ground.

"Thanks," she said.

"What the hell happened?" Benji asked as she looked up.

"Ground gave out," I said. "Think we can get back up?"

Benji reached for a root but it pulled out from the dirt. I joined in the effort but each root I grabbed for either broke or got pulled out from the ground. The dirt was inverted and impossible to climb.

Moshe paroled the edge of the collapsed hole above and then jumped in, landing deftly onto various roots before hitting the ground. She walked around us, inspecting us with some cat arrogance.

"Hey, it wasn't our fault the ground collapsed in," I said to Moshe, but she gave me a sympathetic meow as if to tell me she knew I was just a stupid human.

We couldn't go up, but I realized we didn't fall into a pit but into a cave. I walked a few feet into it and spotted light ahead.

"Looks like we're going spadunking," Eliza said.

"Spelunking," I said and went back to the opening we fell into.

Sherri and Kara were both looking down into the hole.

"What's going on?" Sherri asked.

"We can't get back up, but this is a cave; we're going to follow it. It looks like it heads back in the direction of the raft, and I see a light ahead. We're going to find another way out. Just meet us back at the raft."

"Maybe we should just come down there with you," Sherri said.

"No, too risky. It's a miracle none of us got hurt on the fall," I said. "Just watch out for snakes and stuff and get back to the raft. If you haven't seen us in a while, come back here with some rope."

"Okay," Sherri said and watched me go back into the cave and out of her sight.

Leaving them alone made me sick to my stomach, especially in some island we didn't know. Kara thought this island was a deceiver, and I hoped it didn't just pull its first trick.

The cave itself had a wet, dirty floor, and the ceiling and walls were more roots than dirt or rock. The green and brown vines moved in and out of the dirt like the intestines of some creature. The musty, dank smell helped with the thought that we were walking through the insides of some living creature, waiting to find its digestive tract and escape through its back end. The slope on the tunnel increased as we walked along, pushing us deeper into its belly.

The light ahead turned out to be another sinkhole from the surface. Looking up through the maze of roots left little chance of getting through them, even if we could somehow climb a twenty-foot wall.

Up ahead, maybe another hundred feet, was another shaft of light coming down into the tunnel.

Moshe growled, her deep voice resonating through the cave as if she was a cat ten times as big. Maybe one day she would. I had the impression from her baby-like face that she was still a kitten and not a cat, or sea cat or maybe aquatic feline?

"What is it, girl?" Benji asked.

Moshe looked stiff, and her hair had puffed up along her stiff back.

It hissed, but then I realized the hiss didn't come from Moshe.

"What the heck just made that noise?" Benji asked.

"There's a person, up ahead," Eliza said. "Just past the light."

As my eyes continued to adjust to the light, I squinted into the darkness and spotted the body. She lay on what looked like a large, flat rock, longer than her already long body. She wasn't moving, and I took a deep breath, thinking the worst.

Then I spotted something around her moving and then more things, as if the floor around her had come alive. A few of them moved into the light, and I saw their shiny, green bodies.

"Snakes," Benji said. "Why did it have to be snakes?"

CHAPTER 13

Now, snakes on the ground were one thing. Snakes on the water was another whole kind of terrible, but neither compared to the feeling of being in a cave full of them.

The scaly monsters moved around each other to where I couldn't tell where one began and end. I might have thought it was some thousand-foot-long snake if not for the occasional rise of a snakehead. It would lick the air, tasting our scent, probably deciding how best to wrap its immense body around our neck and squeeze until our heads popped off.

They were a jumble of emotions ranging from anger to curious. There were too many colors and temperatures coming at me for an accurate count.

"I've got a dozen arrows," Benji said.

"I don't know. I once had to kill a poisonous snake, and even after cutting the thing in half, it still came after me, striking," I said. "You ever encounter these, Eliza?"

"No, we never had snakes on my island."

"That's Cass," Aubrey said, leaning forward. "I'd recognize those sexy-ass legs anywhere."

"Cass?" Benji said. "Holy shit, that *is* Cass."

"Is she alive?" Eliza asked.

If she was dead, it had just happened, because she still had color to her skin. I watched her stomach. After a few seconds, I spotted movement from a breath.

"She's alive," I said.

"Cassandra!" Benji said.

She didn't move or respond in any way. Whatever was wrong with her, she was unconscious. Near her, I spotted another creature. It looked like a capybara, the world's largest rodent, but this guy had large teeth sticking out from the corner of its mouth. I would have taken it as dead, but it wasn't stiff-legged like something you might find dead on the road. It looked peaceful, similar to Cass. It lay on its side, with its front paws pulled up closer to its chest, and I saw its chest moving as well with a slow breath. Why it and Cass decided to take a nap in a den of snakes was beyond me, but I knew we needed to get Cass out of there and quick. I could feel the snakes' mood changing for the worse.

"We have to get to her," Aubrey said, pointing her spear at the snakes not ten feet from us now.

"We've got a snake problem," Benji said, stating the obvious obstacle.

"There's another tunnel, off to the left," Eliza said. "We should go that way."

"Oh, hell, I almost forgot," Aubrey set her spear down and swung the bag she was carrying around to her front.

She rummaged through it and pulled out the box of matches.

"Fire," I said, feeling a flicker of hope.

I slid my bag to my front and grabbed some of the bundles of kindling we'd packed and wrapped it around the end of my ax. It would only burn for a few seconds. Then I remembered the lip balm. I smeared some of it on the kindling like a wax. It might only last a few seconds longer, but we'd need all the time we could get.

Aubrey stood by me, holding a match in one hand and the box in the other, ready to strike the match against it.

With the kindling secured to my ax, I extended it to Aubrey.

"We only have one chance at this. Hopefully, the snakes are scared of fire. You three grab Cass, and we'll haul ass down the tunnel on the left. You sure it leads somewhere, Eliza?"

"It feels like the right way to go," Eliza said, not looking as confident as I would have liked.

"Okay, Aubrey, light it," I said as a snake near me lifted its head and opened its mouth.

The match lit, brightening the dark tunnel and giving me a stunning look at the women around me. Even in complete peril, I had a hard time not admiring them. She moved the lit match onto the kindling and it ignited.

I yelled and moved the ax-torch toward the snake. It went back down to the ground and backed away from me. The fear from it wafted up to me like the sweet scent of sugar. We didn't have time to move slow, so I rushed the snake, torch out and yelling. The snakes hurried out of the way of the flames, slithering into hidden dark recesses, and in a few seconds, we got to Cass.

Aubrey shook her. "Cass? Wake up."

Nothing.

"Just grab her," I said, waving the fiery weapon at another snake.

"Of course it has to be the giant we need to carry," Aubrey said, pulling Cass up into a sitting position. "Eliza, you get the legs. Benji, you and I lift the body."

Together, the three women picked up Cass, with Aubrey and Benji each taking a shoulder and Eliza between her legs and grabbing her ankles, facing forward.

"Go," Aubrey said.

A pissed-off, scared snake launched from the darkness, and I swung the flaming ax, striking it over the head right before it got to Aubrey. The snake fell back and slithered into the shadows, and a fresh wave of rage washed over the room like an oven. They were no longer concerned about their safety as much as they wanted to kill us. As long as I had the ax, they wouldn't attack though.

The flame on the ax went out, and the tunnel returned to deep darkness, as if someone had flipped the switch.

"Shit," I said.

"Follow me," Eliza said, pulling Cass's body and by sheer connection, Aubrey and Benji.

I rushed ahead, heading down the dark tunnel right next to Eliza. Behind us, the sounds of snakes filled the tunnel. We crossed under another light shaft and behind us; it gave me a view of the snakes chasing after us.

There were dozens of them, and this time it was easy to see them, as they were all head first and moving in a serpentine pattern. Their big, green bodies were as thick as my leg, and they seemed to fight for position, their rage radiating out as if we were being chased by lava.

"Run!" I said, trying to get the girls moving faster.

I ran to the front and ducked under Cass's butt, lifting her middle onto my shoulder, and ran down the hill as hard as I could. I only hoped Eliza was going in the right direction.

Light appeared ahead, peeking through a thick patch of bushes and leaves dead ahead. I glanced back and spotted a snake just a few feet behind Benji. I braced as we busted through the end of the tunnel, covered in leaves, branches, and vines.

The first thing I could see was the sunlight, and then I realized we had just jumped off a cliff while carrying an unconscious woman.

CHAPTER 14

THE TUNNEL HAD OPENED to a cliff, and before I could make a course correction, Eliza had already fallen, pulling Cass and the rest of us down with her. We slid down the side of the cliff, crashing into the roots, vines, and immense leaves as we did. I held onto Cass, trying to keep her elevated above it all.

We crashed through a thick section of vines and fell another ten feet onto a cushion of foliage. The girls crashed into me, and I had a butt in my face along with an elbow in my stomach.

The girls scrambled to get off me as a snake crashed right next to us. Benji screamed and stabbed it with an arrow. It seemed just as stunned from the fall as we did.

Glancing around us, I spotted the ocean not far away.

"Come on," I said, picking up Cass on my own in a fireman carry while still holding onto my ax.

Another snake slammed into the soft brush around us and I swung my ax, hitting it on the back of the head, sending it reeling back.

The girls grabbed Cass with me, and we took big, high steps, trying to work our way out of the bush as more snakes continuously fell around us now. I kept hearing them smash to the ground behind us.

"Run," I said.

Carrying Cass, we got through the foliage and found a clearer path back toward the beach—the very path we cleared earlier.

Thankfully, Sherri and Kara were at the raft already.

"Untie the raft!" I yelled.

They heard and jumped into action, pulling the rope loose and pushing the raft along the sand.

I took Cass on my own for the last ten feet and placed her as gently as I could onto the raft, then helped push it into the water. I helped the girls get onto the raft as I faced the jungle, waiting for the tsunami of snakes I knew was coming.

"We're on," Benji said, reaching back for me.

I took her hand and jumped onto the raft. She stood next to me and fired an arrow. The arrow flew, and I watched it as it struck the snake in what I would call the snake's neck. It fell to the sand, flopped around, but kept moving toward us, leaving a trail of blood on the white sand.

"Get the sail up," I said.

Sherri and Aubrey pulled the sail up and the wind pushed against the sail, jolting us forward. That's when I saw the snake wave rolling over the green bushes and hitting the white sand. They didn't slow down as they hit the water; in fact, I'd say they increased in speed as they swam toward us.

"What's wrong with Cass?" Sherri said, kneeling next to her and holding her head.

"We don't know," Aubrey said. "We found her like this."

"Oh my God. What do we do?" Kara said, standing over Cass.

"Guys!" Benji said, shooting another arrow at the closest snake in the water.

The arrow lodged in the reptile's body and gave us a flag of sorts as to their location and speed. The arrow didn't seem to bother it.

"She's barely breathing," Sherri said, her ear next to Cass's mouth.

"Guys!" Benji yelled. "We've got a shit-ton of snakes in the water."

They kept spilling from the island as if we had uncorked some kind of nightmare from that tunnel. The ocean waters splashed and foamed as the mass of life moved through it.

"We need more speed," I said, moving to the sail.

"They're catching up with us," Benji yelled.

"We aren't dying to a bunch of snakes," Aubrey said.

"Come on wind," I begged.

As if on command, the wind picked up, pushing the raft faster.

"It's pushing us the wrong way," Eliza said, looking at the distant cave island we'd been on yesterday.

I dashed to the back of the raft and grabbed the rudder. I pushed the rudder into the water, using my strength to turn the boat toward our home.

The raft turned and the sail went limp, flapping in the

breeze. The girls set the sail and the wind grabbed it, but we quickly were getting pulled in the same direction, away from the way we wanted to go.

"They're getting closer again," Benji said.

Behind us, the sea looked alive with green snakes. I sensed them and their anger, their determination to get to us. I sensed some of the fatigue in them, but they had a lot more left in the tank still.

I used the rudder again, and with the same result, the sail failed, and we ended up rotating back away from the way we wanted to go. The wind howled and blew a gust of mist over our raft. I squinted, trying to keep the salt water from my eyes as I watched the snakes. They had gotten closer each time I turned the raft toward home and we lost speed.

We were moving fast through the water now, so fast that paddling wouldn't do much, but we were heading in the wrong direction. I couldn't risk letting those snakes get to us, so I decided to let the wind take us and push us in the fastest direction. The snakes would wear out, and then we could turn and slowly get back home. Even if we lost a few hours, it'd be better than dealing with a mass of snakes.

"We're riding this wind out until the snakes are gone," I said over the wind.

Eliza walked to the front of the raft, and I spotted what she was looking at in the distance. Another island.

"That's my island," Eliza said and looked back to me, terrified. "We're heading toward my island."

"That's where you came from?" Kara asked.

"You made it that far in that canoe you built?" Sherri asked.

"Yeah," Eliza said.

"You got balls, kid," Aubrey said.

Thunder boomed in the distance, and I looked at the dark clouds moving toward us.

"Guess that storms here," I said.

"I thought we could make it back to that cave in time," Aubrey said, looking apologetic.

I felt the notebook in my pocket. I wanted to look at it again. It felt like this mystery I could solve with a fresh look at it, but that would have to wait.

"The snakes are getting closer," Benji said.

I turned the raft a hair, making sure we were pointing right at Eliza's island and then looked back. A snaked bobbed in and out of the water not ten feet behind us. The damn Michael Phelps of snakes was chasing us.

"Tag it," I said, motioning to Benji.

She pulled her bowstring back and held it for a second against the side of her face. The raft bobbed up and down as much as the snake did, making for a tough shot. She let the arrow fly and breathed out. I almost didn't want to take my eyes off of her. Shooting gave her a joy that was hard to describe, but her face brightened after she fired, as if she had released an enormous pressure that had been building and released it all into the arrow.

The arrow struck the snake right in the face. It dipped into the water, disappearing below. Another aquatic reptilian wonder took its place just a few feet behind.

Aubrey and Sherri left Cass's side and went to their paddles.

"We're going too fast for that," Kara said, kneeling next to Cass and securing her.

"Oh yeah, just watch," Aubrey said and swung the paddle through the water.

Sherri matched her and soon they were a flurry of speed, moving their paddles through the water.

The raft didn't move much faster, but it did increase just enough that the closest snake began to slip further and further behind us. I felt the fury in it but also the extreme fatigue. It wouldn't be much longer until it either died from a heart attack or gave up. The snake mass of lesser snakes still held back a few hundred feet. If this wind or these ladies quit, we'd be covered in the green nightmare in less than a minute.

I kept steering, keeping the raft in line with the island even as it wanted to pull off course. The wind gusted and blew ocean mist over us again. I glanced at Cass, thinking the cool splash might jolt her awake like it did in the movies, but she seemed to be in a coma or something.

Even lying down, I could see how tall she was, over six feet for sure, with long legs and a thin waist. She had broad shoulders and muscular arms. She wore a conservative bikini that looked more like a sports bra than a bikini, covering her modest breasts. Her face, while pale from whatever was ailing her, looked pretty, with the larger features of a large woman. I suspected she might be able to row this raft hard enough that we could put away the sail and sit back for the ride.

Eliza's island came into view as we neared it. It was a larger island, about the size of Food Island, with a large, rocky hill on the far left side. The trees were thick but also brown and dead looking. The whole place had a brown cast, as if something had gone through and killed all the greenery.

"What happened here? Everything is dying," I asked.

"I don't know. It's been getting worse for months now. I've never seen it this bad," Eliza said and held her hand over her mouth.

The shoreline was much like Yin Island, with long white beaches. The waves weren't as gentle as the wind continued to whip around us.

"Keep pushing hard until we get close to shore," I said, and the girls complied. "Are there any dangers?" I asked Eliza, searching the dead forest.

"No, not really," she said.

"Good," Sherri said, breathing hard. "I'm sick of wildlife."

As we neared the breaking waves, I looked back and couldn't find the snakes anymore. I searched the waters and didn't feel that rage anymore. They could still be coming, but they weren't close. Then I felt that feeling I hadn't felt since the cave—the sense of something out there watching us. The watchers. They seemed to torment Danforth into a murderous rage, but he never explained any of the dangers or what they even were. Maybe I missed something in the text or there was more to it, but I hated the feeling of being watched. The watchers were getting angrier with each passing day.

"Here come the waves," Aubrey called out as we rose onto the back of one.

We were coming in hot. Maybe too hot.

"Pull the sail down," I said.

Kara and Benji jumped into action and yanked the sail down as we crested over the wave.

"Brace," I said, kneeling down and grabbing a piece of rope to hold onto.

The front of the raft moved down, riding the wave, as the back of the raft lifted up. Kara, Sherri, and Aubrey held onto Cass as we rode down the wave. The raft dipped into the water before bouncing back up and leveling out as the wave pushed us closer to the shore.

Another wave hit us from behind and shoved the raft further. We came to a sliding stop in about foot-deep water, with another waved hitting us, driving us a few inches more onto the shore.

I jumped out, looking for any creatures on the islands or snakes in the waters. Where were the damn sharks when you wanted one? A great white would have probably gobbled those snakes up like spaghetti. I felt a few things on the island but nothing dangerous. Just a few simple-minded things. I wondered what Eliza had on this island.

"Let's pull it up," I said, grabbing the front of the raft.

The girls jumped off, landing in the water, and got to their assigned lift points on the raft. With Cass on it, it was heavier, but we lifted it all the same. We carried it away from the water and up near the dead trees.

Aubrey lay on the sand, breathing hard and looking at the sky. Sherri bent over next to the raft, trying to catch her breath.

Kara knelt down, feeling the sand with both hands. I waited for her assessment of the island. The island had a smell to it that felt familiar, almost like a nutty smell mixed with a hint of smoke. There was a slight has to it as well, as if the sun was burning off the last remnants of fog.

"Something bad is here," Kara said, looking at me with wide eyes.

CHAPTER 15

Eliza went to the tree nearest us and ran her hand along the bark. A few chunks fell off in her hand. She looked at them, confused. A gust of wind roared, pushing at what few leaves were still clinging onto the dying tree.

"It wasn't this bad when I left," she said. "This nut tree hadn't turned yet."

"What happened?" I asked, projecting my voice loud enough to be heard over the wind.

"I don't know. A few months ago, the island started rumbling, and then there were a few cracks in the ground where steam would rise and then trees and plants started turning brown, dying."

Aubrey got closer to me and said, "This storm is going to be hitting here soon, and we need to get Cass somewhere safe."

The wind kicked up, sandblasting us from the beach. I held my hand close to my face, trying to block the onslaught. Cass still lay on the raft with Kara and Sherri covering her face and body as best they could.

"Do you have a shelter?" I asked, though what we needed was a rescue helicopter and a hospital. None of us were adequately equipped to deal with whatever was wrong with Cass. I didn't want to think of the worst, but I couldn't help it.

"Yes," Eliza said urgently. "It's not far."

"Everyone grab their supplies and follow Eliza," I said, getting next to Cass. "Sherri, you want to help me with Cass?"

In less than a minute, we had our bags and weapons and headed into the dead forest. I held Cass from under her arms while Sherri had her feet. Thankfully, she was lighter than she looked. She weighed maybe a hundred and forty pounds. Each time she breathed, the six-pack on her stomach formed, and I felt her firmness of her muscles in my hands. Another athlete—my guess was a volleyball player or perhaps a swimmer.

Moshe ran around us, darting off into the forest before coming back. She seemed on edge, and maybe it was just the storm, but as I carried Cass, I kept my senses open, feeling for a creature with murderous intent. I felt a few things in the forest, but nothing malevolent.

Eliza walked briskly ahead, sometimes slowing to feel a tree or run her hand over them as she looked at their dead limbs. Each sign of death on the island visibly upset her, and I could only imagine how much each of these trees meant to her.

There were different types of trees along a dirt path covered mostly in brown leaves. Some trees still held what looked like nuts and even one dead fruit tree that had dried remnants of what might have been an orange at one point on the ground.

We neared the rocky hill on the far side of the island, and in front of it stood a shack. Maybe shack was too harsh, but it landed in-between cabin and shack, with the wood structure attached directly to a steep rock wall behind it. It appeared to be mostly constructed with a mixture of branches, woven together tightly and then layered with a thatch. The roof was of similar construction and sloped toward the front door. The front door itself looked like a thinned log, slid behind the rock next to it. I imagined they could slide the wood, and my theory was confirmed when Eliza lifted the door and slid it to the left, with the rock keeping it in place.

A gust of wind ripped through the forest, sending a branch falling within a few feet of Kara. She jumped back from it, and we all looked up. The trees were massive, and the tops of them swayed in the wind, their branches creaking at the strain.

"I wasn't expecting anyone," she said, standing at the door with her long hair whipping in the wind and a hint of color blooming on her cheeks.

"No judgments here," I said, adjusting my grip on Cass. I really wanted to get inside.

Eliza stepped in, hugging her bag to her chest, and I walked in backward, angling Cass's body carefully through the doorway. The wind slowed considerably once inside, and I was impressed at how well the cabin blocked the weather. The ceiling held of another layer of wood on it, almost like paneling, and the walls were of a similar material. It was actually awe-inspiring, and it gave me a good idea of what could be built if proper time and materials were applied.

It appeared to be one room with a bed at the far end, which carried on the built-by-branches look. A chair and a table were built similarly. I hurried Cass over to the bed with Sherri's help, and we lay her down on what looked like cotton. The bed creaked and popped, as if screaming out at the weight being put on it.

Sherri went to Cass's face and brushed back some of her dirty blonde hair from her face.

"Whoa, what's up with the stick people?" Aubrey said.

"Umm, I just…uh…it got lonely here and I…" Eliza said, turning a deep shade of red.

I hadn't noticed, but near the bed, there were a few… sculptures. They were crude representations of the human form, made from bent branches and a batch of what I thought was old pine needles on their heads. The faces were formed like a child might a snowman, with walnuts for eyes, a small chunk of wood for a nose, and a couple of branches, painted a soft red, for the lips. They stood about five feet tall and appeared to have apposable arms with stick fingers. The legs and feet were also bent branches that seemed larger than humanly possible but were able to keep the figures standing on their own. One appeared to be a woman, with longer hair and two coconuts for breasts. The male had short hair but no anatomical features to speak of.

"You made these?" Sherri said, getting closer to the female.

"Uh, yeah, just… you know, passing the time," Eliza said, still red and not looking at any of us. In fact, she kept looking out the door and I suspected she wanted to run out of there.

Eliza moved to the open and I thought she might just run out in the storm but she pulled the door close and the cabin fell silent. There were no windows in the cabin but the walls had enough cracks between the paneling, that light got through, giving us a warm light as if the room was lit by a candle.

"These are amazing," Sherri said. "If you brought these to New York, with your story behind them, you could sell these for a fortune I bet."

"Sell them?" Eliza said, looking confused.

"You know, for money," Sherri said and touched the women's coconuts breast. "This must have taken forever."

"I made them a while ago," Eliza said, glancing at me and then at Sherri. "After my mom left, I really didn't have anyone to talk with, so I created things— friends and objects." She gripped her bag and looked down at it.

"Hey," Aubrey said. "This one time, when I was a kid, I tried to convince everyone that I had a friend named Penelope that only I could see. We'd perform surgery on my stuffed animals with an emergency stuffing replacement procedure. *Penelope, I need cotton, stat.*" Aubrey laughed.

"Really?" Eliza asked, brightening up a bit. "I thought this might be weird or something."

"Oh it's weird, but you're my kind of weird, Eliza," Aubrey said.

"Me too," Sherri said. "I think what you made here is awesome."

"Thanks," Eliza said. "I'm glad you like them. I don't really need them since I have you guys now. You guys are so much better to talk with…. I really can't believe I found you. These days with you have been the best days of my life."

"Me too," Sherri said. "Snakes and sharks and all."

"Yeah, well, being chased by water snakes, twice as long as I am, doesn't quite make it to my top ten of awesome days, but pretty close," Aubrey said with sarcasm.

Thunder boomed outside and rattled the cabin. We all looked at the ceiling as the structure creaked and groaned under the pressure of the outside wind.

"Is it waterproof?" I asked.

"It usually is. It needs patching sometimes," Eliza said.

I kneeled next to Cass and studied her face, looking for any signs that something had hit her. Her face had bits of sand on it, but no bruising or blemishes. I brushed some of the sand off her cheek, making sure nothing got in her eyes. I moved my hands through her thin, light brown hair and made it down to her shoulders, feeling her scalp for any damage. On the back of her head, I felt a lump.

Aubrey, seeing the look on my face, ran her hand next to mine, feeling it as well.

"She took a few good headers while we transported her. Especially when we fell from that cliff," Aubrey said.

"A knock on the head wouldn't do that anyways," Kara said.

"Unless it put her in a coma," Sherri added.

"We need smelling salts," I said. "Kara, you had the first aid kit."

Kara went to her bag and pulled out the small, white bag with a red cross on it and handed it to me.

I opened it the bag, sorting through the supplies until I found the small tube of smelling salts. I brought it over to Cass's face and broke it open. I got a good whiff of the ammonia as I passed it under her nose. It brightened me up, and I took a deep breath, blinking my eyes from the odor.

Cass's hand moved and pushed my hand away. She groaned and rolled to her side.

"Cass!" Aubrey said. "Wake up."

She didn't move.

Sherri shook her, pushing on her shoulder rather hard, but she didn't respond.

"Wake up, sweetie!" Sherri said. "She's not in a coma… people in comas don't move. It's like she's heavily sedated or something."

"Wait," I said, spotting something on her side. "Look at this."

On her side were two red dots about three inches apart. I got close to her body, looking for more, and I found another pair. I rolled her over and looked at her other side and spotted another two. Each set came in a pair and was roughly the same distance apart.

"What are they?" Sherri asked.

"Bites and I bet from those snakes," I said, pointing to one bite. "Look, each one is like the others, coming in a pair."

"Oh my God. You think she's been bitten multiple

times?" Benji asked.

"Constrictors aren't poisonous though," Sherri said.

"We don't know what those snakes were. They weren't like any snake I'd ever seen."

Aubrey sat on the bed, looking at her legs. "She has red indentations on her legs."

They were in a series of lines, across her legs. They were about a half inch wide and wrapped around the outsides of both her legs.

"Constriction marks I bet," I said, feeling them to make sure they weren't hot with fever. They were cool to the touch and I felt the groove bumps in her skin. "They must have dragged her to where she was by her legs."

"How long do you think she's been like this?" Aubrey asked.

"Couldn't have been long," Sherri said. "She would have, you know, soiled herself if it'd been for days."

"Gross, Sherri," Benji said.

"It's true," Sherri said.

"Okay, so do we think she was poisoned?" Aubrey asked, raising a brow.

"Look at her bites," I said, pointing at two of them. "If they were poisonous, like a rattlesnake bite, the skin would be red or even blackened around the bite. But these bites look more or less as if she was poked with a clean needle."

"So why isn't she waking up?" Aubrey asked.

"I don't know what else we have to go off of here but remember that capybara looking thing lying next to her?" I asked.

"No," Aubrey said.

"I remember," Benji said. "That brown, hairy thing about the size of a small dog."

"Yeah," I said.

"Wasn't it dead?" Benji asked.

"That's what I thought at first glance, but then I saw it breathe, and it looked peaceful, like it was resting on the floor with its snake buddies, but when we grabbed Cass and made all kinds of commotion, the thing never moved."

"You think whatever happened to that thing happened to Cass as well?" Sherri asked.

"Yes, and I think the snakes could have been storing her, like a spider does for her young."

"Storing her, for what?" Benji said hesitantly and braced herself.

"Snake babies," Aubrey said. "Maybe when their snake babies are born, they'd eat Cass and whatever else the snakes brought down there for them," Aubrey said. "Or suck their blood like some vampire snakes. Who knows what these islands are capable of holding."

"Snakes don't suck blood," Sherri said.

"And pigs don't swim across oceans, and the bird from *Up* doesn't exist, but they're all here," Aubrey said. "Do you really find vampire snakes such a leap after seeing what we've seen?"

"Okay, you got a point," Sherri conceded.

"So you think the snakes were… storing her?" Kara asked, looking horrified.

"They must have some kind of anesthesia," I said. "She reacted to the smelling salts but never awakened."

"Like Sleeping Beauty," Benji said, placing her hand over her chest. "What's going to wake her up?"

"My guess is time," I said. "From the number of bites on her, I think they've been at this for a while on her. Could be any minute now, or hours, until it wears off."

"So, what are we supposed to do with her?" Sherri asked.

"We wait," I said. "And hope she gets better."

"And if not?" Benji asked.

"Let's not think about that now," I said, and right then, another thunder blast from outside rattled the small building.

"Holy smokes that was close," Benji said, looking at the ceiling.

"I've been in here for many storms. It should hold up fine," Eliza said and then opened the bag she had against her chest.

She reached in and pulled out a chunk of wood that had been smoothed out and almost looked like a statue of Buddha.

"This is Mr. Wood," Eliza said, holding him out. "He's been with me for almost every storm I can remember. He has the power to protect me."

Sherri gasped and held her hand over her mouth. "That is so adorable."

Eliza scowled and stuffed it back in her bag. "It's not adorable. I'm not some kid, you know. I'm a woman, like you, and just because I don't know what you guys are talking about half the time doesn't mean I'm not an adult with adult feelings…and desires." She eyed me.

"Okay," Sherri said, holding up her hands. "I didn't mean it like that. I can't imagine what you've been through, growing up here and then losing your mom.

Raising yourself in a hostile place like this and still turning out to be a whole human? Sweetie, I am in awe of you and your innocence."

"Sorry, Sherri," Eliza said, pulling Mr. Wood back out and then gazing up at me. "And I'm not that innocent."

I glanced to Benji and stowed her urge to talk about Brittney Spears.

"Dude, you're a grown ass woman just like the rest of us. You're nineteen. All kinds of shit you can do back in the States," Aubrey said. "You could buy cigarettes, guns, lotto tickets…hell, you could even buy a hooker outside of Vegas."

"For a hand job?" Eliza asked, looking at her nails. "You guys must get handjobs all the time, because your nails look great. Why would you need to be an adult, though?"

The snickering was surprisingly subdued.

"Just for safety reasons," Aubrey got out.

"Oh," Eliza said, as if that was a perfectly reasonable answer.

Rain started pouring down on the island, and we all looked at the ceiling. It peppered against the ceiling, creating a steady drone of noise. It quickly rushed off the roof and smacked the ground outside. We all stared at the ceiling thinking the same thing. There was no way that ceiling wasn't going to leak but it didn't. After a minute of steady rain and a dry ceiling, I found a new respect for Eliza's craftsmanship. She'd be invaluable for shelter building when we got back home.

Thunder crashed nearby, and the girls jumped in surprise.

Benji had her hand over her chest, looking at the front door as it shook from a gust of wind.

"This is getting worse," Aubrey said.

"It will hold," Eliza said, not looking as confident in that statement as the first time. "And I think I have something for Cass."

Eliza knelt next to Cass and pulled out a round, blue stone from her bag.

"Cass, I know you don't know me, but I hope you can hear me. My name is Eliza Brown. You're in my house right now, and I want to give you something that has helped me get through every sickness I've ever had. Her name is Mrs. Granite. She will help you get better and get back to us. I want to get to know you, Cass, so please, let her guide you back to us."

Eliza slid the stone into Cass's hand and closed her fingers around it. I wasn't sure how, but Cass kept her grip on the rock, maybe even tightening on it.

A flash of light streaked through the cracks in the walls, followed almost immediately by an explosion of thunder. Outside, it sounded like gunfire, and then something crashed into the ceiling.

Dead branches and a good section of a tree smashed through the ceiling and halfway into the house. Kara dropped to the ground just in time to miss getting crushed by it. She scrambled away from it as the wind and rain poured into the house. Sherri and Benji screamed, and Eliza stood there, dumbfounded at what had just crushed part of her house. Moshe hissed and bolted across the room with unbelievable speed, ending up gripping the wall near the ceiling on the opposite side of the room. She hung on the wall like Spiderman and hissed at the wooded intruder.

With the ceiling broken open, the fury of the storm dropped onto us. Wind gusts pushed the rain into the house. It roared with noise, shaking the tree branch near Cass's feet. The storm outside had come in, and Cass was right underneath it all.

CHAPTER 16

"HELP ME WITH THE BED," I said, and pulled Cass away from the opening so the rain would stop hitting her feet.

"Screw you!" Aubrey yelled at the tree that rudely decided we needed a sunroof. "I swear...this freaking-fracking island is trying to make us miserable as it can. If we ever get back to Yang Island, we're never leaving again. I'll live off slugs and sweet water and croc embryos before leaving again!" she screamed, and the storm seemed to respond with another howling gust and thunder that all but drowned out her threats.

We stood on the far side of the cabin and stared at the destruction.

I leaned down, close to Eliza and asked, "Are you okay?"

She looked up at me with tears building in her eyes. This house was more than just four walls and some wicker furniture—it was her home for her entire life. She knew nothing else but this. It had given her comfort and might have been a good reason for keeping her sanity. Now, half of it was destroyed, and it wasn't like we could go to Home Depot for supplies or put on Facebook that she needed a team of volunteers to help rebuild. Fixing this would be a long process, and one she likely would never complete. This was the death of her house, and I saw it all over her face.

Her face crumbled into a cry, and it broke my heart. I pulled her close to me in a hug, and she buried her face in my chest. I felt her body shaking as she sobbed. The other girls were scared and looked from Eliza and me to the opening in the ceiling. I just held onto Eliza and I felt her hand go behind me, and up my back, gripping me tightly.

Moshe finally climbed down from the wall and paced near the rain, as if thinking she might be able to fight the thing that had given it such a fright.

"I should have kept that damn blanket," Aubrey complained. "Stupid Lieutenant Dan."

"Ha," Benji said, pointing at Aubrey. "Forrest Gump."

Aubrey rolled her eyes. "This is going to be like us on the shrimp boat, you know."

"You think?" Benji said, looking excited.

"Who wanted the comfort of some house anyway," Sherri said, looking just as excited as Benji. She skipped below the hole in the ceiling and let the warm rainwater pour over her body. It rained down her face and over her chest. "Now this is a real adventure. Us versus nature." He raised her fists to the open sky.

"You're insane," Aubrey said.

"I'll take this over Yin," Kara said quietly.

"It's only water," Sherri said, jumping in a circle,

hands up and welcoming the rain over her body. Her feet stomped in the growing puddle under her.

Eliza looked out from my chest at Sherri and wiped her nose, laughing while she still held tightly to me.

"You okay?" I asked again.

She looked up at me with red-rimmed eyes. "You guys are my new home. I don't need this place. I need people like Sherri in my life," she said, releasing me, setting her bag on the ground and joining Sherri, splashing in the water puddle and smiling.

Sherri took her hands, and they danced in the rain.

The floor to the cabin had been graded at a slight tilt, and most of the water pouring in from the ceiling ran out of the house. We were getting wet, but at least we weren't going to be swimming anytime soon.

I glanced down at Eliza's bag next to me and spotted more items in it. Different chunks of wood, rocks, and some tied-together stick figures of humans. That was her bag of friends, or *protectors,* as she had called Mr. Wood and Mrs. Granite. Also, Mr. Rope, who had actually saved our lives. I had wondered why she held that bag so close. For her, those items were clearly more valuable than this house. They were her family, and I knew each one had a name and function for her.

While Eliza wasn't on the ship with us, in a way, she was. Rebecca had been the captain, and it didn't take an artist's imagination to see that Eliza was the thing Rebecca had been searching for in the seas. I wondered if Rebecca was out there as well, on some island. Would she be coming here to find Eliza? Or did she suffer a similar fate to Cass and end up being trapped on an island? Or had the islands turned her into something terrible, like the shadowy figure I watched in the forest? I felt that creature though. I didn't feel people, or at least, none of the ones I had encountered so far. There was a puzzle to figure out there, but I had too few pieces, and trying to figure out the picture at this point just hurt my head. Better to watch and enjoy the two nearly naked women dancing in the rain.

Benji moved next to me. "Do you think another tree is going to fall?" Benji asked, looking at the ceiling above us.

"What are the chances of two trees falling on us?" I said, brushing the comment off as I nervously stared at the ceiling.

In truth, in here seemed safer than most anywhere else on an island of trees. At least the roof over our heads would stop most falling objects.

Kara moved up to the other side of me and leaned against me, putting her arms around my waist as we watched Sherri and Eliza dance in the rain. I reached over her and put my arm around her, kissing her head.

"She's a special person, isn't she?" Kara asked.

"They both are," I said.

"Hey, what about me?" Benji said and put her arms around my chest.

I reached over her shoulder and kissed the side of her head.

She looked up at me.

"Sorry," I said, not sure if I had crossed some line with the physical contact of lips on her head.

"It's okay, you can kiss me," Benji said, reaching up and giving me a soft kiss on my lips before returning to holding me with a big smile.

"Oh my God, I'm going to fuck you two if you don't fuck each other soon," Aubrey said and then went to Benji and cuddled up against her.

Moshe paced near my feet, meowing. Then she jumped in one mighty leap to my shoulder and sat there like some kind of pirate's parrot.

"Come on, Moshe," I said. "Get down, girl."

She meowed, licked the side of my head, and jumped back down.

After a little while, Eliza and Sherri came back out of the rain, laughing and soaked from head to toe. They both looked incredible, dripping wet. I admired each of their bodies with Benji and Kara on my arms, but I had been thinking of a difficult question for Eliza.

Eliza caught my stare and tilted her head, watching me.

"What, Jack?" Eliza asked, hands on hips and water dripping from her long hair that reached to her waist.

She was a sexy little thing, and I hoped she didn't hate me after asking this.

I took my arms off Kara and Benji against their protests and stepped toward Eliza. I wasn't sure how to put it without sounding like an asshole, and I just hoped she took it for what it was: something that was going to help the group.

"Eliza, can we strip this cabin for parts?" I asked.

CHAPTER 17

THE STORM TOOK full advantage of the opening in the roof and sent a steady flow of water and wind upon us. This offered us little chance of sleeping or even resting, so we worked through the evening and well into the night.

At the center of Eliza's house sat most of our efforts. Eliza had obliged my request, but I could see on her face the pain as we pulled off a wood panel or dismantled her table.

Eliza had gone back to holding the bag against her chest, as if we might want to take apart Mr. Wood for a new ax head. I didn't like destroying a childhood memory, but I had to think of our shelter back on Yang Island. We could desperately use this kind of stuff, and I didn't think Eliza was going to leave us, so in the end, this was bringing part of her home back to our home. She would always have it with her.

I reminded her of this at some point in the night and she smiled, thinking on it, and then for the rest of the night, enthusiastically helped tear her place apart.

Aubrey called the rain ending about ten minutes before it happened, and we settled into various spots around the cabin to sleep. Kara, Aubrey, and Benji slept next to me, while Moshe curled up at my feet. Sherri slept on the bed with Cass, spooning against her, while Eliza slept on the floor, next to the bed.

I thought I heard some cries in the night, but I was so tired from the day that I quickly fell back asleep if they were real. I dreamed of half men, half snakes chasing me while a fish-man watched the whole thing like a god, laughing at all my efforts. I couldn't remember if I got away or not.

In the morning, the sun rose and the light of what we had done, spread across the cabin. Being the first to get up, I noticed Kara's hand resting on my crotch while Benji lay her face on my shoulder. I eased Kara's hand off me and then tried to not wake Benji, but as I moved, she opened her eyes.

"Sorry," I whispered. "Didn't want to wake you."

She rolled her eyes and sat up. "What, don't want to spend time with me," she whispered, and then looked over to Aubrey behind her, who stirred awake and looked disappointed at what she saw.

"Still here," she said with a sigh. "This place smells like a wet dog."

The tree that had crashed into the house yesterday still dripped onto the floor. The morning sun had heated it up and it steamed, which I suspected added to the smell. That and the mud and wood on the ground.

"We did a number on this place last night," Benji said.

We did, and looking around, I felt bad for what Eliza

was going to wake to. It was one thing seeing it in the dark, and a whole other thing seeing it in brilliant daylight: Every panel missing and stacked on the floor, the table and chair both dismantled for transport. Even the firewood was stacked next to the "go" pile, along with various knives she had made over the years. One thing left untouched was her stick-figure parents with coconuts tits and red painted lipstick. It seemed to be an unspoken agreement that those were going to guard what was left of Eliza's old house.

Living so tightly, it was hard to move without disturbing another person, and a conversation, even in whispers, would be heard. Soon, all the girls were awake, except our sleeping beauty, Cass.

At least she didn't look worse in the morning light. Her tanned skin looked perfect, and once she got going again, I knew she'd be a great addition to our tribe. It also made me think about our shelter and maybe the need for a few different rooms. I tried to map it out in my head, given the placement of the trees, and thought I had a good idea of what we could do. Of course, we had to get back to Yang Island first.

"Good morning," Sherri said with a yawn, then gave Cass a few halfhearted shakes before getting off the bed.

"We should get going," Eliza said. "I bet we could get back home before nightfall." She got up and went to the front door and slid it open. She then went to the pile and picked up a handful of wood.

"What?" Eliza asked.

"Nothing," I said. "You heard her, let's get going."

I grabbed some wood and walked out of the house with it. On the outside, the storm had done a number on the forest, with branches littering the ground and even a few trees toppled over, the most notable of which was resting halfway through the cabin.

The beach had debris washed up on it, driftwood and bits of seaweed. The waves had died down, and I didn't think they'd give us trouble on leaving. Thankfully, the raft looked unharmed. It sat on the sand right where we left it.

Eliza set the wood down next to the raft, and I did the same. Right behind us was everyone but Sherri and Cass, carrying more of the wood.

"We are going to make an awesome shelter with this," Benji said, setting her wood down on top of mine.

"We should get the raft closer to the water before we weigh it down too much," I said.

We all took a corner and carried it to the water's edge, where the waves would wash around it but not take it into the sea.

We dedicated the four corners of the raft for the storage. It would make the raft cramped, but we could keep our assigned stations and hopefully balance the weight. Over the next hour, we gathered the rest of the supplies we'd stripped from the cabin, and then gathered our final and most precious cargo—Cass. I had actually expected her to be awake by now, and her continued unconsciousness was concerning.

We carefully placed her near the center of the raft with her body hugging the mast.

"What are we going to do with her?" Kara asked, shaking her head as she stared at Cass.

"We're going to do what we can for as long as we

can," I said. "Eliza, is there anything else on this island that we can A: fit on this raft and B: could use?"

"There used to be food all over these trees. There might be some deeper into the forest. I also had a few chickens that free-roamed the island. Not sure if they're still alive though."

We were getting low on food, and the idea of something different piqued my interest.

"Benji, can you Sherri and Aubrey tie off the raft and collect any food from the trees, while Eliza, Kara, and I search for the chickens?" I asked.

"Chickens," Benji said, wide eyed in excitement. "Chickens would be amazing out here."

"Yeah, sure, no problem," Sherri said. "You guys smell smoke?"

I took a whiff and did smell it, like burning wood. I took a few steps back and spotted a trail of smoke coming from deeper into the forest.

Leaving the raft, I followed Eliza into the forest where the smoke started to become thicker, not bad enough to choke on but a subtle haze.

"Something is eating this island," Kara said.

"What do you mean?" I asked.

"Even since the time we've landed here, I can feel the change. The good parts of this island are losing a battle against the bad, and it's getting more powerful by the hour. I think it won't be long until this island is a horrible place like Yin Island."

"Well, that's comforting," Eliza said.

"Sorry," Kara said. "What's your intuition telling you?"

Eliza laughed. "It told me to get the hell off this island months ago—a journey that led me to you guys. But I feel as if there's something still on this island for us. But half of me feels like we need to get out of here as soon as we can and leave it alone."

I frowned at the admission. If there were something else on this island, we'd need to find it. It could be another sister or someone else. I still hadn't seen Mario from the ship. He was co-captain and the engineer. I wondered where he was in all of this.

As we traveled deeper into the forest, I saw Kara lagging behind and slowed to let her catch up.

"Something's bad this way," she said.

"Yeah," Eliza said. "I'm getting bad vibes as well."

"Probably just the smoke," I said. "But if there are chickens somewhere on this island, then we've got to risk it. A continuous supply of eggs could change everything."

"Yeah, I guess,' Eliza said. "I hope Henrietta is okay."

"Henrietta, the chicken?" I asked.

"Yeah, she's like Henrietta the Fifth if I get technical."

"What's with that name?" Kara asked. "I mean, is a chicken born with that name or something?"

"I don't know, but she has a couple friends, Poly and Opal. All three should be here somewhere. Oh, and Hank, the rooster."

"Well, we should find them all," I said.

"Not sure how Moshe is going to feel about that," Kara said.

We pushed through the barren forest but didn't spot any chickens. The smoke thickened and I developed a burning sensation in my throat. I had to see what was creating this smoke though.

Then through the smoke, we found it: a tree that had split through the middle and each section lay to the sides of the massive stump at the bottom. In the heart of the tree, hot embers crackled bright red with heat. I might have thought that this tree was a victim of a lightning strike last night, but I had seen this before, and it looked exactly the same. This same tree had been on Yin Island.

The island rumbled with an earthquake and a branch from a tree crashed to the ground behind us.

"This is so bad," Kara said, staring at the tree.

I had the urge to just lay before the tree and give up on everything. The girls could find their way back home. They would get rescued eventually and then none of this would matter. I was probably getting in the way of them getting rescued. They'd be better off without me.

"It just doesn't matter," Eliza said. "I mean, I've never even seen a man naked in my life, and now here comes one, but he's covered in girls that are so beautiful and dynamic. What could I even offer him? I'm like a candle against the sun."

"Exactly, I'm holding everyone back," I said, not really hearing what Eliza had said.

"We need to leave," Kara said, but she wasn't moving, and tears spilled from her eyes. "There's something in the tree." She spoke through gritted teeth.

"Eliza's right. It doesn't matter," I said, looking at the red embers.

"I didn't say that," Eliza said, but I was lost in the tree.

The embers, they didn't look that hot. Maybe I could

touch them. I took a few steps forward, but I felt so tired. Perhaps I could just lay down on them and take a nap. Cass knew what was best, just to sleep through this whole mess. I could just wake up on some Disney Cruise a week from now, and Mickey Mouse could be giving me high fives while I lose at a bacon-eating contest. Of course, is there any real loser in a bacon-eating contest?

"Jack!"

I could hear them chanting my name. This would be better.

"Jack!"

A hand grabbed my arm and swung me around. Another hand swung at me, but I reflexively blocked it.

"Kara?" I said, holding her raised hand in mine. "Did you just try and slap me?"

Tears fell from her eyes, and she grabbed me with both hands, pulling me.

"We need to get away from it," she said, but I looked back, wondering why.

Why do anything? This whole world was lost, and what could I do about it? The watchers were probably the real rulers of this world. They could have it. I would leave them and whatever else was in that cave. I'd leave them alone.

"We need you," Kara said, pulling on me.

Eliza grabbed my other arm, and they both pulled me away from the tree. With each foot, I realized more about why they were taking me. The tree. It was terrible, just as Kara had said.

Glancing back, I spotted the smoldering tree through

the smoky haze and hated it. It made me want to give up, and I would never give up. What the hell had happened?

"I'm okay," I said to Eliza and Kara, but both of them kept pulling me with all their strength. "Hey, it's me, I'm okay. I'm better now, thank you."

They stopped and I pulled my hand free from them.

"What the hell, Jack?" Kara said, crying and hitting my chest with soft punches. "You were saying crazy stuff, and you wouldn't respond to us."

"We need to leave this place. The chickens will just have to find a way," Eliza said.

"Something bad is building here, Jack, and we need to leave before it finds you again," Kara said.

Right then, a chicken clucked and scratched at some nearby leaves in search of food.

"Henrietta!" Eliza said, rushing over to the chicken and picking it up.

With chicken in hand, we rushed back to the raft.

"We need to leave," Kara said.

"What happened?" Sherri asked. "Have you been crying?" Sherri looked to me for answers.

"There's something bad in the forest, just like Yin Island," I said.

"It's eating this island," Kara said.

"Dude," Benji said. "You found a chicken too?"

In Sherri's hands were two chickens.

"Opal and Poly!" Eliza said.

Moshe walked off the raft, growling at the chickens.

"Moshe," Benji said, kneeling down and shaking a finger at the cat. "These are our chicken friends. You are not allowed to eat them, okay?"

"Can we leave, please?" Kara said.

"The rooster?" I said, sensing the forest but coming up with nothing.

"No, Jack," Kara said. "We need to leave now."

"We gathered a bunch of nuts too," Sherri said.

"That's awesome," I said, scanning the forest for the elusive fowl.

I hated leaving a resource behind, but Kara glared at me. If I made a move away from the raft, she might tackle me to the sand. Eliza would probably help. I had to cut bait from this island.

Moshe meowed at me and then stared at the chicken in Eliza's hands.

"Moshe, no," I said, and the cat backed away, averting her eyes from the chicken. I sent a simple thought to Moshe that the chickens weren't food. I wasn't sure if it worked but the sea cat seemed uninterested in the chickens suddenly.

"Chicken cage," Eliza said, stuffing the chicken into Benji's hands.

"What?" I said, but Eliza was already running into the forest.

"I'll be right back."

I quickly inspected the tie-downs the girls had done, and it looked good. They had pulled some of the rope off the raft and then tied it off to the bundles of wood and supplies. The design kept the integrity of the raft, integrating the wood piles into it. Pretty smart, actually.

In less than a minute, Eliza came running back holding a cage made of thin branches in her arms.

"A chicken cage," she said, trying to catch her breath.

Eliza stuffed the three chickens in the cage and tied the cage off at her corner of the raft.

With Cass and chickens on board, we dragged the raft to the water. We struggled to get the raft into buoyancy, but once we did, the girls jumped on board.

Aubrey grabbed my hand, helping me up after I shoved us past the first wave.

"Open the sail," I said, and Benji and Kara raised it up.

The wind took hold of the sail and pushed us past the waves. The larger logs we used on the bottom helped greatly with cutting through the waves and getting out beyond them.

Soon, we were on the open ocean. I glanced back at Eliza's island and saw the plume of smoke rising from it. When Yin Island had that same plume, it drew the attention of the ship and the shadowy figure that ran it.

I reached out into the ocean, feeling for the creatures, and came back with the static of a tame sea. It didn't mean I could relax, but at least there wasn't some ravenous shark or killer whale out there. In fact, the ocean seemed lighter, as if fewer creatures were swimming around down there. Maybe the storm shuffled them around.

"Can we make a stop at that cave island?" Aubrey asked.

"Why?" I asked.

"I've been kicking myself ever since leaving that blanket and shoes. We can't be leaving supplies. This might be our only chance at this."

"I don't think so," I said. I had an urge to visit the island as well, but not for resources.

"Oh, come on. We need a blanket," Aubrey said. "I can

wash it out, and we could even boil it back on our island."

"It's not a bad idea," Sherri said. "Hell, I'd take that jumpsuit as well. We could make all kinds of clothes out of it."

"So now we're grave robbers?" Benji said. "Gross."

"I was actually confused on why we didn't take it," Eliza said. "I mean, it's not like that guy needs them anymore."

"I'm with Jack," Benji said. "I don't want some dead guy's clothes touching my skin." She gave a shake of revulsion.

Aubrey got next to me, touching my hand that held the rudder.

"Plus, I'd like to be under a blanket with you. You get me that blanket, and I'll make it worth it, over and over," Aubrey whispered.

"What do you think, Eliza?" I asked, and I think she really knew I was asking. What was her gut telling her?

She stroked Henrietta through the cage and said, "I don't know. It's just a blank when I think about going there or not. That's strange…for me."

"Well, it's not a bad thing then, and it's on the way. We'll just grab the blanket and shoes, but not the jumpsuit." I glanced at Kara, and on her right arm was lyrics from the song "Jumpsuit." "Some things should be left on that island."

Kara and I had shared in each other on that island, and in that way, I had a great memory of getting to know a fantastic woman a little better, but I did something else on that island that I had an urge to check on—to see if it had even been real.

"Okay," Sherri said with a sigh. "Cass could use a blanket, anyway. Her heads always bouncing around on hardwood."

"Okay, we'll stop by the island and grab the stuff," I said, not liking it, but it was hard to argue the logic.

We could use Danforth's stuff, and he wouldn't miss it. His book and lasting memory sat in my front pocket. Tapping it, I thought about his descent into what seemed like madness. Was this gift a disease? Was it eating away at me? Were these watchers just an early symptom? Danforth said he killed them, but they kept coming back, and in the end, he wrote he knew it all and knew what he had to do.

The dates placed it seventy years ago, but the story felt fresh to what I was experiencing. Plus, we both touched what was deep below in the cave. We shared more things than I wanted to.

As we neared the cave island, I felt a change in the ocean, a silence. I closed my eyes and reached out, but there wasn't anything but Moshe and those chickens. Moshe seemed devious—not a huge surprise, given her interest in the chickens—while the chickens were just a blank page fluttering in the wind.

"I don't like this," Kara said, looking at the cave island.

"Me either," Eliza said, sitting near the chickens and giving Moshe suspicious looks.

Thankfully, the cat seemed to have lost interest in the chickens and lounged near the edge of the raft, licking herself.

"It's just a grab and go," Sherri said. "We buried him

right on the shoreline."

A hundred yards off the shore, I felt them. A watcher, maybe several of them. I paced around the small space I had on the deck and scanned the waters for dark shadows. They were closer to the shoreline, I felt that, but I couldn't see them.

I grabbed the scope and scanned the waters. Nothing.

"What's up?" Sherri asked.

"Nothing," I said.

"Doesn't seem like nothing," Kara said.

"No, I mean that I don't feel the static of the sea. The creatures are gone. The only thing I feel is the watchers."

"What?" Sherri said, looking into the waters below.

"I haven't felt this vacant of an ocean since Tar Island," I said, finally able to place where I'd felt this before.

"Should we still land?" Benji asked.

I shook my head and said, "Yeah, we'll just make it quick. Sherri's right. We can't pass up on stuff like this."

The waves rolled by us, pushing the raft toward the familiar coastline with its too-coarse sand and a cave that shined with the brightness of silence.

The raft slid onto the shore, and we jumped into the water, pulling it just enough onto the sand that it would stick but close enough that it would be easy to push back in.

Lieutenant Danforth had been buried at the back of the beach, right next to the rocky cliff.

With a knife in hand, I jogged toward the spot we buried him and stopped at the hole in the ground.

"Where the body?" Aubrey asked.

"We put it right there," Sherri said, pointing at the hole.

I spun around, looking for the thing that did this, but I felt nothing but the watchers out there in the waves. They were watching me, and seemed nervous. They should be nervous, because I was sick of them spying on us.

"There's footprints!" Kara exclaimed, pointing at a footprint in the sand near the hole.

Benji knelt down and touched the sand.

"You feel anything?" I asked.

"It was compressed not long ago. Maybe a few hours," Benji said.

"How the fricker-fracker could you know that, Benji?" Aubrey asked.

"Me?" Benji said, pointing her finger at Aubrey. "Who knew about the storms and even knew exactly when they were ending last night?"

Aubrey crossed her arms and looked away, lips pursed. "I wanted that blanket."

"Hey guys," Sherri called, walking toward the cave. "I see drag marks here."

Once I saw them, they weren't hard to follow, like two lines in the sand. So Danforth had been taken.

"We shouldn't go that way," Eliza said.

"Is that your intuition talking?" I asked.

She bit her lip and looked at the cave ahead, then shook her head. "No, but that's just it—I don't feel it on this island, Jack. Something is wrong here."

"It could be a hog that dug him up and dragged him back to the cave," Sherri said. "We can't just give up now. I sort of need to know what the hell happened here."

"Everyone, get your weapons, and let's make this

quick."

In a minute, we all grabbed our weapons. We followed the trail over the rocks and indeed, the two drag marks from the grave went right into the cave.

"This feels like the start of some horror movie. Freaking Pennywise could be in there, dancing away, getting us to float or some shit," Benji said, bow in hand.

"It also could have been a person," I said, pointing to the footprints near the drag marks. "In and out, okay?" I said.

It wasn't like we hadn't done a hundred other dangerous things; what was one more?

I entered the cave with a spear in hand, leading the way. I heard a deep bass tone and saw the ceiling vibrate with luminosity as we entered. The drag marks faded away as the sandstone was too hard to leave marks. I walked up the hill, hearing another bass tone, as if some kid in his car was on the street doing a bass test.

"What's that noise?" Benji asked.

"I don't know," I whispered.

I resisted the urge to reach out to feel for what might be making that noise, because deep down, I had an idea that if I did, there would be consequences.

The plateau was just as empty as we left it, and I stared at the doorway. Another boom and the room darkened.

"Something's down there," Eliza whispered.

"Jack," Kara hissed, but I didn't respond.

I walked down the back side of the plateau and went to the doorway. Laying on the floor was Lieutenant Danforth, exactly as I first spotted him. It was as if we had never moved him. Even his shoes were back on his feet.

"What the fuck?" Aubrey said.

Another boom and this time it was clear where it was coming from. The small hallway that had been filled with concrete.

"Who did this?" Kara said. "Because sure as hell wasn't a boar."

"We're not alone here," I said, again resisting the urge to reach for what was below.

"What do you mean?" Benji asked.

I took out Danforth's journal and held it up. "The watchers he mentioned in the book."

"Yeah, the ones he kept killing?" Kara said.

"Shit drove him crazy," Aubrey said.

"Well, I feel them, right now, in those waters out there."

"Shit," Benji said. "We shouldn't have come here."

"This is just part of it," Sherri said, looking at the ceiling. "We came here for a reason."

Another boom, and this time I thought I heard a crack. What was down there?

"Screw this," Aubrey said. "Grab and go, remember?"

Aubrey pulled the shoes off Danforth and then yanked the blanket.

I mentally slipped and reached out to below the cave. The creature was right there, as if our minds were close enough to touch, as if it had been waiting for me and my connection the entire time. It felt ancient and beyond rage, more of a lunacy that didn't have reason or cause. As if something had broken inside it, and it just wanted to destroy.

Our connection scared it, though, and it broke it off, and I felt nothing.

Another boom and another. They kept coming now at a constant pace like a person beating on a drum. The sound of it all sent the cave into complete darkness and the deafening bass drummed through the cave so loudly that I could barely hear the girls screaming.

I dropped my spear and grabbed Benji with one hand and Eliza with my other.

"Everyone grab hands," I said.

That's when I heard another cracking in the rock.

"It's breaking," Benji said, pulling against me. "I can stop it, I think."

"No," I said, yanking her with me. "We need to get out of here."

The sound of running water could be heard between the thumps and cracks. Then I felt the warm water run past my feet, rising up to my ankles and then my calves in a matter of seconds. Whatever had broken, it was filling the room up with water, and quickly.

"Shit," I said. "Run."

I held onto the girls and took big steps through the water as it poured from the doorway. We ran up the bank, getting out of the water and looking down on the doorway as I made sure we all got out. Moshe hissed back at the doorway and shook the water from herself.

The room lit for a brief second, but it was enough to see that the water had reached the top of the doorway and was on its way up the bank. Once it reached the top, it would be a waterfall back down the other side.

We ran down the backside, sliding down the sandy part

and rushing up the other side and out of the cave. The roar of water came out of the cave along with a steady breeze of air as the water pushed it out of the cave.

"What the hell was that?" Eliza asked.

I felt it again. It was angry, trying to get through.

"It's getting loose," I said.

"What?" Kara asked.

"Nothing good," I said.

"We got the blanket and shoes," Aubrey said, holding up her trophies. "Now let's get the hell out of here."

We ran back to the raft with a sense of urgency. I could feel the creature or creatures now—one was squeezing and changing itself. It didn't make much sense, but that's what I felt from it.

In record time, we got the raft back on the water. Benji and Kara went to the sail while Sherri and Aubrey went to paddling.

In less than a minute, we were past the waves and back into the open ocean. I looked back, watching the cave. When I felt a release from a creature, I knew something had gotten through. It wasn't strong, though. It was weakened, almost dead. Just as we started to move too far away from the cave for me to be able to see it, I spotted the water spilling from the mouth of the cave and something came out with it.

In the mix of the water, I saw tentacles, and within moments it was in the ocean. It was hungry and searching for food. One thing I noticed was the absence of the watchers. They were gone.

I just wanted to get home, but then I felt the creature. It was following us.

CHAPTER 18

"WHAT THE HELL HAPPENED BACK THERE?" Aubrey asked.

The girls' attention was on me, and they looked scared. Hell, I was scared too and felt responsible for that thing getting loose. What was it? Maybe an octopus or a squid. I knew from some research that an octopus was one of the smartest creatures in the world and found extraordinary ways to escape enclosures. They could camouflage themselves or spray out ink in the water to disorient a predator.

"I think something got loose from the place," I said. "It had tentacles and came out with the water."

"Yeah, I saw it too," Benji said. "I say we just get home as fast as we can. We have enough to worry about with Cass."

The wind blew against the sail, and the girls paddled in unison, making a steady whoosh sound. I steered the raft, watching the island behind us get smaller.

"It's following us," I said, trying to decipher how far away it was but it was…blurry.

"Mr. Tentacles?" Benji asked, looking back at the waters behind us with the bow in hand.

"Yeah," I said. "It's fading, though. I can barely feel it now."

"Well, fantastic," Aubrey said. "Just what we need, another predator in the waters coming after us."

One thing I didn't feel was the loud static of the ocean. It wasn't silent anymore, but it was just a low hum. The storm must have done a number on the sea.

"Whirlpool," Sherri said as she got up from paddling and pointed ahead. "Move to the right a ways, and we'll miss it."

I couldn't see the maelstrom, but I didn't need to. I trusted Sherri with my life. I turned the raft in the direction Sherri said. In a few minutes, we passed by the swirling water.

After a while, the wind became strong enough to give Aubrey and Sherri a reprieve from rowing. Aubrey went to Cass and knelt next to her face. She touched her cheek with the back of her fingers.

"Cass, can you hear me?" Aubrey lifted Cass's hand. "She's still holding the rock."

"Mrs. Granite," Eliza said, sitting next to her chickens in the pen, probably to make sure Moshe didn't yank one from that cage. The cat had gone back to staring at the chickens.

"Yeah, Mrs. Granite," Aubrey said, and then took Cass's other, free hand and held it in hers. "Cass, if you can hear me, squeeze my hand."

We all watched, and Aubrey's eyes lit up with excitement.

"I can feel it," Aubrey said. "She's squeezing my hand."

"That's good, right?" Benji asked.

"Yeah, it means she still in there, and she can hear us," Sherri said.

"Cass, squeeze my hand once for yes, twice for no," Aubrey asked.

I reached out to the creature that had escaped and felt it no more. I hoped it had found easier prey and got distracted in the ocean. Or better yet, a great white had gobbled it up like a snack.

"I think it's gone," I said.

The raft dipped down into the water on one side and the girls gasped, grappling for a handhold as the raft tilted hard to one side.

I jumped up and stepped toward the front. A tentacle wrapped around the front right balsa wood log. I crouched down as I grabbed for the nearby spear.

"Shit. It's here," I said, pointing at it.

The girls all jumped into action, grabbing their weapons and staying in their positions. I wish I had more time to admire them, but another tentacle went up and slapped the deck. It grabbed one of our bags, ripping it loose from the deck. Aubrey stabbed the tentacle that was the size of my leg and grazed it. Moshe launched for the thing's limb but it snapped back into the ocean like a rubber band, pulling a dry bag in with it.

"That was our first aid bag," Aubrey groaned.

The raft shifted again. This time the rear of raft sunk near Sherri.

"Shit," I said and moved closer to the remaining bags near the center. "Sherri, spear it."

Sherri moved and spotted the tentacles wrapping around the log. She thrust a few times, stabbing creature each time. It uncoiled its grip from the raft and dropped back into the sea. The raft righted itself and slammed back into the water.

The breeze pushed against the sail, giving off a soft rippling sound as it moved over the blanket. None of us moved as we stared at the ocean around us. I reached out, trying to feel it, but as, only found a hint. The thing wasn't pissed off with hot waves of rage. It felt calm, and patient. As if anything we did for the next hundred years wouldn't be inconsequential.

"Is it gone?" Benji asked, an arrow still primed for release in her bow.

"No," I said, moving in a circle around Cass and the remaining bags. "It's going to hit us again. Get ready."

The raft moved along in the water, sending a small wake behind us and to the side. The sunlight sparkled on the surface, dancing with yellows over the dark blue water. The waves splashed softly against the raft, and I listened to the girls breathing as we waited.

The water on my side bubbled, and I spotted the thing in the water, maybe five feet below the surface. It looked like an octopus, but bigger, with long tentacles stretching out from its body. It stared at me with black eyes. It hated me—I felt that, and it wasn't the same thing I felt in the cave. This was something different, but similar, as if it came from the same family.

"It's over here. I have eyes on it." I raised my spear, waiting for the thing to get in range so I could skewer it and hopefully get our bag back.

It moved under the raft and out of my sight. I leaned over, trying to track it, when Eliza screamed. Two tentacles had wrapped around the chicken cage. Moshe jumped and dug its claws into the creature, biting down and drawing blood. The cat was too small to do any real damage, though.

Eliza had her knife out and slashed at it. That's when I heard a splash from the other side of the raft, and a dark purplish creature grabbed ahold of the raft with the rest of its body, pulling itself out of the water and grabbing Sherri with one of the long tentacles. It slung around her calf and pulled her toward the sea. She screamed and dropped her spear in the fall.

I jumped across the raft as an arrow flew by Sherri, hitting the octopus in the body. It looked gelatinous, the arrow seemed to absorb into its body. I wasn't aiming for the body. I was aiming for a limb. I stabbed the spear down as I landed next to Sherri. The spear went through the tentacle and stuck into the bamboo. The creature pulled, but it was stuck to the raft.

It let Sherri go, and she jumped to her feet as another arrow blasted into its body. Then Aubrey hit it with a spear. I felt a fear spike in the creature as its injuries mounted. Sensing its situation, it went into a reckless attack against us. It grabbed a stack of wood, breaking it from its bindings and yanking it into the waters.

It grabbed for another bag, and Sherri, Aubrey, and I

all jumped on the thing's limb, pinning it with our weight to the deck. I had my knife out and sliced at it, cutting through it. It let go of the bag, and another tentacle slapped at Cass's immobile body before grabbing her by the leg and lifting her leg up. I sliced at the thing, cutting through it with a few sawing motions before it yanked it back.

It reached out again, this time grabbing me around my neck. I felt its muscles and cups pressing against my throat as I stabbed at it over and over again.

Another arrow hit it in what I'd call the face. Benji had been busy, because no fewer than a dozen arrows now stuck in the things body, making it look like some nightmarish pin cushion.

"Die!" Benji yelled as she fired another.

She only had two more on her, though.

Sherri pulled at the tentacle squeezing the life from me and then wrestled with it as it flung her into another pile of wood. I stabbed it again and then pulled my knife against it, ripping through it. The thing let go of my neck, and I collapsed to the deck, gasping for breaths. Kara and Aubrey both threw their spears while Benji fired another arrow into the monster.

It let go of the chicken box that Eliza had been fighting it over. A few more of its tentacles flailed in the air, grabbing at stuff unseen. Then it turned from a purple color to a gray color as it stopped moving entirely. Its appendages slid over the deck and toward the ocean. I ran to the edge, looking at it in the water and not feeling a thing from it. It was dead, but I also spotted our bag, curled up in one of its arms.

"Damnit," I said, half considering jumping into the water.

Sherri had a hand on me, holding me back. "Sweetie, no. It's not worth it," she pleaded, but I pushed forward, and Aubrey then had hands on me as well.

"Jack, don't," Aubrey said.

"We beat you!" I screamed, the bloody chef's knife in my hand.

The girls let me go, and Sherri plopped down on a pile of wood, laughing.

"That was some crazy shit, right there," Sherri said, raising both hands and howling at the sky. "I'm so alive!"

"That was some Twenty-Thousand-Leagues-Under-The-Sea kind of shit," Benji said, holding her hand over her chest and leaning forward.

"Everyone okay?" Kara asked.

"I'm going to have bruises," Sherri said, rubbing her leg. "But I'm okay."

"I'm okay," Eliza said, putting some pieces of the chicken cage back together.

Moshe meowed and paced in front of me, staring down into the dark sea. The carcass had fallen into the darkness of the sea. Already, I felt the static of the ocean growing, as if the creatures knew it was dead as well. Good, they can gorge on the monster and erase it from the waters.

It had taken our first aid kit, and our broken flashlight, and the bag that held it all.

"I can see our island," Benji said, a spark of hope in her voice.

I saw our island as well, and it felt like coming home.

Behind us, only a speck of the cave island could be seen. I knew that we hadn't seen the worst of what that island could deal out. All the more reason to build a strong house, so these things could no longer get to us. And all the more urgent to find the rest of the women lost to these islands.

"Guys," Kara said. "Cass is moving."

CHAPTER 19

OUR SLEEPING beauty didn't fully awaken, but the poison had subsided enough that some motor functions were now happening, though without much meaning behind them. Her arms moved, as if reaching for something unseen. Her lips parted in a mumbling of whispers that even when we put our ears close to her mouth, we couldn't decipher.

Eliza steered the boat toward our island as we kneeled next to Cass.

"Get her some water," I said, and Benji handed me one of the water pouches. I tilted it and wet her lips with the liquid. Her arms moved in what looked like a desire to grab the drink. The fist holding Mrs. Granite grazed the pouch.

"Cass," I said, putting the edge the water pouch against her lips. "Here is some water, but drink it slowly."

I eased some of it into her mouth, and she gulped down a few sips before I took it away. I wasn't sure how long she had been without any liquids. If I gave her too much, too fast, it would come right back up, and she'd be worse off than before.

"Island's coming up," Eliza said.

I lay Cass back down and put her head on the blanket pillow we'd made for her from Danforth's blanket.

"Let's drop the sail and row it in," I said.

We rowed the raft onto the beach and then jumped off, pulling the raft high up onto the sand. Benji, Sherri, Aubrey, and I carried Cass to the platform, while Kara set the blanket down for her to lie on. As we set her down, her eyes opened.

"Cass," Benji said, getting close to her face, but Cass seemed to look through her.

The island rumbled more than it ever had before. I had trouble staying on my feet as the island rocked. The trees shook and shallow waters rippled and writhed like bathtub water with a rambunctious child in it.

The girls held onto Cass, making sure she didn't bump her head as the earthquake vibrated the platform.

It stopped after a few seconds and the island seemed to ring, like a bell for a few seconds more and then nothing.

Kara stepped out from the sand she had sunken into and knelt down, touching the island.

"Something is wrong with our island. I feel something building in it and…it's getting worse."

"What do you mean?" I asked.

"I felt something so subtle last time that I wasn't sure if I was mistaken, but this time I feel it clearly, like pressure building," Kara said, getting up and rubbing the sand from her hands.

"Anyone else feeling anything?" I asked, looking around at the girls.

"I do," Eliza said in a shy whisper.

"Well, what is it?" Aubrey asked.

"I'm not going to, but I have an urge to leave this island," Eliza said, hugging her bag of protectors. "I felt it the second I stepped onto the sand. Even before that quake."

"Do you think what happened to Eliza's island is happening here?" I asked.

"I don't know," Kara said.

"Cass," Benji said, touching Cass's face. "She's gone unresponsive again."

"At least we got some water down her," Sherri said and then stepped toward the forest. "Speaking of water, do you guys notice how dry the forest is looking?"

I walked to the forest edge. We were on the narrow section of island the geyser usually didn't reach. But from there, we could easily see where the moisture gradually increased as the plants were larger, greener and always had a wet, slick look to them. Now, the plants that were usually dripping wet were completely dry.

Before we left, the geyser had gone the longest time not erupting since we had arrived on the island. We had joked it was Old Faithful at one point.

"What if the geyser still hasn't erupted?" I asked. "What if that is the pressure Kara is feeling? What if it has something to do with what Eliza is feeling?"

"We should check out the geyser," Sherri suggested.

"I agree," I said.

"I'll stay here with Cass," Aubrey said, brushing back the hair on Cass's face.

"Think my chickens will be okay?" Eliza asked, holding the cage and eyeing Moshe.

"I'll watch them," Aubrey said, extending her hands.

Eliza handed the cage to Aubrey.

"If the chickens give you any trouble, just give 'em a good shakin'. That'll settle 'em down for ya," Benji said with a Midwest twang.

"What?" Aubrey asked.

"Napoleon Dynamite?" Benji said, looking affronted.

"I swear, Benji… I wish you had spent more time watching Survivor or some Bear Grylls show than these other movies. Might be of some use out here then."

"Are you kidding?" Benji said. "There isn't anything more important than keeping up your spirits in a situation like this."

"Amen," Sherri said. "Nearly everything can have a positive."

"Tell that to Cass," Aubrey said. "At least when she wakes, I'll have someone that isn't fucking Marry Poppins out here on my side of things."

"Hey, if she's anything close to as awesome as you are, Aubrey, we'll be damn lucky to have her," I said.

"Ah, shucks, Mr. Sawyer," Aubrey said. "Now go on. Find out what's wrong with the only good island out here."

"Will do," I said and took the rest of the girls into the forest.

It had rained a lot when we were at both the other islands, and it was safe to assume that this island had a similar deluge, but the plants seemed dry, as if they hadn't had water in weeks. I touched a few green leaves and broke them open, searching for the scarce moisture in them. As we got closer to the pond, the dryness lessened, but it still wasn't what we'd typically seen on the island.

Then we saw the pond itself, or what would more accurately be described as a sand bowl. The pond that was once the size of a large swimming pool, filled to the edge with its glorious liquid, was now barren. The waterfall that had continually fed the pond and creek was nothing more than a dark, smooth rock overhanging the pond now. It was as dry as the rest of the rocks around it and the sandy bottom.

"Our water," Benji said. "It's gone."

The very source of nearly all of our water since arriving on Pela. We had some water stored—we could maybe get by for a few days—but this water was everything out here. It's ease of access allowed us to concentrate on other things, like building and rebuilding our camp and raft, and rescue. I had big plans now that we were back home and had some decent materials to work with, and now this. I knew of a few other ways we could look or even make drinkable water, but nothing was as easy as dipping a bag into an ever recirculating pool of water within a minute of camp.

"Hopefully, the geyser has something," I said.

Even a small pool of water would be immensely helpful. We got up to the geyser platform and stared into an empty hole in the ground.

"Well, shit," Kara said. "I loved this water too. It was one of the things that got me through it."

Seeing the emptiness shocked me, even though I

suspected it. I felt the hot rocks under my feet and kneeled down, feeling the hot air coming off the rocks below.

"Still thermal," Sherri said.

"I can feel the heat down there," Benji said, touching the rock under our feet. "Lower, they're much hotter though."

"Is there water there?" I asked.

Benji shook her head. "I don't know, but there is pressure there. I can feel it in my chest, if that makes sense."

"This whole island is pressure building," Kara said, as if she understood exactly what Benji meant.

I used my extra sense and felt below, but it came back as blank as the girls did. There wasn't any kind of animal responsible for this, but on these islands, who knew what was possible.

"What do you think, Sherri?" I asked.

"My guess is something got shook loose down there and blocked this spring up. Now it's boiling and building down there, pushing up at us and causing these quakes. I bet the whole island is heating up. Might explain the plants struggling as well. Their roots might be getting cooked."

"I think you're right, and that means the water isn't gone but trapped down there," I said. "Can you tell what's going on with the water below?"

Sherri shook her head, looking confused. "I'm not sure what you mean."

"You can feel the water, Sherri. Like I can feel the animals, Kara the island, Benji the rocks and Aubrey the air and weather."

"You guys noticed that?" Sherri said, looking shy.

"Hello," Benji said. "Mrs. Whirlpool finder here."

"It's just a little crazy to think it's real though, don't you think?" Sherri asked.

"It was and it is," I said. "These extra senses have saved our lives many times now. From Benji moving rocks and Eliza warning us of a danger, to you helping us avoid the whirlpools."

"The first one almost killed us," Sherri said. "Sorry, I knew something was wrong ahead, but you know, you just tell your gut to shut up and stop being paranoid. Thinking you have some kind of… *power*…is a little more than hard to swallow."

"I didn't want to believe it either, Sherri," Benji said. "But when I saw Jack stuck in that cave, about to be eaten by those birds right in front of me, I knew I would do anything to save him. Including letting go and grasping my power with both hands, even if it felt completely insane. Jack is here because of that."

Sherri looked nervous and got closer to the edge. She closed her eyes and held her hand over the hole. I knew this technique, and I used it often with the animals. It seemed to help when you shut down one sense and allowed the other one to work. I noticed that the more I used this extra sense the stronger it got, and I could feel things further away. Even from up there, I felt the ocean's static…and a watcher.

Damned watchers. I would deal with them later. They didn't seem to be an immediate threat, but I was irritated to know they were still with me.

"I feel it," Sherri said, opening her eyes in excitement. "It's so hot down there that the water is more or less compressed steam. It's trapped, but if something gives, it's going to blow out."

"Like a kernel of popcorn ready to pop," I said, staring at the hole. "Benji, do you feel any weakness down there? Maybe we can release some of the pressure?"

"I don't know. I can feel it out," Benji said. "I'm not really good at this, you know."

"Hey, you were incredible back in that cave. You saved my life down there, and I know you can do this as well," I said.

Benji didn't look that confident, but she took a deep breath and touched the hot rock under our feet.

About a minute passed and then I felt a vibration in the rock and a whistling sound.

"Oh shit," Benji said as her eyes shot open. A strain came across her face.

The ground rumbled, and I heard rocks cracking under us. Benji kept her hand on the rock and had an unblinking stare into the hole.

A gust of steam blew from the hole, missing us by a few feet, but we felt the hot air from it.

"Whoa," I said. "Did you—"

"Run," Benji said and I was about to ask why when she screamed it again. "Run!"

Kara and Eliza took a few steps back.

"We need to go," Eliza said, rushing down the rock. "Now!"

The steam blew from the hole like a train whistle, getting louder with each passing second.

"I'm not leaving you, Benji," I said, trying to block some of the heat from the steam from her.

Kneeling next to her, I saw her face straining in agony. When I used my sense, I felt a strain, if I tried hard enough, but nothing like what she was going through. Had I not been pushing my gift to the limit? Benji's hands were starting to shake, and tears were welling in her eyes.

"I can't move," Benji said, a tear flowed down her face. "I'm holding it back so you can get away."

"I'm not—"

"We're not—" Sherri said, kneeling next to Benji and using her hand to block some of the heat from hitting her face.

"I can't hold it for much longer, Jack, and when I can't, we're all going to die," Benji said.

CHAPTER 20

ONE TIME on my dad's construction site, I had been in charge of helping an excavator dig a deep utility trench for an apartment complex. It was a stupid job that required about as much skill as a stop sign, but at least it was outdoors, and there was a soothing feeling watching heavy machinery digging through dirt.

Now, what I didn't know was that Dig Alert had missed a major eight-inch gas line running right through where we were trenching. This main line had about five hundred pounds of pressure sealed in it. A typical house only had a few pounds of pressure.

The excavator hit the line, tearing through the metal pipe, gouging out several inches from the top. All the pressure escaping through the small hole made it sound as if a 777 jet engine had been dumped in the hole and was blowing out of that trench. Thankfully, the operator wasn't a smoker and nothing immediately exploded. Later I was told if it had, it would have sent me to the moon and leveled a city block.

The sound of that gas escaping that pipe made me run faster than I'd ever had ran in my life. At that moment, I was sure I was going to die.

The steam and water escaping from the hole in the ground sounded much like the gas pipe we hit, and I was beginning to understand that it was just as deadly. The difference was that I had a person that I was not leaving alone to face this. I wasn't running for my life but staying for hers. She needed me, and the very least, I wasn't going to let her die alone. Neither was Sherri and I didn't even try to get her to leave. I saw in her eyes the same thing that I felt.

Kara and Eliza had fled, and I knew they went to warn the others. I hoped they would be safe from this.

"Jack, please," Benji said, shaking from the effort.

Sweat dripped from her face and spit flew from her mouth as she spoke.

I put my hand on her shoulder. Her skin felt hot to the touch, and her face had turned a deep shade of red. I didn't think it was from the heat but rather the strain of whatever she was going through. It didn't escape me that I asked her to do this, and I would do whatever I could to make sure that she wasn't harmed.

"Benji!" I yelled. "We're going to jump for it all at the same time. I need you to keep your mind on whatever it is your holding for as long as you can."

"I can't!" she screamed, and Sherri held onto her other shoulder.

"We'll grab her and run with her, Jack," Sherri said.

Benji was small, but still, she wasn't a stuffed animal.

We'd have trouble moving fast with her, but if Benji could hold on for a few seconds even…

"Straight toward the woods," I yelled over the jet of constant steam, and Sherri nodded. "Benji, we're getting you out of here. Hold on."

The muscles on her neck were bulging out, and her mouth was open as if she was screaming but she nodded. She heard me.

"On three," I said, grabbing Benji under her left leg and Sherri did the same on her right. I placed my hand on her back and got ready to lift and run. I screamed the first number as loud as I could to be heard over Benji's now audible scream and the roar of steam blowing out.

"One, two, three!" I said and lifted Benji.

We couldn't be gentle. This was a matter of life or death, but I still felt bad in handling Benji so rough. Bruises would heal, and I could apologize to a live Benji later on. If we lived through this.

With Sherri's help, Benji felt light and we both had her tight in a near cannonball position as we jumped from the rock. The whole motion took less than a second. We landed partially down the bank and we kept running hard.

"Sorry," I heard from Benji.

That's when I heard the explosion and the ground rumbled. I wasn't sure if a shockwave or the earthquake caused us to fall but we all fell, rolling over the ferns near a tree. I scrambled to my feet, finding Benji and Sherri right next to me.

Glancing back, I only had a second to see what was coming at us. Before, when the geyser had blown, it wasn't anything more than what Old Faithful looked like in

Yellowstone, but this plume of highly pressurized water and steam looked kind of like those Bikini Island videos where they tested nukes in the water. The nukes would cause a column of water a thousand feet across to shoot up into the air.

The exact size and width of the water column weren't as important as the fact that I knew we had no time to move any further from it, and we were most likely going to die like lobsters at a restaurant.

In my last moment, I covered Sherri and Benji with my body in the hope that I could take the hottest water and spare them a grisly death. I was face to face with Sherri. My God, she was so beautiful, and if I had to die, I couldn't have asked for two better women to be on top of when I did.

Sherri wasn't looking at me, though. She had that same strained look Benji had, with her hand out and her face contorting and coloring with effort. Then the water crashed down around us with the force of a wave.

CHAPTER 21

I TENSED, expecting the boiling water to hit me in the back with the forces of a north shore wave. The tension in me built as I closed my eyes tightly. If I pressed them tight enough, I hoped I wouldn't be blinded. Seconds went by, and I heard the water splashing around me and felt some heat, but not much more than a blast from a hairdryer. I dared a peek.

The steaming water poured around us, but didn't touch us. It moved around us as if we were water repellent.

Looking down at my patriotic wonder, and seeing her face in a contortion of pain and panic, I asked, "This is you? You are doing this."

She didn't need to answer, and maybe she couldn't, as she focused on something unseen above me.

Then a rock hit the bush near us, kicking up some sand. I tensed again as more rocks hit the island and spread over against the girls. Sherri might be protecting us from the water but I doubt that protection extended to the falling rocks.

It sounded like a meteor shower hitting the sand and water as the super-heated rocks, spewed from the geyser, landed around the island. I only hoped Sherri could hold on a moment longer and that my body was large enough to block any object landing on us.

Benji hadn't moved or spoken, but I felt her chest moving with breath under me.

We lay there, holding each other for what felt like a long time but it might have only been a minute or two, and when the sounds of rushing steam and falling rocks subsided, I lifted up a few inches, looking around us.

The forest, one used to heated water, hadn't fared well against this next onslaught. The leaves of the nearest trees had been stripped away. The ferns and bushes had been compressed down, as if some giant with wide feet went stomping through. There were a few twigs still sticking up, but most of the wreckage had been carried out to the sea with the heated wave. I glanced up into the sky and there was only a column of steam rising from the geyser hole.

Somehow, we lived through it.

The two girls under me, the marvelous Sherri and the incredible Benji, were alive. I was alive, and I lay back down with them, hugging them tightly and laughing.

They both put weak hands on my back and hugged me.

"Are you two okay?" I asked, searching their bodies. I noticed a few red marks on my arms.

"I need to lie down for about a month," Benji said.

"I'm right there with you," Sherri said, chest heaving with heavy breaths.

"Sorry, guys," Benji said. "When I went feeling down there, I dislodged something, and it was like I popped the champagne cork on that thing, and when I tried shoving it back in the bottle, it sprayed all over all of us."

"Then it burst," I said. "It was my fault. I shouldn't have had you do that. I wasn't thinking of the consequences."

"No, it was my fault. I was trying to show off for you," Benji said.

"You can't impress me any more than you already have," I said, looking into those blue eyes of hers and not the Sponge Bob blues on her tits.

"Hey, I did some shit as well," Sherri said, sucking in quick breaths.

"Yeah," I said. "How did you do that?"

"Well, I couldn't let my friends die, now could I? So the water and I came to an agreement that it wouldn't touch us."

"An agreement?" I asked.

"I can't explain it because I don't understand it, but that's what it was," Sherri said.

"Crap, you think the others are okay?" Benji asked, breathing hard.

I got to my feet as the hot fog spread over the island. I heard the waterfall behind us going again and smiled in relief. One problem solved, but if these islands had proven anything, it was as one problem went down, five more would show up.

I helped Sherri and Benji get to their feet. They both draped their arms around me. What they did was not only the most incredible thing I'd ever seen, but it also wiped them out. They leaned on me on the way back to camp.

We crossed the forest, which had taken the heat blast remarkably well. The fog had thickened, and a few stones the geyser sent out were steaming on the forest floor. Other than that, the leaves were still on the trees and the forest floor still held the wide variety of leafy greens and ferns.

"Oh my God," Kara said, running toward us. "Are you guys okay?" She rushed to Benji, looking over her body.

"Just tired," Benji said. "Jack here saved our lives, again."

"Well, that isn't exactly true. Sherri and Benji are the real heroes," I said.

Aubrey came running to us with a spear in hand, looking scared and angry. When she spotted us, she stopped an expression of relief washing over her face. "You guys made it. The way freaking Eliza was talking… we thought it was all over for you guys. I'm going to kick her ass for scaring me like that."

"Sorry," Eliza said, standing behind Aubrey and looking at us with unblinking wonder. "I didn't expect… what I mean is, I had a bad feeling about this outcome."

"Sweetie, that just shows that even your hooker's intuition isn't infallible," Sherri said. "How's Cass?"

"You guys have got to see this," Kara said.

We followed her back to our camp, and I stopped cold at the sight of the platform we had constructed. A rock had crashed right through the platform. The logs were sticking up and the branches were scattered around it in broken pieces.

Cass, thankfully near the edge of the platform, looked unharmed and asleep.

"We almost lost her," Kara said, holding her hand over mouth as she looked at the wrecked platform.

The black rock sitting at the bottom of the splintered wood steamed as it sat halfway buried in the sand.

"Eliza saved her," Aubrey said. "She pulled Cass over a few seconds before that explosion."

"It just seemed like she'd be better on this side," Eliza said softly as she seemed to take an interest in the sand near her feet.

"You women…" I said, almost getting choked up but and then recovered. "You women are truly the best women I've ever known. You continue to put your lives on the line to save those around you. Eliza, I am sure you knew that there was also a chance you could have been hit by that rock."

"There was a fifty-fifty chance," Eliza said, now taking an interest in her hands, not looking up. "At least, that's what I was feeling at the time."

Aubrey went and put an arm around Eliza, squeezing her small body against hers.

"And to think I didn't like you at first," Aubrey said.

"You didn't like me?" Eliza asked, looking up at Aubrey.

"Oh, that's right, you've never been around other women besides your mom," Aubrey said with wide eyes. "Let's just say that Jack is right. These are some of the finest bitches in the world. Back on the mainland, there are some downright wrecked skank bags that wouldn't offer you anything more than vapid comments and shit-talking. What we have here is special. I'm sorry I didn't think you were going to be part of that at first."

Eliza blinked, and I wasn't sure she understood the brown-haired beauty.

"She means we're chill, and we like you," Benji said.

"And most other bitches out there aren't," Sherri said.

"You poor girl," Kara said. "When we get rescued, your only comparison for men is going to be Jack and us girls. You're going to be in for a huge disappointment in the human race."

Eliza's gaze swept over us and stopped on me. She once again seemed to undress me with those eyes, a look that seemed to amuse Sherri and made Benji look away.

"If you are the only people I find in my life, I will be happy. I can barely keep up with this many," Eliza said, keeping her eyes on me. "I've never experienced the feelings I have. This is all so new to me. It's overwhelming at times, but I can't have wished for anything more in my life than what I have right here and now with you all."

"Ah," Aubrey said, squeezing Eliza again.

"And we're lucky to have you, Eliza," I said.

"You guys really like me?"

"Yeah, I like you, Eliza. I could put on conditions like you are incredible for what you've been through or what an amazing woman you turned out to be, living on an island by yourself, but that's bullshit. We like you for who you are right now, and that's a smart, beautiful soul that cares for the people around her even at the expense of herself," I said.

She looked away, turning a shade of red.

"There's things that you make me feel, Jack, when you talk to me," Eliza said. "I'm not sure if this is normal…but it's nice."

"I have a feeling we need to have another talk, Eliza," Aubrey said.

"What talk?" Eliza asked.

I cleared my throat and noticed Cass looking pale and sweating from her face, with more beads of sweat on her chest. I let go of the girls and walked to Cass, kneeling next to her as Kara did.

"She's not looking good," Kara said.

I touched her head and pulled my hand back.

"She's warm," I said, feeling the sweat on my hand.

"Get her away from that rock," Aubrey said.

"It's not the rock. She has a fever. It might be a reaction to the poison leaving her body. Like a junky going into withdrawals."

"So she can ride it out?" Benji asked.

"Withdrawals can kill you. I think this is the early signs, but we need our first aid kit. It has ibuprofen in it," I said, looking at our raft.

"Fucking tentacle monster took it," Aubrey said, pacing behind us.

"Shit," I said, and felt Cass's hand.

It was just as hot as her head and sweaty. She had to be pushing a temperature of at least 101. She wasn't in any danger at that temperature, but I suspected it was going to get worse before it got better.

"She's going to okay, right?" Kara asked, looking at me with a panic building in her.

"I don't know, but we need to get something soon to get this fever down," I said. "Do you guys know anything… maybe something natural that can take a fever down?"

Kara shook her head and looked to the others.

"I don't know," Aubrey said. "We studied some origins of medicine from plants, but I don't remember them talking about a fever reducer."

"Think guys," I said, trying to remember anything from my life that might help.

Back in the States, something that was so readily available, cheap, and effective, didn't really have much need for a natural remedy. I thought of the various trees and plants used to make recreational drugs, but I came up blank for anything that would help Cass.

A fever that got too hot for too long could do all kinds of bad things to her as her body struggled to survive. If we had a freezer, we could get her in ice, but no such things existed out here, and this island was warmer than most. Especially now, with the warm fog flowing through the island.

I hadn't even thought much about the platform we had to rebuild. The rock had destroyed it, but that seemed unimportant compared to helping this woman laying on what was left of it.

"Holy shit," Sherri said with her hand on her forehead and looking surprised. "My dad told me this on that camping trip. I had this headache, or at least I told him I did, but I mostly just wanted to go home. But he cut the bark off this tree and made me a tea with it. It didn't taste great, but the headache I had, went away."

"What tree?" Aubrey said.

"A willow tree," Sherri said.

Aubrey lit up and said, "There's some willow trees on

Food Island. I remember seeing one near the lagoon. I thought it was so strange that it was there."

"Holy shit," Sherri said again. "You think it'll work?"

"It has to," Aubrey said, glancing at Cass and then to me.

"Okay, then, let's get the raft in the water," I said.

CHAPTER 22

THE HEAT from the latest eruption had sent a fog blanket over the island, so thick that we couldn't see more than twenty feet around us. As we got onto the beach, I could see the fog around the island also rose high into the sky, well beyond the trees, and made the island seem as if it was sitting high up in some cloud.

"We all can't go," I said, as we pushed the raft into the shallow water. "We can't take Cass, and some of us will have to stay here in case boars or something else comes here."

We removed all the wood and aluminum from the craft and kept only a couple day's supply of water. The rest of the supplies would stay on the home island.

"Well, I need to go to make sure you know what tree to even get," Aubrey said.

"Yes, I agree, and Benji, if you're up to it, I could use your bow for those birds," I said.

"You have my bow," Benji said, and bowed.

"You're so fucking weird, Benji," Aubrey said with a smile.

"Weird and proud," Benji said.

"Then the rest of you stay here and see if you keep her cool," I said and then jumped onto the raft. "And if she wakes, see if you can get some water in her. Just keep it slow, not too much too quick."

"Okay," Kara said, not looking that happy about it. "Just keep safe, guys. Keep him safe as well, ladies. Sort of a unique asset out here."

"Oh, I know about his assets," Aubrey said, grabbing my ass and laughing.

"Hey," I said and slapped Aubrey on the ass.

"Oh my God, you just spanked me," Aubrey said.

"Keep acting up and I'll do it again," I said.

"Is that a promise? Kind of hot," Aubrey said.

"Now I want to go," Sherri said, pouting on the shoreline.

"We'll be right back," I said.

"You're lucky I love Cass. Otherwise, I'd be fighting to be on that raft right now," Sherri said.

"I'd kick your ass anyway," Aubrey said playfully.

Sherri pushed at the back of the raft, sending us into the shallow waves.

"Be safe and come back," Sherri said.

We paddled into the tame waves.

Eliza watched us as we left the shoreline and went over the first few waves. She looked concerned, and I wondered if it was her intuition or if she was just concerned for us. She probably felt both. She waved, and I waved back.

After a few minutes, we were on the open ocean.

Leaving the girls back on the island wasn't something that was easy for me, but we had to get used to the idea of splitting up as we found more survivors. Plus, moving Cass around didn't make sense. Still, I didn't like leaving them, and I was already missing them.

"Like old times, eh?" Aubrey said. "Just the three of us."

"Yeah, it was just us three for what, like one hour?" Benji said, reflecting on the brief stint we had as a trio.

In a way, it felt like a homecoming. Benji and Aubrey had approached me on the party cruise with a sultry walk and hunter eyes. They were drunk at the time and probably just wanted a little fun with the deck boy. We had kissed, and I realized that I hadn't really kissed Benji since then. We had shared a peck in Eliza's cabin, but nothing like that first kiss on the deck of the boat. This felt like a grievous error that needed correcting soon.

Aubrey and I had taken things to another level, and then some with Sherri, but Benji had been more reluctant since arriving on these islands. On the ship, I had been attracted to Benji right away, with a strong physical connection. Even in a sea of beauty, she was still one of the most stunning women I'd ever seen. That body of hers. The hair. The comical bathing suit that covered a few things. Yet those few mysteries left made it seem as if she had on a snuggie.

That was then. Now, I had a different attraction to her. She was still all the other things, but those were beneath the person I knew her as now. She was braver than I could ever be. She saw the world in the most beautiful way, with humor and kindness. She recited movies and TV shows that I loved as well. Usually, that'd become annoying after a while, but with her, it just fit her. We shared the same taste in pop culture. I enjoyed and understood most of what she quoted.

Even now, as we make a medicine run across the ocean, she still took my breath away.

She glanced back at me, and I smiled.

"What?" she asked.

"Nothing," I said and looked ahead at Food Island.

"Just keep an eye out for anything with tentacles," Benji said, tapping her temple.

I nodded but I didn't feel anything in the ocean but the static. Not that it was a guarantee. I had missed that tentacle monster. Another could be on us at any second. For now, though, I enjoyed the sweet static. Oh and the watchers. It felt like bitter flakes over ice cream but there they were. I didn't get the sense that they would hurt the girls on the island, but I didn't like it, all the same. Eventually, I'd have to deal with them, whatever they were. That much I knew. That was what Danforth knew as well.

"You feel anything?" Benji asked.

"Nothing dangerous," I said.

"Good," Aubrey said. "That will be a freaking first."

I did wonder where the sharks were. We hadn't seen one since leaving Eliza's island. It was as if something was keeping them back from us. Even the tar remnants on the raft only prevented them from ramming our raft, for the most part. They still swam around us. The other thought was they were scared of something. I wasn't sure how to feel about that. It was one thing to have sharks to deal with, but it was a whole different thing to have what sharks feared in the water. I would keep my mind open and hope nothing from below would come up to get us.

The large raft cut through the water with ease, and the breeze blew across the sail, allowing us to just watch the seas as we traveled. I began to think of the new materials we now had and what would be the best uses for them.

The wood panels would obviously go onto the new shelter we'd be building but I thought about the aluminum panels we'd pulled off the plane. There wasn't enough to sheet a whole roof but perhaps we could use some of them for that, or even to waterproof a wall. One panel would probably be an excellent surface to cook on. I wondered if we could shape one into a pot. That would allow us to make soups and boil water.

"Eliza wants to see you naked," Aubrey said.

I coughed and choked on my spit. "What?"

"We haven't really told her about the details of… you know," Aubrey said and then poked her finger through a hole she made with her other hand.

"Oh my God, Aubrey," Benji said, covering her mouth.

"Oh please, like you don't want to as well," Aubrey said.

Benji glanced at me and then turned away.

"She seems a little naïve about things in that department," I said. "I'm not sure it would be appropriate for me to be the one to show her things."

"What?" Aubrey said, appearing shocked. "She's full woman, trust me. She's also nineteen, like two years younger than you. And she's hot as hell. She's like a small, female Tarzan out here. All feral and shit. You don't like her in that way?"

"It's not that I'm not attracted to her," I said and tried to think about what it was about Eliza that was making me hesitant.

Aubrey was right. She was this hot little thing that truly amazed me becoming the woman she was when she had been by herself for so long. If I had been on these islands alone for that long, I would have swum into the ocean like Danforth in an attempt to escape. In the late of the night, sitting in her cabin, looking at the world she created around herself, I think I felt sorry for her, and I hated that.

The mannequins she made of her parents and all the protective stones and wood she gave names to seemed like a healthy way to deal with the crippling aloneness she must have felt every day. I came up with a theory about how she made it with her mental state still intact, and I thought it was due to her power. She probably knew, deep down, that we'd be here one day, and if she just lived long enough and did the right things to stay alive, she'd find us. It was a little grandiose, thinking me and the girls were her reason to live, but if I looked into that bag, I wouldn't be surprised to find thirteen tokens inside. One for me, and then one for the twelve women that came from that ship.

"She is cute. I want to get my hands on that hair, though. It needs some help," Benji said. "Poor thing. I can't even imagine what she's been through out here, alone. I mean, at thirteen, I was hating on my mom for not letting me get more money on my Xbox account."

"I was doing pageants between track meets," Aubrey said.

"You did pageants?" Benji asked.

"My mom was super pageant freak. She put me in track just so to make sure I had this banging body."

"Sounds like I should thank your mom someday," I said.

"Yeah, well, the pageant thing didn't exactly work out for me when I kneed a judge in the balls for getting handsy," Aubrey said.

"No?" Benji said, looking shocked.

"Yeah, some guy in a Member's Only jacket creeping in the back went to 'help' me with my outfit. His hands went places, and then my hands went places, and then my knee as well. Floored the fucker."

"Good for you." Benji said.

While this happened many years ago, I felt my blood boiling, and my hands closing in fists. I wanted to find this man and hurt him for hurting my girl. I would start with breaking those grabbing hands of his.

"Yeah, well, I got in trouble for that. Bullshit. After that, I wasn't really down for the pageants anymore and dedicated myself a hundred percent to track just so I'd have an excuse to get away from my mom," Aubrey said.

"You've never told me any of this," Benji said.

"I'm sorry that happened to you, Aubrey. If we get rescued, I will hurt the man that hurt you."

"Okay, deal," Aubrey said, shaking her head and smiling. "What are you going to do about Eliza though, for real? Even if we are alone for a few minutes with her, she asks a lot of questions about men and you and what it looks like and why is she feeling this way when she looks at you and on and on."

"You know you don't have to tell me everything," I said. "But Eliza is a special woman, and I will treat her as such."

"Just play doctor with her, Jack," Aubrey said. "Let her see it."

"Jesus, Aubrey," Benji said.

"Bitch, please," Aubrey said. "I'm not sure who's thirstier, you or Eliza."

"I haven't seen this in Eliza," I said. "She seems more confused and excited about everything than wanting to see me naked."

"I'm not sure about that, Jack. I can see her animal side building each day she's around you. She has new feelings, and they are directed at you. If you aren't interested, we'll tie her up at night and make sure she leaves our Jack for us."

"Don't tie her down," I said. "Let's just get to the island and help Cass out, okay?"

"Fine," Aubrey said.

The island wasn't too far off now, and I kept an eye on the sky and the tree canopy. After a few minutes of watching the treetops, I'd only spotted two birds. Before there were hundreds. It'd only been a few days since we were there last. Where had they all gone? There wasn't enough time for their young to hatch and fly away.

The rocks blocking the lagoon in appeared, and I steered the raft to the left of it, on the sandy beach.

"Where'd the birds go?" Benji asked.

The raft slid onto the sand, and with just the three of us, we were only able to pull it slightly out of the water.

"I don't know, but I saw a few up in the trees. So let's move low and fast. Grab and go."

"We should grab some mangos," Benji said.

"A few other things as well," Aubrey said. "We can't waste this chance on collecting food."

"Okay, we'll grab what we can on the way," I said.

We climbed over the rocks, which had blocked our view of the magical lagoon. When we got to the top, I saw the horrifying scene below and then knew what had happened to all the birds.

CHAPTER 23

BELOW US, in the once-pristine lagoon that I had personally considered one of the wonders of the world was now sullied with the dead, floating foul. The vibrant and protective birds were now in varying degrees of decomposition. Some were near featherless, their gray skin showing underneath. Many looked mangled and broken, as if they all went through some churning machine that broke them and spit them out into this lagoon.

"What did this?" Benji asked, covering her nose and mouth.

The smell of them wasn't as strong as I would have thought. Some of the bodies were bloated, while some of the birds looked relatively fresh.

"I don't know," I said, looking into the forest, thinking of the animals that were capable of this.

"Freaking disgusting," Aubrey said, pinching her nose. "That smell, oh my God."

"A pack of tigers?" Benji said, as if throwing out the ridiculous.

"Moshe," I said. "Full-grown versions."

"No way," Benji said. "There is no way she'd be capable of this."

If Moshe were indeed nothing more than a kitten, then at some point she might be the size of a 150-pound mountain lion—more than capable of taking out a bird or two. But this was near-genocidal. It would take a pack of them, working in unison and quickly. That didn't explain why they were here, in this lagoon, though.

Could the watchers have done this? I felt them, not far off the shore. They were nervous about us again, and curious. They were pissed off as well. Complex emotions seemed to be growing every day with them. Whatever it was that I was doing, they didn't seem to like it.

In the forest came a crunching sound, something that wasn't concerned about how much noise it made. It got louder, coming closer. We all watched the forest bushes rustling and listened to the broken branches and leaves getting trampled.

Benji had her bow out and pulled the string back with an arrow. Aubrey got ready with a spear. It moved slowly through the underbrush, and I spotted a dark green shape. We were still on the rocks that flowed out into the sea, protecting the lagoon and also keeping the dead birds in place.

Before, when there was this kind of death ready for the taking, the crocs had descended on our island to take it all. They were ravenous, and I couldn't imagine they wouldn't do the same with these birds unless they were somehow not edible to them.

"Whoa," Aubrey said as the body of another dead bird emerged from the bush.

Its head flopped around on a loose neck and its body was held by large mouth. As the croc emerged from the forest, I recognized the beast and had a sickening thought about what these birds all were.

"That's the croc I was telling you about. The one from the cave I saw a while ago," I said.

"That was in the cave we went into?" Benji asked, lowering her bow and leaning forward in awe of it.

"That is a straight up Jurassic croc," Aubrey said. "Is this like a nuclear waste site or something? Because that doesn't look natural."

The first time I'd seen the beast, it had been partially showing from its cave, but now it was on full display. I was dumbfounded at its size. It had to be thirty feet long. The bird in its mouth looked as small as a turkey. It moseyed along a path down the beach, toward the lagoon.

"We were in the cave with that thing?" Benji asked again.

"Yes," I said, feeling the creature with my extra sense.

It was annoyed and tired but didn't seem to notice or care about us. It felt old, as well, as if it'd been there for as long as the island.

"You think it killed the birds in the cave, when, you know, we drew them all in there?" Benji asked.

"I think most of the birds must have gone into the cave after us. I felt the croc near the entrance, but it was sleeping when we passed by. I suspect the birds made a lot of noise coming in and awakened it. It might have gone right to the entrance and blocked any exit the birds might have made."

"Jesus," Aubrey said. "I mean, the birds would probably try to fight that thing, but it would just kill them one at a time."

"And now it's cleaning its cave out," Benji said.

The croc carried the bird and swam into the water before spitting it out and going back to shore. The new deposit joined the crowded space.

A bird flew above, circled once, and flew back into the forest. If there was ever a showing of pure carnage, this was it. The birds wouldn't likely land down here, and I felt better about getting the bark and even the food now. I think avoiding the massive croc wouldn't be too much of a problem.

We waited until the croc had waddled back into the forest and then we jogged over the chunky rocks and onto the sandy beach. With weapons in hand, we trotted down the beach toward the woods.

"I remember seeing one over here," Aubrey said, referring to the willow tree.

Just a dozen feet in, she spotted the tree and ran up to it.

"Okay, just cut some of the bark off. A few pounds will give us a good supply," Aubrey said.

"Okay," I said and went to slice some of the bark off.

"We'll get some fruit," Aubrey said.

"Mangos. We're getting mangos," Benji said.

"Stay close and keep an eye out for…anything. We don't know if our theory about the croc is right. There could be something else out there."

"We'll be all right," Aubrey said, pushing Benji forward and into the forest.

I mentally reached into the forest for any creatures and felt a few things I was reasonably confident were the last of the birds. Some were scared, but still had a protective feeling, as if they had young in those nests up there. *Good, you guys stay up there, and we'll be down here.* There was another feeling in the forest, but it came and went, as if there was a stealth to it.

The urge to call out to the girls and bring them back was strong, but they were grown and strong women. They could handle trouble if they found it.

I glided the knife around the willow tree, peeling back the bark and stuffing it into my bag. If this would help Cass's fever, I'd be shocked. I was used to popping a pill. God, I hated that stupid octopus for taking our first aid bag. Those were things we weren't going to be able to easily replace, if not impossible. I should have taken those scissors in there and the pills. Instead, we were risking our lives on Food Island. Home of the monster croc, pissed-off giant birds, and now featuring a Lagoon of Death.

The feeling of that stealth popped into my head again. It jerked me back from the tree, and I scanned the forest. The girls were out of sight but I thought I heard Aubrey's voice. I wanted to call out to them, but I sensed that this creature was looking for us and that making noise wasn't the best action.

With a couple pounds of bark in my bag, I grabbed the spear I'd leaned against the tree and headed in the direction the girls went. I found them quickly not two hundred feet from the willow tree.

I breathed out, seeing they were fine. Benji was walking around a mango tree, touching the fruit as a person might at a grocery store. When she found one to her liking, she plucked it from the tree and put it in her bag.

Aubrey stuffed oranges in her bag without much consideration.

I rushed up on them, feeling the creatures in the forest. They were getting closer.

"We need to go," I whispered.

"What?" Benji said, pulling another mango off the tree.

"There's something in the forest. I think it's hunting us," I said.

"Crap," Aubrey said, scanning the nearby forest.

Benji pulled a few more mangos off the tree in a rush.

"Be quiet and follow me," I said.

We weren't more than a few hundred feet from the shoreline and another couple hundred from there to the raft, but I sensed them. Maybe three of them now. They weren't being as stealthy and were moving faster. They were breathing in, trying to get our scent. Good, that probably meant they hadn't spotted us yet.

I jogged through the forest, constantly looking back for the girls and for the predators that seemed to be tracking us now. Then the three stealthy creatures emotions shifted in an instant, and a clarity hit them.

"They've found our scent," I whispered as I cleared a bush.

"What are they?" Aubrey asked, staying close to me.

"I don't know, but they're predators. I don't think we're going to make it to the raft."

They were much closer now, and I felt them more

clearly. They weren't hungry or angry but they were hunting us. They seemed to enjoy rushing after us, as if it was a sport of theirs. They fed off each other's energy and moved faster. My God, they were fast.

I jogged onto the sandy beach of the lagoon and knew we only had seconds before they'd be on us.

"We have to hide," I said, going into the water.

"No freaking way," Aubrey said in an angry whisper.

Benji didn't say a word, just went right into the water with her bag of mangos.

"Shit," Aubrey said, looking back and then getting quietly into the water with us.

I walked as fast as I could, shoving a bird carcass out of the way as I got to waist-deep water. Aubrey and Benji stayed with me, walking through the water right next to me. The smell, when we were up on the rocks, was bad, but down there in the water, the stench was enough to make me gag. Decaying bodies had a specific smell, but water amplified the smell of decomposition and accelerated the deterioration of the body.

The water had a film on the surface, like oil, and the feathers that floated did little to soak up the surface slick. We pushed past more carcasses until we were surrounded by the bloated, dead birds.

"I can't swim," Benji said, gripping my arm tightly.

I took her into my arms and held her right in front of me, her back to my chest. I used one arm to stay floating and kicked my legs hard to keep us both up. I really didn't want to dunk my head into the water around me. The oil on the water slicked up my neck and the birds kept bumping into us.

Aubrey pushed one away, and I saw her hand sink into the bird. She yanked it out, a gelatinous, reddish goo attached. She went pale and threw up onto the water next to her.

She pushed the vomit away from her and looked as if she might throw up again.

My gag reflex kicked in, and I looked away. I felt Benji tensing in my arms as she gagged herself. I glanced at the beach, between two carcasses, and spotted them.

"They're here," I said, and was damned glad we'd hid.

On the shore stepped out three large cats. They were of the same type as Moshe and with similar coloring, but as big as lions. Two hundred pound cats. They had found our scent and went to the edge of the water.

They were repulsed by the smell of decay and backed away from the beach. They made a clicking sound with their mouths and looked at each other. They were smart cats, and I could tell they were thinking about where we might have gone, because the trail had gone cold. From the slick look of their fur, I had no doubt these were water cats, just like Moshe. If they spotted us, they might not decide to wade into the putrid waters, but I wasn't going to bet on it.

Benji tightened up in my arms, and I felt her gagging. If she hurled, it would get on us both, but I wasn't letting her go. Thankfully, she kept it down.

The three cats paced the shoreline then spread out, running up and down the beach. They would pick up our scent and then lose it again. They were having fun trying to find us, and I felt the pleasure of it for them.

"Just leave, fuckers," Aubrey whispered so low I

barely heard her and then she wiped her mouth on her shoulder

My legs were starting to hurt as I kicked hard, trying to keep Benji and me up. I knew one thing for sure: before any shelter was made, or weapons, I was teaching Benji how to swim. I don't care if the geyser blew right on us, we were spending some time back at the pool on our home island. Not knowing how to swim in a world of mostly water was going to get her killed and maybe me, too.

A few more minutes passed, and my energy started to flag.

The bird's bodies thankfully continued to give us good cover. They floated a good foot and half to two feet over the water, blocking those things from being able to see us properly. I used my swimming hand and pushed a bird away from my face.

It's wet feathers peeled off from the bird, and I wiped them off my hand in the water. The simple effort of pushing the bird away almost sent Benji and me under the water.

Benji kicked her legs and paddled her arms. She kept them under water, making for silent movements, but she grabbed and kicked at the water, like she might be doing some strange dance. It helped some, but I was wearing out quick.

The cats made a barking sound and converged right on the spot we left the forest and moved down to the beach. I could feel them thinking—plotting and getting excited as one of them sorted the trail out. The cat at the center looked out into the water, searching for us.

"Don't move," I whispered to Benji.

She went still, and she had been helping a lot more than I imagined. We dipped under the water, and I felt the scum of the surface coat my face like an oil painting. With a burst of frantic kicking, I got us nearly instantly back onto the water, but in the process, I made a splash.

The cats heard it and zeroed their attention to our area of the lagoon.

"Shit," I whispered.

One thing I knew is that these cats were more deadly in the water than on land. I'd seen Moshe firsthand, taking on a whale. If they got through the grossness of the waters, they'd be on us in seconds, and there would be little we could do to defend ourselves from such a predator.

Then a rustling came from the forest, and I felt the presence of our most unlikely savior.

Captain Croc appeared with another bird in its mouth. The cats hissed at it as it entered their space and puffed up their fur. The croc spat out the bird on the beach and rotated its massive body toward them. The cats jumped back from it and kept moving back as the croc lumbered toward them.

The croc knew no fear, while the cats were terrified of the beast, that terror was tinged with a kind of arrogance that might overpower common sense.

Sure enough, one of the cats jumped up, clearing the croc's mouth and landing on its back. It bit at the thick scaly skin, but it might have well been trying to bite into steel. The croc rotated its head back, snapping at the cat.

The more agile cat moved, avoiding the large mouth. The other cats moved around the croc, confidence building at the success of their kin.

"We need to leave now," I said.

It didn't really matter who won this fight—both resulted in trouble for us. Either the cats went into the water to search for us there, or the croc would grab the bird and swim into the lagoon to dispose of the bird. In the process, it might find a more appetizing meal in us. Plus, I didn't have much left in me.

With me still holding Benji around the chest, I swam backward and away from the island. Looking back as I swam, I spotted the lagoon's narrow opening into the ocean. Just fifty birds were between us and it.

The dead birds seemed to gravitate toward us, as if they were performing some sick postmortem joke on the humans trying to get by. Maybe this was their revenge, their haunting on us. I knew if we got through this, I wasn't going to forget this swim anytime soon.

The surface here wasn't just the oily slickness from before but also the occasional string of entrails leading out from a bird, like seaweed might from the ocean floor. I wished I could say it didn't touch me and wrap around my neck, but I'd be lying. I heaved and Benji heaved, but we both kept it down.

I couldn't see the battle on the beach, as the birds were now too thick between them and us, but I saw the ocean and heard the soft waves. I'd never wanted to be out of something more in my life. The clean ocean water looked like heaven, and I swam hard, trying to end this nightmare of grossness.

We got to the edge of the lagoon, and we were able to scramble over the rocks where the water was just a foot deep. I kicked off the rocks, with Benji in my arms, into the clean ocean water. We kept swimming near the outside of the edge of rocks as they rose from the water, and soon we were able to run down the edge of the rocks as they were tall enough to block the cats' view of us.

We got back to the raft, groaning as we struggled to get it back into the waters. Finally, I felt it break free from the sand when a wave washed up against it.

"Now!" I yelled. "Push as hard as you can!" The raft launched into the sea and I jumped on after the girls, using my spear to push us off and away from the island. A hundred feet into the ocean and away from the birds and cats and crocs, I took my first deep breath and ran to the edge of the boat.

At the front of the boat, I lay down and hung over the front. Scooping water, I splashed my face and neck and the rest of my reachable body, trying to get the vomit and residue of death off of me. Then I looked up at Yang Island.

"Oh shit," Aubrey said, seeing it at the same time as I did.

I jumped to my feet, dripping, still not quite clean, but I didn't care about the dead bird on me or the near-death experience we'd just had on the island behind us.

A long, deep blast of the horn confirmed it. Parked right at Yang Island was the big ship, the Veronica.

CHAPTER 24

"GET TO THE PADDLES," I said as I backed up into the mast. I worked my way around it to the back of the raft.

The ship was back, and my girls were in danger. We had to get there as quick as we could, because if it left and took the women I swore to protect, there was virtually nothing I could do to catch it. It had mechanical engines that were of this time, while we were paddles, poles and wind, technology as old as recorded history.

Aubrey and Benji jumped to the sides and paddled. I used the pole and pushed off the back, and we all propelled the raft forward. The wind blew against us, slowing us.

"Did we bring the scope?" I asked.

"No," Benji said. "Are they going to be okay?"

"We'll make sure they are."

The fog still covered the island and even spilled out past the shores and partially around the ship. The cover of fog might help the girls hide but it might have also hindered them from seeing the boat. It hadn't blown its horn until the moment we got onto the raft. Eliza was with them though. She had to have known about this ship, like she did last time, and would have moved the girls to safety.

Cass would make things more difficult, but not impossible with the three of them able to move her. They were strong women, and they could carry her to the falls. They could hide.

The three of us paddled and pushed hard. We got to decent speeds, but it still felt as if we were floating through tar. I needed to get to the shore.

I reached out, but we were too far for me to feel anything on the island. In a few more minutes, we were getting closer to the ship. It seemed massive and was partially covered by the fog of the isle.

I pulled up my pole up and told the girls to stop paddling. The raft moved forward on its own momentum. I slid my pole into the water and pushed us ahead.

"What are we doing?" Aubrey whispered.

Many things were going through my head, and I reached out again, trying to sense the thing from this ship. It wasn't on the ship. I felt its hunger and knew it was on the island. This was the second time this thing had been to our island in a few days. It wasn't going to stop. It knew of us, and even if the girls did hide and evade this thing, it would only be a matter of time until it caught us off guard and took us. I couldn't allow that.

"It's not going to stop," I said. "We're going to have to stop it."

"Hell yeah," Aubrey said, gripping her spear.

"If we can deal with the octopus, we can deal with this… *kidnapper*," Benji said, referring to how the thing took Eliza's mom. Which was a strange thing to think about, as the ship was captained by the very person that kidnapped her. Or at least that was a theory.

We got closer to the Veronica, or what I thought was the Veronica. It was the same type of ship, but the back of the boat that held the name had been burned off and covered in black soot. Much of the ship had been scarred with flames, and it looked much older than Veronica. Rust showed in areas, and the paint had faded to a slim resemblance of the boat I had been a deckhand on. I had spent hundreds of hours on that ship, but sailing up to it on the raft, it seemed massive.

Our raft felt like a log in the ocean compared to this vessel. If it had a captain in the bridge, they could have run us over, and there would be little we could do about it. The steel hull would rip through our lightweight wood and bamboo like nothing. The propellers would chop us up and spit us out the back.

Getting on the boat appeared impossible as well. The walls around the boat were a good ten feet high—too slick to climb and too high to jump. Well, at least for us. Sherri might have had a chance. Fortunately, I knew where the ladder was. We just needed to get around the back side of the ship to get to it.

I scanned the island, looking for the girls or the shadowy figure, but I didn't see any movement in the thick fog. I gasped as I felt the shadow man's mood change to one of excitement, and there could only be one thing that excited it in that way—it had found them.

We could rush the island and fight it on the shores, but I was afraid the thing might slip right past us and get on the ship. Once on the ship, we were done. We weren't going to see the girls again. If we got on the ship, we might be able to intercept any attempts at it taking someone. Hell, for all we knew, all the girls were already on the ship, and it was just collecting more now.

"We're getting on the boat," I said.

"What?" Benji asked. "That's insane. There could be more of them on it."

"It's alone," I said. That much I knew. The boat was empty.

The raft glided up next to the large ship, and I pushed off the ship, making sure we didn't collide. Looking up at the hull, all the way to the railing, I realized that if we could procure this ship, we could sail right off these islands and back to the regular world. With this ship, we'd have a real chance of getting back home.

Moving along the boat blocked our view of the island. I used the pole mostly to push the raft down along it and to the stern while pushing off the metal hull as needed to keep us from colliding. I wasn't worried about damage to the raft, but if we hit the boat, it might sound like a bell going off. The sound could alert the creature to our presence. The best thing we had going at the moment was the element of surprise. I didn't want to give that up.

"There's a ladder on this side," I said, using the pole to push the raft around the hull.

Near the back of the boat, the engine rumbled, and the smell of exhaust blew out from the pipes. It was idling and the propellers weren't moving as the water was still behind the boat. The boat moved slightly up and down with the waves. How it wasn't grounded was a mystery to me.

We were about twenty feet offshore now. As we rounded to the side of the boat facing the island, I spotted the long ramp leading into the water from the deck. The thick fog went past the ramp and all the way to the shore making the island trees hazy at best. The boat and ramp swayed with the ocean waves and the rocking boat. That's when I spotted the shadow in the fog.

It carried a tall, athletic woman on its shoulder, jogging through the sand. I thought it might see us—we weren't well hidden near the back of the boat—but it was focused on its prize: Cass.

"It's got Cass," Aubrey said, and Benji had an arrow pulled back.

"Too risky with it holding Cass," I said, touching Benji's arm. She growled and lowered her bow.

The thing jumped onto the ramp, and in a second, it was up and onto the ship.

"Shit," Aubrey said. "It's got her."

"Not yet it doesn't," I said.

The ramp got yanked onto the boat in two motions, and a few seconds later, I heard a steel door slam shut. I pushed the raft up next to the ladder that was more like recessed rectangles on the side of the hull. I grabbed the first rung and started climbed as I heard the motor revving up. Behind the boat, the propellers cut through the water, kicking up sand and foam while pushing the ship forward.

Benji ran to the front of the raft and jumped, grabbing onto a rung below me. Her feet kicked out, and for one heart-stopping moment, I thought she was going to fall into the water. She held on, though, and pulled herself up against the boat and got her feet on the ladder. She looked up at me with terror as the ship began quickly moving away from the island.

Aubrey stood on the raft, watching our departure. There was no way for her to jump onto the ladder, and we were already too far and going too fast for her to catch us. I watched as the fog thickened around her, and I wanted to yell out to her. I had too many things to say to Aubrey, and I couldn't say any of them. I knew she'd survive on that island. They all would. As she faded into the fog, it felt like a goodbye.

CHAPTER 25

THE WATER RUSHED BELOW. Benji looked up at me, a frightened but determined look in her eyes.

I climbed the ladder and got near the top. I slowly rose up over the edge of the deck to get a look. The deck had been cleared. The bolted-down chairs and boxes were gone. The deck had also peeled up in places and looked dull with age and neglect. The long ramp was the only thing on the deck. The bridge windows were coated with either a white film or blackened with smoke. If anything was up there, I doubted they would be able to see us.

The shadow creature wasn't on deck, though.

I crawled under the railing and slid on my stomach onto the deck. I helped Benji and pulled her onto the deck with me.

"It went inside with her," I whispered.

Benji nodded. We got to our feet and jogged toward the door under the bridge. This was the only door leading into the boat. I stopped at the closed door and noticed a bloody smear near the handle.

"Blood," Benji whispered.

"It's not hers," I said. "It can't be."

Benji had an arrow nocked and ready.

"If I get a clear shot, I'm taking it," Benji said.

"Okay," I said and pulled my knife out.

I'd seen the way the thing cut through birds. It did so with speed and precision. The last thing I wanted was an up-close confrontation with it. Benji's bow would be the ideal way to deal with this thing.

Standing next to the door, I hesitated and looked to Benji. She was taking slow breaths, holding an arrow in the string, ready to pull back and fire.

I turned the handle.

CHAPTER 26

The door creaked, and I winced from the sound. I only opened it far enough to fit through and then slid into the boat. I moved in quick motions with a knife if hand, prepared to stab as needed, but there wasn't anyone or anything there.

The insides were as bare as the outsides, with only one light still working in the lower hall. I searched for the creature and felt it, faintly. I couldn't tell if it was above or below. On the left was a set of stairs leading up to the bridge, but I had a feeling things were deeper in the boat.

The floor was wet, and the steel showing through the paint looked corroded, as if it might not hold our weight. It flaked and cracked as I took a step on it. The steel walls once had white paint over them, but now the steel showed more than the paint. The stairs leading up to the bridge had a handrail that had fallen off in several sections.

"This isn't the Veronica, is it?" Benji whispered.

"No, I don't think it is," I said. "Or something drastic has happened to it."

"Up or down?" Benji asked, seeing me look from one staircase to the other.

To the right of us was a staircase leading down into the boat. It curved and had walls on either side, blocking us from seeing more than ten feet down into it. I noticed a few drops of blood heading that way.

"Down," I said and walked to the staircase, holding out my knife, which seemed to be sadly lacking in the weapons department, given what we were facing.

I wanted a damned machine gun down there. Plus, a hottie in a Sponge Bob bikini and a dude in shorts and a white button-up shirt didn't elicit a response of fear from anyone.

The steps were steel, and the white paint had worn down through the middle of the steps. I took one step at a time, thinking this shadow thing might come around the corner at any second.

Fortunately, I knew this ship well and pressed on, around the corner and down into the next floor. A few lights were on, but it was still dark and wet. The ship must be littered with holes, and the ocean spray from above leaked down into these lower floors. Rebecca would have never stood for such a lack of maintenance. A boat wouldn't last long with this kind of deterioration, and I was surprised to hear the hum of the motor below. If they couldn't bother with leaks and paint, I doubted they maintained the engine either.

The area ahead looked as bare as the rest of the boat. This area had been mainly the living quarters, storage, and kitchen. There used to be a table in the far back. Mario, Chef Frank, and I would play cards on that table and eat sandwiches. Now the area looked as bare as the rest of the boat.

I walked around the corner of the stairs and down to the hall with the living quarters. If I turned again, the stairs continued down to the next floor, leading into the engine room, fuel tanks, and more storage. On the Veronica, this floor mostly acted as a storage floor. I often wondered why she held so many supplies, but now it made sense—she was preparing for her and her daughter. Probably bringing every possible supply to help them live on these islands if they couldn't get back out. This was sheer speculation, as I was never allowed to look into the storage bins.

A light in the hall crackled and then went out, further darkening it. I stepped into the hall, walking on my tiptoes, trying to make as little noise as possible. I sensed the creature somewhere on the ship, but I still couldn't pinpoint it. Maybe the steel was messing with my ability, bouncing it around like an echo. I wished I could feel Cass, but she was blank to me, just like the rest of the women.

Benji had her bow raised and ready as she stepped off the last step next to me. If I had been properly trained in an assault on a ship, I might have known what to do, or how to clear a room properly, but I was a deckhand and former construction worker. Most of my knowledge came from fictional sources starring Tom Cruise or Dwayne Johnson. I neither had the looks or the Hollywood luck to pull off such personas, so I stepped forward, hoping the monster didn't jump out and get me.

We neared the first door. Fear bubbled against my throat, and I found it hard to breathe. The soft drone of the motors became the only sound around me. Each step I took, I labored to make as quiet as I could. I anticipated the monster would be in this room. I moved to the open door, but the room was as empty as the rest of the boat. This room would have had a bed and personal effects. The single light showed the peeling paint and rotten floors. I suppose the creature could be hiding behind the door, but it didn't strike me as the hiding type. If we ran into it, it would be a fight for our lives.

On the opposite side of the hall was a mirror image of the empty room, with varying degrees of white paint showing. We moved down the hall that opened up into a larger storage area. Here there were a few steel boxes that I thought were bolted straight down to the boat. Typically they held things the coast guard required, like extra lifeboats, life jackets, flares, and such. I didn't know about all the regulations, but I remembered the coast guard doing a few checks on the boat, to the great annoyance of Captain Rebecca.

Beyond that was the kitchen and a small dining room. What I was interested in, though, was the boxes. The floor leading up to one of the boxes showed wear, as if there was a path to it. The lid looked worn from use as well.

I approached the box with Benji behind me, looking out for any surprise attacks. I pulled the metal latch up, unlocking the lid, and then pulled the lid up to its locking position over me. Inside the box were smaller boxes that looked like they were carved from single blocks of wood. They had symbols on them, like hieroglyphics, but I wasn't sure. They could have been drawings of a satanic cult, for all I knew. Ancient languages and cultism weren't part of my skill set. I took one box out.

"What is it?" Benji asked, looking at the box in my hands.

"It's heavy," I said, hefting the box in my hands.

Much more substantial than the wood would be alone. There was something in the box, like a lead brick. I found the edge of the lid; the seam was almost invisible. I wedged my fingernail in the slit and pried the top open.

Inside the box was a black, shiny stone, shaped like a teardrop and about the size of half my thumb. It sat in a bed of red cloth. I reached in for the stone, and Benji grabbed my hand, stopping me.

"Don't touch it," she said, staring at the stone. "Set it down."

I complied and set the box on top of the pile of other boxes. Benji, visibly shaking, moved her hand over the open box and the stone and then closed her eyes.

She jerked her hand back as if she had been burned or bitten, and her eyes went wide from terror. Her lips thinned as she bit them, and her face turned red, eyes brimming with tears ready to drop. She wanted to scream, and it was taking everything in her to stop that reaction. I took her hands, but she seemed unharmed. Confused, I stared at her, hoping for more information.

"Close it," she said in a low, screechy voice. "Hurry."

I shut the lid over the box and then closed the compartment as silently as I could.

I hadn't felt anything from the stone, but Benji was connected to the earth in ways I wasn't. Her ability let her see into rocks and stones. Whatever she felt from that stone had sent her to the edge of a panic attack. Her face went from red to pale, and she leaned forward, with hands on knees, breathing hard, as if she'd been holding her breath the whole time.

"You okay?" I asked, touching her shoulder.

She jerked away from me and straightened back up, looking terrified and pointing at the box.

"We have to destroy them," she said. "All of them."

CHAPTER 27

I HAD an urge to open the box back up to see what I missed.

"What's in the box?" I whispered and retook her hand. This time, she let me hold it as tears welled in her eyes.

"Seven," she said.

"What?"

She shook her head, dismissing the comment. "Remember the tree on Yin Island, the smoldering tree?" Benji asked.

"Yeah, the same tree was on Eliza's island as well," I said.

Both islands shared a tree that had been split down the middle and burning as if by a lightning strike. They burned from the inside out. Red embers filled the insides of both trees and sent a trail of smoke rising into the sky. They also both changed the way I felt about things. As if they were the greatest downers around. Around those trees, I wanted to give up and just lay in a hole. I felt worthless and powerless. When I opened the box, I didn't feel any of that. It just looked like a smooth black stone. The kind you might find at some rock store in northern Arizona.

"On Yin's tree, I felt it, and you did too, but I was too scared of it to really feel it, if you know what I mean. But on this stone, I hadn't felt anything until I reached out to it and went into it."

"What was inside?" I asked.

"Hell," Benji said. "It's rotten, and is pure evil, but dormant like a seed or a..." She tapped my hand holding hers as if coming to a great realization. "Like the rock at the end of the Time Bandits, the one the parents touched and disintegrated."

"*'Don't touch it, it's evil,'*" I said, quoting the movie.

"Can you be any more perfect?" Benji said, staring at me with those big blues. "I think if we went to the smoldering trees and cut through them, we'd eventually find one of those stones in it." She pointed to the box in disgust.

"You think shadow man is planting these stones on these islands?" I asked.

"Look at what it has here," Benji said, still pointing to the steel box. "It's using them to spread its evil onto the islands. I bet Kara's island, Yin, had been taken out by one of these, and then Eliza's island was next. Jack, I believe there is one on Yang as well. Remember the plants and the earthquakes? Our island is changing."

"How can a little stone do any of that?" I asked.

She pulled her hand back from mine and covered her forehead. Some of the color had returned to her face as she glanced at the other boxes.

"It's concentrated wrongness, Jack. It doesn't take

much. Like a drop of poison that kills an elephant," Benji said. "We need to destroy them."

"Let's check the other compartments as well," I said.

A protest built on her face, but she didn't say anything as I went to the compartment less traveled and opened it. To my surprise, it held a folded up, inflatable life raft and some life jackets. The red ditch bag wasn't there, as it had been on the Veronica, but these supplies were definitely something we could use. Hell, I wanted this whole damn ship.

"Okay, we'll destroy them," I said. "But first, we need to find Cass."

We left the box of evil and headed for the kitchen area. Visions of Frank working in the kitchen came back to me, but what I really wanted was some pots and pans. Good God, it would be amazing to have some cooking supplies. Of course, it held nothing. Drawers and cupboards were empty, and even the stove was gone. The kitchen seemed better off than the rest of the boat. It had a dry floor. The white paint still covered most of the walls and cabinets. Even the stainless steel counters were gleaming clean.

"We should check the engine room," I said.

Leaving the middle floor, we descended to the engine room. At the bottom of the stairs was a steel door with a window in it. I looked into the adjacent room through the window and didn't see Cass or much of anything besides the motors and pipes running everywhere.

I opened the door, and the noise of the engines flooded us. I quickly went inside the room with Benji and pulled the door closed. If the shadow had been listening, it might have noticed the spike of the engine drone. I waited, feeling for it, but I didn't sense any urgent change in it.

The engine room smelled of burning oil and hot metal. The constant drone of the motors made it near impossible to speak to each other, and it was hot, really hot, probably pushing a hundred degrees. I'd been down in the engine room a few times with Mario to make some simple repairs. Once a fuel line had cracked, spilling diesel over the floor. I spotted the same black hose running along the wall toward the motors leading directly from the fuel tanks. The only difference seemed to be these small black boxes over the fuel line.

I walked through the engine room, crouching down under the beams and low ceilings until I was sure there wasn't anyone down there. The last thing in the world I'd want was to leave the ship with Cass, only to learn later that Kara, Sherri, or Eliza had been hidden on the ship somewhere.

We moved back to the engine room door. In one quick motion, I flung the door open and jumped into the stairwell with Benji, shutting it just as quickly behind us.

"I hated that room," Benji said, wiping some the sweat from her brow.

Her whole body glistened with sweat.

"There's one place left," I said. "The bridge."

That wasn't entirely true. There were many rooms around the ship for more storage and other utility rooms for waste and water, but they were too small for two people to be in, and I doubted the shadow monster would stuff Cass in a wastewater room.

We walked up the stairs with more speed than coming

down, and Benji practically pushed me past the middle floor. She kept looking back, as if one of the stones were going to jump from their boxes and launch at her.

Back where we started, I stared at the stairs leading up to the bridge. Blood smeared across part of the handrail. It had to be up there; I felt it. It was hungry but satisfied, as if it was watching its meal being cooked. This was a disturbing thought and made the urgency of ending this all the more significant.

One thing I thought we still had was the element of surprise. What we were going to do with that, I wasn't sure yet. Eliza could probably tell us what she felt we should do at this point, but we didn't have her. I had to trust my own hooker's intuition.

I stepped onto the first tread of the staircase leading up to the bridge's door. Benji had her bow in hands, an arrow at the ready. She took slow breaths and stared at the door. I saw her in this zone mode before. She was a state champion archer, and there wasn't a single person I'd rather have on my side at that moment.

We climbed the stairs, reaching the metal door leading into the bridge. It didn't have a window on it, so we'd be going in blind. Taking a deep breath, I gazed at Benji. She had an unblinking stare at the door.

"I'll open," I whispered near her ear. "You shoot."

She gave me the slightest nod as she kept her focus on the door.

There would be no countdown and no second chances. I turned the handle and flung the door open.

Before the door stopped moving, Benji let go of the string. I watched the arrow launched from a bow she made from bamboo and string. She was already reaching from the second arrow as I moved crouched down, into the bridge.

The shadow figure stood behind the helm controls and didn't look back as the arrow struck it in the center of its back. I heard the second arrow fly over my head, and as the figure dressed in black spun around to confront us, the second arrow hit it in the chest. It fell to the floor with a knife in hand. A bare human hand. This wasn't some monster, it was a person wrapped in black fabric.

"Cass!" Benji cried.

The volleyball player lay on the floor in front of the shadow man. The shadow crawled to her, putting the knife against her neck.

"Hurt her and the next one goes through your eye," I said.

"Jack?" the shadow said, and then pulled down some of the black fabric, exposing his face.

"Mario?" I asked, leaning forward.

"You know him?" Benji asked.

"He was on the ship with us, Benji. He stays below deck, so you wouldn't have seen him."

It really was him—Mario from the Veronica, the engineer and back-up captain of the ship. He was the shadow man?

"You shot me," Mario said, pulling the arrow from his chest while keeping the knife on Cass's neck.

"What are you doing?" I said. "Let her go."

"I can't do that. I need her," Mario said, and I realized I could feel him.

He was the shadowy figure and all the hunger I felt

was in him. He wanted to kill us and eat us, but not our flesh. He wanted something else from us. He desperately needed Cass and even us.

"Let her go, or we will be forced to stop you," I said.

He showed his teeth and looked demonic. "I want to die," Mario said. "Kill me. I don't care."

"We don't want to kill you," I said. "Get back from her, and we can help you. We have first aid, and with this ship, we can all get out of here."

Well, we had some bark in a bag back on the island. A sea monster took our first aid kit.

"Good luck with that," Mario said and tried to pull the arrow from his back but couldn't reach it. "She's almost ripe," Mario said, rubbing his knife blade across Cass's face. "You've got a ways to go, Jack—you were always a good, sweet boy—but it won't take long to ripen you as well. Her though"—he spit on the floor while keeping his brown eyes on Benji—"she's so sweet it makes my teeth hurt. But she will ripen as well. They all do in the end. The king is coming for them all."

"What are you talking about, Mario?" I asked.

"You'll learn soon enough," Mario said with a laugh. "I'll show you what was given to me down below. A present wrapped up just for you."

"We've seen your sick rock collection," Benji said with an arrow pulled back.

Mario didn't like this revelation, and his face contorted with anger. I felt it like a hot wave radiating out from him. Why could I feel his emotions and not the ladies?

"You have gifts as well, don't you?" Mario asked. "I

woke on this boat and knew I had a job to do. The king commanded it."

"The king?" I asked.

"Oh yes, the great king. He's the one that gave me my gift," Mario said, looking up.

"What's your gift?" I asked.

"Being an asshole," Benji answered for him.

Mario laughed and hearing that laugh I knew, disturbed me. "I'm the reaper. The collector. I work for him, getting him what we need and preparing for him. These islands will soon be ripe, as well, and then he can come here."

"Mario, please, just get back from Cass, and we can figure this out," I said, sliding my knife into its sheath.

Mario coughed into his hand. Blood stained his palm and ran down his chin. He showed us his palm and gave us a bloody smile.

"I was promised immortality," Mario said, looking at his hand and then to me.

For the first time, I felt the sourness of fear from him. He was confused and conflicted.

"Jack," Mario said and coughed again, producing more blood from his mouth. "There will be another. If you want to live—if you want them all to live—then you need to find the king before he finds you. Only his fingers tips reach this far out but soon he will close his fist on this part of the sea." He took his knife off Cass's throat and leaned back to the helm, where he stumbled forward, slammed his hand on a button, and fell to the floor. "Now get the fuck off my ship."

"Is this the Veronica?" I asked. "Where's Rebecca?"

"This is not the Veronica. Rebecca has that." He laughed and coughed, then spit blood on the floor.

"Where is she?" I asked, taking a step toward the dying man.

"She's be in his grasp, same as you," Mario said, spitting out blood as he did.

Benji slowly stepped toward Cass while keeping an arrow pointed at Mario.

"What do you mean?" I asked. "How do we get out of here?"

He laughed again, and it sounded wet. He coughed again and whispered. "You can't leave. I've tried so many times, only to end where I started. He promised me…" Mario fell to the floor, and the emotions emanating from him ceased.

"He's dead," I said.

"Should I pop him one more time to be sure?" Benji said, her hands shaking and welled-up tears in her eyes.

"No, let's get Cass out of here—"

A rumble came from below the ship and the hum of the motor slowed to a stop.

Benji lowered her bow and looked at the floor. "What was that?"

"Nothing good," I said, running to Cass.

Mario lay near her, and I got an up-close look at the man. A man. His eyes were still open and looking at something over my shoulder. He resembled Mario, but he also looked as if he had taken on a transformation. The skin around his eyes was dark and seemed to hang from his bones. Mario had to be in his mid-twenties, but he looked as if he could have been in his late thirties now.

There were creases at the corners of his eyes and stubble that looked as if it had a hint of gray in it. His blood pooled up below him, slowly moving toward Cass.

I slid my hands under Cass and lifted her up. I put her over my shoulder, feeling her limp body flopping around on me. I gave her one adjustment and went to the bridge door. Benji was there, pushing it open for me.

She stared at Mario.

"He would have killed us," I said. "He would have killed Cass, and the rest of us, in time."

"I know," she said breathlessly.

Benji had killed the man, and I wished I would have been the one to do it. I should have been the one to hold that burden.

I carried Cass down the stairs, and that's when I smelled smoke, like burned plastic and rubber. There was smoke in the air around the lower staircase. I went to the deck door and opened it. I set Cass down on the deck and went back in.

"The engine room's burning up, I bet," I said. "He pressed a button right before he died."

"You think he set off something?" Benji said.

"I think he sabotaged this boat," I said, and now wished that we had killed him quicker. This boat would change everything in our situation. We could have stocked it to the brim and then set sail for back home. We could have lived in this boat. We could have done a million things with it, and Mario was trying to take this away from us.

"Stay with Cass," I said and ran downstairs.

The thicker smoke below made it harder to breathe,

and I pulled my shirt over my mouth. The smoke wasn't coming from the middle floor, it was coming up from the engine room. Back on the Veronica, there was a fire extinguisher right next to each staircase, but here there was only a hook on the wall that once held it.

This ship was too important. I had to risk it. I ran down the next flight of stairs to the engine room door. The window was filled with yellow flames, and the fire had burned the rubber seal around the door. Noxious fumes escaped the engine room from around the door. I held up my hands, trying to block the intense heat from my face as I stepped back up the stairs. The ship couldn't recover from this fire, and I had no way to stop it.

"Son of a bitch," I said, pissed off.

I started coughing as the smoke went deeper into my lungs. My shirt filter wasn't working for shit, so I decided on speed and ran to the box in storage. I opened the box and grabbed one wooden box from the lot and then closed the door, securing the latch. Then I went to the next box and pulled out the inflatable life raft and three life vests.

The smoke had thickened in the room, and my lungs burned with the acrid smoke. With goods in hand, I ran to the stairs and up them, carrying the heavy inflatable.

Benji was at the door and rushed to me, helping me with the raft. Getting out of the door, I took a deep breath of the fresher air and then bent over in a coughing fit, dropping the items onto the deck.

"What the hell, Jack. You got one of the boxes?"

"We should have it to study it. It might help us find the one on the island," I said, coughing several times.

"Or it could become the one on our island, Jack. These

things are evil and transformative. It could be manipulating you right now into thinking it has value."

I glanced back at the door we came from. Smoke poured out from the opening now and rose from the various vents above, creating a plume of smoke over the boat.

"It's important, Benji, that we understand something about what is going on here. Each time we learn something, we learn we know nothing. This stone could start our understanding of what's going on here and maybe help us get out of here."

"All we need is each other, Jack. I already understand that stone. It's meant for nothing but pain and destruction."

"Mario said it was preparing this place for the arrival of something," I said.

"Mario had gone insane. I didn't need an extra sense to see that in him. He was delusional. The king was something he manifested in his own mind."

"These stones aren't delusional," I said. "How could he have made these?"

"It could have been his gift. Do you really think all these gifts we're getting don't have a dark side? Maybe a very dark side."

Benji picked up the box and threw it into the boat. It disappeared in the thick smoke but I heard it clatter across the floor and down the stairs.

"You didn't have to do that," I said.

"Jack, that was the box we opened. It was already getting to you."

Cass groaned and rolled to her side.

"Cass," Benji yelled, getting close to her and touching her face. "Her fever is worse and she's shaking."

"We got to get off this boat."

I looked out into the ocean around us. I quickly saw where we were, near Tar Island. This was great.

"You're right. I shouldn't have grabbed that box, but I need to go back in. Get the raft inflated and be ready to jump ship."

I didn't wait for her response or protests—just ran back into the ship.

CHAPTER 28

In a couple minutes, I returned out of the ship, coughing madly as I breathed in the clean air. The raft was quickly inflating and spreading out over the deck next to Cass and Benji.

"It's done," I said, pointing toward Tar Island.

Benji looked behind her at the island that seemed as nasty as any of them. Maybe the worst.

"You're ramming this ship into that island," Benji said, an incredulous look taking over her lovely features.

"Yeah, the fire should burn it out, but after the fire, this could be a gold mine of material for us out here."

"Jack, I don't want anything from this ship and neither should you. This ship should sink to the deepest part of the ocean and rust away there."

"It's too late, the course is set, and it's time for us to get off this thing," I said and could tell Benji didn't like what I'd done.

That was okay, when we had steel and other items scavenged from the wreckage, she'd forgive me.

With the raft fully inflated, I took a second to study it. It was shaped like a donut, with a teepee-like tent up the middle. It had an inflated floor across the middle and probably could hold ten people. The red color made it easier to spot from the sky, and it had reflective tape around the borders for the night. I unzipped the door and peeked inside. It had a soft bottom and was otherwise waterproof inside. This was a damn good grab.

Getting a life jacket on Cass, we carried her and put her in the raft. Then we brought the raft to the lowest part of the boat, about ten feet above the water.

"We can hold onto the top and lower her into the water," I said and glanced at the island we were sailing toward with gusto. We weren't more than a quarter-mile away now. We might have a couple of minutes before this boat slammed into that tar pit.

I broke the rusted railing and slid the raft to the edge. We grabbed the top of the raft, which was probably six feet high, slowly slid it off the ship. We lowered it, getting all the way down on our stomachs, but it wasn't enough for the raft to touch the water.

"Drop it," I said and we both let go.

The raft hit the water with a thud, and Benji and I got into our lifejackets and jumped. I impacted the water right next to Benji and plunged under the water only a few inches before the buoyant life vest pulled me back onto the surface.

I grabbed Benji, pushing her over the edge of the donut-shaped raft. She grabbed the ropes around the raft, and I pushed on the bottom of her foot, getting her into the open door. Then I grabbed the lines, and Benji's hand reached out, grabbing my wrist. She pulled me in as I climbed, and my momentum pulled us both into the raft. I landed on top of her, soaking wet but smiling.

She shook her head, smiling as well.

We did it. We got off that ship and got rid of the shadow figure. The ship!

I got off Benji and stood at the door. Benji got up next to me, and we had a view of the ship that seemed just like the Veronica but different in every way but the shape. The ship's fire had breached the deck and the middle floor. Flames poured out from the now-broken bridge windows. Mario's body was in there.

Then the ship hit the ground. The front of it rose up and then it listed to the right side. The smoke began to cover the vessel, obscuring a clear view of it.

"Good riddance," Benji said. "Those stones will hopefully burn up or fall into the tar."

"Yeah, good riddance," I said, but really, I wished we had that ship intact. No damn shark or whale would stand a chance against us in that.

Black smoke started coming up from the ship now, rising high into the sky.

"At least Aubrey's got her smoke signal now. Anything in few hundred miles will probably be able to see that," Benji said and then hugged my side, putting her face against my wet chest.

"You okay?" I asked, touching her wet hair.

"I will be," she said, and then let go of me. "Found a couple paddles inside."

She went inside and pulled out two telescoping paddles. I took one in my hand, feeling how light it was.

Modern machining in all its splendor, with a mix of plastic molds and aluminum. This was a significant order of magnitude better than what we currently had.

We unzipped more of the tent around the raft and went to each side of the raft, and then we paddled. I felt for the creatures in the ocean, but as when we left cave island, they were gone. I felt a few hints of things here and there, but something had spooked the sea again. Maybe it was the ship and the fire.

This inflatable raft would be no match for a shark. We needed to get back to our island as quick as possible.

With our island in sight, we paddled hard. I needed to see the women's faces. I had to know they were all okay. I paddled harder.

As we neared the island, I felt a familiar creature. The watchers—several of them, near the island. I sucked in a breath, angry at their presence. I want to scream at them, asking them what they wanted and if they would just leave.

They were curious as ever, with an underlining emotion of concern and anger. It was almost as if we did something wrong or something they didn't like. A complex emotion, and I was starting to wonder what they really were. Danforth had killed them, seemingly in great numbers, but he never really described what they were or why he killed them.

He said they kept him from leaving, and he wouldn't be free until he killed them all.

I checked my shorts pocket, feeling for the stone I took and realized it was gone. I searched my other pockets, and even my underwear, but the stone wasn't there. It must have slipped out when I jumped off the boat. It was probably at the bottom of the ocean. Perhaps Benji was right, nothing could be gleaned from the stone. It was what it was, evil.

"I see Eliza and Aubrey," Benji said, beaming with a smile as we neared the shore.

THE FOG still covered the island in a thick blanket, making it difficult to see much past the sandy beach. I spotted our bamboo raft and a few shadowy figures behind Aubrey and Eliza.

We paddled hard, both wanting to get home and hopefully get some medicine into Cass. I looked back at Cass in the life raft. She hadn't moved while we'd been in the raft, and looked pale and sweaty.

At the shoreline now stood Eliza, Aubrey, Sherri, and Kara. They were all there and looking well. I felt a great weight being lifted off my chest. We all made it. We were all alive.

They were jumping up and down, hugging each other as they waved and yelled to us. We got to the small waves and felt them rolling under the raft, pushing us the last bit onto the beach. We kept paddling, and I couldn't stop smiling. We'd made it; we'd *all* made it.

The life raft skidded up onto the sand, and the girls pulled us further onto dry land. I jumped out with Benji, and together with the girls we pulled it all the way out and onto the dry sand. This raft weighed nothing compared to the one we built.

The women surrounded Benji and I, hugging us and peppering us with questions. I didn't say much, waiting for the hubbub to lessen.

"We found out who the shadowy man was," I said, and they all quieted down. "It was Mario, from the Veronica. I knew him. We worked together, but he wasn't the same man anymore. He went on about some crazy mission from the great king to kidnap people and destroy the islands for him."

"He was insane," Benji said, Sherri's arm wrapped around her, still hugging her friend.

"Unbelievable," Aubrey said. "If that was Mario, then who the hell took your mom?" She looked at Eliza.

"I don't know," Eliza said. "Maybe Mario killed the person that took my mom and assumed the role. It doesn't matter, because he's dead. He can't haunt us anymore. He can't take any of you away from me."

"Oh, and we beached the ship onto Tar Island, where it's completely in flames."

"I thought we saw smoke," Kara said, looking back at the sky.

Even through the fog, a trail of black smoke could be seen. It had risen high up into the sky, where it started to flatten out and get carried away in some high current. That trail of smoke might reach far enough for someone to see it. They could follow it right back here.

"I want to hear every detail about this," Kara said, looking fierce. "You scared the crap out of us."

"Sorry," I said. "Why don't we take care of Cass first? You still have the bark, I hope?" I asked, looking to Aubrey.

"Better than that. I've been steeping it since I got here. It should be ready by now."

"Great, let's get Cass to the platform," I said.

"What's left of it," Aubrey said.

We gathered Cass and commented about how hot she felt. She groaned and moved slightly as we carried her to the platform, settling her as best we could on the small remaining section. She opened her eyes and locked in on me for the first time. I froze, looking at her pretty, light brown eyes.

She hit me in the face. Not that hard, but the surprise of the attack was worse than the hit itself. I stumbled back as she swung at me again, and the startled girls leaped into action, grabbing her arms.

"Cass!" Sherri said.

"It's us," Benji added.

"Yeah, don't be hitting our man. He's Jack from…the deckhand, from the boat," Aubrey said.

Cass grumbled a few incoherent words and closed her eyes.

"Cass," Sherri said, shaking her friend back awake.

"Where am I?" Cass asked, looking at the trees above us.

It was the first intelligible thing I'd heard from Cass, but her voice sounded weak and dry. Aubrey rushed to a bag of water near the fire and brought it over, shaking the contents as she did. She handed the bag to Sherri who brought it to Cass's lips. Cass grabbed for the bag but Sherri pushed her hands away.

"Easy," Sherri said. "Let me help you."

"It won't taste good, but you need to drink it, Cass," Aubrey said.

With Sherri's help, Cass drank some of the water from the bag. Sherri pulled it away, making sure she didn't take too much too quickly, and then gave her a bit more.

"That should be enough," Aubrey said.

Cass lay back down, and her body relaxed against the platform as she slipped back into sleep.

"Let her sleep," Sherri said. "We'll keep a watch on her, but it's mostly out of our hands now."

"You okay, Jack?" Benji asked, putting a hand on my back.

"Yeah," I said, probing my cheek. "Is she normally aggressive?" I thought of what Mario had said about her being near ripe.

"She's a bit rough on the edges, but a kind person," Benji said. "I think."

Aubrey laughed. "Rough around the edges. If that bitch hits our man again, I'm throwing hands, coma or not."

"Chill out, Aubrey," Sherri said, touching the side of Cass's face. "She's been through a lot. Who knows what's going on in that pretty head of hers?"

"Great, now that that's all taken care of, you can tell us what happened on that ship," Kara said.

"And *you* can tell us what happened on the island?" Benji said.

We sat together near the platform, and I told them what happened with as much detail as I could remember. Benji would add things, especially when it came to the evil *Time Bandit* rocks, as she called them. Kara seemed very interested in the stones and the connection to them and the island she landed on. Beyond that, they didn't have many questions, but comforted Benji as her voice cracked when she told them about shooting Mario.

"So you think this island has one of those stones on it?" Kara asked, putting the pieces together.

"I didn't say that," I said.

"I am," Benji said. "There's one on this island, and I'm pretty sure he planted one on Eliza's island as well."

"How? If he wasn't here then?" Kara asked.

"I don't know. We arrived at this island at different times," Benji said. "Maybe Mario got here at a very different time."

"You think he—or it—sabotaged my island?" Eliza said.

"It seems a strong possibility," I said. "Benji felt the stone in the boat, and it had the same horrible feeling that the tree had."

"He's destroying the islands," Kara said, tapping her chin. "Turning them into something awful."

"In preparation for something, for his king," Benji said. "See, I told you. Insane."

"Yeah, but where do these stones come from? You said he had a bunch of them," Eliza asked.

"I don't know," Benji said.

"How about we stop talking about this depressing shit, and we can tell you about our heroics when we faced this insane man?" Sherri said.

"Please, I'd love to hear it," I said.

The girls told us their encounter with the ship and the shadow, mostly told by Sherri with Kara and Eliza adding stuff in. They actually fought him off, stabbing him with a spear, and then in the melee, he got to Cass, flinging her over his shoulder and running back to the ship. That was when I had arrived.

"Is everyone okay?" I asked.

"Yeah, some bruises and such, but nothing serious," Sherri said. "I tell you what though, fighting for my life with these women was amazing. These islands keep giving us the craziest lives, and my whole body tingles just thinking about some of the things we've seen and done."

"You're probably thinking of the things Jack's done to you," Aubrey said with a scoff.

"You're not wrong," Sherri said, putting a hand on her chest and rolling her eyes back in pleasure.

"What's Jack done to you?" Eliza asked, looking from me to Sherri.

"You know what," Aubrey said, getting off the platform and putting an arm around Eliza. "I think it's time for that detailed talk I've been threatening you with."

"What?" Eliza asked, walking with Aubrey. "There's more?"

"Maybe we should start with what hand jobs really are," Aubrey said.

Eliza nodded her head, looking at her nails.

"Wish I'd had an Aubrey to tell me how it was, back in the day," Sherri said.

The cool ocean breeze blew through our camp, our home, and carried away some of the warm fog with it. It gave us a bit more time to see the two young women walking into the forest. My parents had never sat me down and explained the way things worked between men and women. The school system had tried, but there was a lot of giggling and jokes. I think it would have been cool, though, to go on for as long as Eliza had without the physical knowledge of boys and girls, and then to have a friend like Aubrey explain things to you. My generation was thrown into the internet fire, eyes burning.

"I threw up when I saw it on the internet for the first time," Benji said. "I was like, twelve, and thought that I would never want anything like that happening to me."

"I had an older boyfriend in high school," Sherri said.

"I dated this guy in a band," Kara said, rolling her eyes. "Don't ever do that."

I didn't like hearing that there were other men in their past, but I had other women in mine. Now, we had each other.

"What are we going to do now, Jack?" Kara asked, moving up against me and putting her arms around my waist.

"We've been here for what, a week now?" I said. "I think it's time we start preparing for a long-term stay here. We still haven't seen a plane in the sky or a boat on the waters beside Mario's since we've been here. I think this place is some undiscovered, lost archipelago. We may have to rescue ourselves off these islands, and that could take a long time."

"Too bad we couldn't have pirated that ship," Kara said.

"I tried," I said.

"We have more materials than ever and tools," Sherri

said. "We can kick the shit out of building a new shelter here. That last one is too small, anyway."

"Yes, a new shelter, and I think we can make the raft bigger with a massive sail from the Danforth's parachute. We can also have walls around it as well, for more protection."

"We're out of water purification tablets," Benji said. "I think I can make a simple sand filter with a couple of bags. We can use some charcoal as filters, too."

"Yeah," I said. "Water is the most important thing, and if we're going to be here for a while, it's best to find a long-term solution to safe drinking water."

"I can build a kiln," Kara exclaimed, as if coming to a great realization. "The aluminum! I can bend it and puncture holes into it for more air. I bet I could get it hot enough to fire clay bowls and plates."

"That would be amazing," Sherri said.

"You said you saw clay near the pond, right?" I asked, looking at Benji.

"Yeah, at least I think it is," Benji said, looking into the forest. "Jack, maybe you can come with me, see what you think it is?"

"Sure," I agreed and then looked to Kara and Sherri. "Start breaking down the existing platform, keeping the broken pieces as well, and start piling them up here. When we get back, we can start laying out the new shelter. Something higher up that can withstand a big cat attack."

"Aubrey told us about what happened on Food Island," Kara said, looking grossed out. "The pond is full of warm water. You two should get cleaned off. Aubrey already did."

"Yeah, I'd scrub everywhere if I was in that filth you described," Sherri said, shuddering.

"Not a bad idea," I said and sniffed my shirt. It mostly smelled like smoke, but under that, there was a hint of a dead-bird-decaying-in-the-ocean.

"Oh God, I bet it's in my hair and everything," Benji said, bringing her hair over her shoulder and looking at it with a disgusted expression.

CHAPTER 30

WE DID INDEED FIND some clay near the stream from the spring. It would take some work to get it out, and Benji talked about purifying it, but the important thing was that it was possible. The idea of being able to make stuff from the clay drove my imagination wild. We could have some real storage options, and actually eat off something that wasn't a rock or a leaf. I couldn't believe the simple things from civilization that you missed, like having something to hold food with.

"The water's warm," Benji said, standing on the edge of the pond and putting in her toes.

She probably needed a proper cleaning as much as myself. Well, maybe more, with all that hair. My God, she was stunning. She pulled her wavy blonde hair over her shoulder and onto her tan chest. The bikini was starting to show some wear. I really wanted to find them some clothes to wear, beyond the swimsuit edition. As much as I enjoyed seeing their nearly naked bodies regularly, there was a practical side to having more clothes. If we were staying here for a while, then I had to think of winter. Even a mild one might affect a person wearing less than a square foot of fabric over their body.

Another task, I supposed.

Getting clothes seemed like a near impossibility, so I didn't dwell on the how and where we'd accomplish this task. A stable shelter would provide some protection. Then I thought of an indoor fireplace. The clay could be fashioned into blocks or bricks, and we could build a brick fireplace with a flue.

I started to picture the way I wanted our home to look like and imagined a large shelter, maybe with a few rooms. Big enough for every girl on that ship.

That was one thing that Mario mentioned—that we better find the girls before he did. I took a deep breath and knew that we'd still be searching for the rest of the women out there. They could be at the bottom of a cave, with a pit of snakes, waiting for someone to help them.

"You have your thinking face on," Benji said. "Why don't you enjoy this water and stop thinking about stuff for a minute?"

She was right, as usual. I had this insanely beautiful woman right in front of me, standing at the edge of a tropical steam bath, surrounded by lush greenery and topped off with an amazing natural waterfall that cascaded over a large rock and into the pool. That was all thanks to Benji, who removed the "cork." We would have been in real trouble if we hadn't gotten the water supply back up and going. Once we had clay pots and a good way to filter the water, we could store a week's worth of water.

"You're thinking again," Benji said, dipping lower into the water.

I had a gorgeous woman wanting my attention, and I was thinking of shelter and fireplaces. Sometimes I felt dumb.

"Sorry, got a lot to think about," I said, and swished my foot in the water. "It is warm, almost hot."

It was warm as a hot tub, and while the fog over the island had lessened, the pond steamed.

Benji stepped deeper into the water, laughing as she got below her waist and finally dipped in almost to her shoulders. She leaned back and got the back of her head into the water, running her fingers through her hair. I wasn't immune to the pleasures of seeing such a beautiful body. When she arched her back, her neck and breasts were accentuated. Another moment where Benji took my breath away.

When she came back up, her usually big hair was tight against her head, and the warm water dripped over her face.

I jumped into the water with a cannonball.

It was even warmer than I thought, and deep. I hit the sandy bottom with my feet and jumped back to the surface.

"It's so hot," I said, wiggling around and hoping my body would get used to the heat quickly.

"You're such a baby," Benji said. "This feels nice, and I think I needed something hot to get this feeling off my body."

Getting used to the hot water, I unbuttoned my shirt and let it float in the water. Hopefully, the hot water would clean it as well.

"Why don't you come over to me," I said, wading in the deeper water.

Benji was about ten feet away. She eyed me, perhaps questioning the intentions of my invitation.

"I want to teach you to swim," I said. "I'm not even sure how you've never learned."

"I hate big bodies of water. When I was little, I was at my cousin's house, and I thought I was all hot shit and could swim. Well, it turns out, I *couldn't* swim, and the first thing I remembered was my Aunty Mary giving me mouth to mouth and me puking up water."

"Wow, that's awful," I said. "So after that, you just never went back into the water."

"No, I did. I just didn't swim. It's amazing what you can fake. I don't think anyone really knew I couldn't swim."

"Until you fell off the ship," I said.

"Yeah, then you saved me."

"Well, why don't you try to swim to me right now?"

"I don't know," Benji said. "I think I've been through enough today."

"There is no time like right-now time," I said. "Now get your sexy ass over here."

"Oh, forceful are we?"

"When I have to be," I said. "I won't be able to live with myself if you drown out there."

Benji didn't answer but looked to the shore.

"Benji, come to me," I said.

"I'm not a dog," she snapped.

"I know."

"Fine," she said with a drawn-out breath. "But just make sure I don't drown."

She pushed off the bottom and flailed in the water, splashing, and kicking. For a second, I thought she might recover and start at least treading water, and then her head started dipping under. I rushed to her, grabbing her and lifting her up so her head was out of the water. Her hands slapped at me until she found something to grip, the back of my neck, and she pulled tight against me. Then she wiped the water from her face and looked scared.

"I got ya," I said.

"Don't let go," she said as I swam us to deeper waters.

"You know, you've been the water several times now. This shouldn't be nearly this scary for you," I said.

"Those times when I went into the ocean, I just knew you were there, and it wasn't scary, because I knew you had me. In here though, I feel like I'm on a test I know I'll fail." She laughed. "You must think I'm such an idiot."

"Of course not. Sometimes I think you don't know how amazing you actually are."

She turned back to face me, and her expression went from jovial to serious. She held me in her gaze.

"I like you, Jack." Her face turned a light shade of red but she kept her gaze on me. "I mean, like, I *really* like you. You always make me feel good about myself."

"I like you too, Benji," I said. "Now, I'm going to turn you around."

She gripped me tighter.

"I won't let go," I said. "I just want you to try and stay up by cupping your hands and pushing the water down like this." I demonstrated a basic paddle.

I turned her around so that her back was facing me, holding onto her waist with one hand and keeping us afloat with my feet and my free hand.

"Paddle," I said.

She moved her arms, and at first, they were spastic, but after she knew I was going to let go, I could feel her relaxing. Her movements were slower but effective, scooping the water and pushing herself up with each stroke. I felt her getting lighter in my arm, so I loosened my grip off her, just a few inches.

"There you go," I said. "You're swimming."

"Don't let go," she said in a panicky voice.

"I already have. You're doing it on your own."

She spun around, screaming in fear and grabbed me in a panic.

"I'm so stupid," she said, laughing into my ear as she hung onto me.

"Stop it," I said. "Now that you have an idea of how to stay up and floating, let me show you how to swim on your back."

I moved her around as I went to the shallow waters where I could stand on the sandy floor. Reaching under her, near her butt, I lifted her up like a newlywed over a threshold. She laughed nervously as her face neared the water. She was feather light in the water, and I held her there, letting her float at the surface to get her comfortable with the position.

"Okay, now you kick with your legs and reach back, and push through the water," I said. "See, you're doing amazing!"

"Oh yeah," she said, reaching back and touching the back of my neck.

She pulled herself closer to me, rolling over in my arms and bringing her other arm over my shoulder. Her gaze went to my lips, and she leaned in to kiss me. I bent over, holding this magnificent woman in my arms, and kissed her. She caressed my face and kept kissing me. I got lost in a live fantasy all of my own. I opened my eyes, just to make sure this was really happening.

I felt her tongue slide across my lips, and then she pulled back with a sweet smile and a small laugh.

"We should get cleaned up," Benji said. "My hair is still gross and stuff."

I held onto her. I was pretty sure she had spoken words, but her kiss had sapped me. I stood frozen with her, wanting more of what she was giving. I sucked my lip, tasting the saliva she left there.

"You okay, Jack?" Benji said.

"What?"

"Can you put me down?"

"Oh, yeah, sure," I said and set her down where I knew she could stand on the sand.

"Sorry, I just feel dirty and need to clean myself," Benji said and dipped her hair in the water. "I would kill for some nice bath soap. Something with a bakery scent, like mango cupcake or red velvet."

I watched her, and I was pretty sure she knew I was watching, as she moved up and down in the water, fanning out her long hair around her like some halo while keeping her wet chest above the water. She straightened up and brought her hair into a ball and wrung it out. The water dripped down her chest.

I swam over to her, putting my hands around her waist and kissed between her chest, sucking the water off her. I wanted to taste every inch of her.

She laughed and pushed me back.

"Oh, I know of something," she said, climbing up the beach and getting out of the pond.

She pulled some leaves off of a nearby bush and then grabbed some sand off the beach.

"What is it?" I asked her absently while I watched her reenter the water.

"Soap bush," Benji said with a big smile. "Plus the sand over there is like powder, like real cosmetic grade shit. Here, turn around. I'll do you first."

I turned around and felt her hands on my back. Her touch gave me chills, and I savored this slow build with her. With Kara, it had been a rush—a fantastic rush that I loved—but it was also nice to just play. I wasn't sure how far Benji would want to take it, but I was thrilled to play ball with any of the bases involved.

She rubbed my back and neck, and I felt the lather of the soap bush and the granular texture of the sand. After my shoulders, she pulled at my hair and I leaned back, putting my hair into the water. Her fingers moved through my scalp, and she stood over me, looking down at me with that pretty face. Her hair cascaded over me and she bent down, kissing me once again as she held me in the warm water. Her hands went to my chest and stomach, washing, rubbing and exfoliating me.

"Let's get you into the shallows," Benji said.

I moved with her as she stayed behind me, as I had with her earlier. She moved lower, sliding her hands down my stomach and then into my shorts. She touched me, and I was at full strength down there. Her hands rubbed me, feeling me everywhere. She kept moving down my legs and even ducked under the water to reach my feet.

She popped up next to me with a big smile. I floated in the water as if I was floating in the sky. I was high on her. She could be my addiction. I wanted her in every way, but she was so resistant to my advances earlier that I didn't want to push it along. This was going to go at Benji's pace and at Benji's distance.

"Now it's your turn," I said and grabbed some of the leaves she left at the shore.

I dipped the leaves in the water and rubbed my hands together. She watched me, holding her hair in one hand. Once I had a nice lather, she turned, pulling her hair to her front and looking back at me over her shoulder.

The hot water steamed, creating a slight mist between us. I think it helped in the creation of the lather but there was still plenty of bits of leaves and small stem in the mix. Reaching back to the shore, I grabbed a small amount of sand and mixed it in.

Up closer to her, I noticed she had a few freckles on her shoulder. I spread the lather over her back, feeling her perfect skin. I worked my hands lower, struggling under and around the back of her bikini.

"Take off your top," I said.

She looked back at me, smiling with a raised eyebrow. Then she lowered the bikini strap off her shoulder and doing the same on the other side. She slid the bikini top down into the water and kept it near her waist. Her breasts were out of my sight as she kept her back to me.

I messaged her bare back, mixing my harder scrubs with a softer touch.

"That's nice," she said.

"I'm just getting started," I said.

The crystal clear water gave me a perfect view of her body in the water. Just above her ass, she had two perfect dimples that I slid my thumbs over before moving back up to between her shoulders. The lather was gone, but I felt hints of sand over her body. Taking things a bit further, I moved my hands around her waist and to her toned stomach.

She had her hands over her breasts but she let them drift down, and I slid my hands up her stomach, and just knowing that I was about to touch those breasts that I had imagined and pictured more times than I could count, I nearly lost it. My fingers slid up until they reached the bottom of her breasts, and then I kept moving until I had them cupped in my hands. Her nipples were hard, even in hot water, and I spotted goose bumps along her shoulders. I kissed the back of her neck and heard her release a quick breath.

I spun her around, and she gasped, but didn't attempt to push away or cover herself. I feasted on the sight of her topless body and brought her tight against me, kissing her. She moaned and kissed me just as hard. Her hands were roaming my chest, and moving around to my back and neck. She had one hand touching the waistband of my shorts, and I moved to the edge of her yellow bikini bottom, pushing it down a few inches. Then she grabbed my hand and took a slow step back from me.

She looked at me as if she wanted all of me. She was out of breath and stared at me. "I can't do this."

"Hey, that's fine," I said, taking her hand in mine. "Is it something I did or am doing?"

"No," she said, shaking her head. "I want you, like *really* want you, and that's the problem. Sex isn't something that I've ever enjoyed. It's been…I had a boyfriend that… he wasn't friendly, and then I had a date in high school that ended with me drinking too much and pictures…"

Tears spilled down her cheeks, and seeing her hurt like that just broke my heart. I wanted to go back to the world just so I could find those that hurt her and kill them all. I wanted them to feel ten times the pain they inflicted on my girl.

"I'm so sorry, Benji," I said.

"Don't give me pity. I don't like it, and it's one of the reasons I don't talk about it. Everything is fine up until the moment that I think sex is going to happen, and then I panic." She looked pale, as even thinking about the moment triggered her.

"I like you, a lot," I said. "We don't need to have sex to have a connection. Seeing those, out for me to touch and admire, was more than I could have ever hoped for in my simple life." I offered a friendly smile, and she looked down at her tits.

"They are nice," she said, and then brought her hair over shoulders and covered them. "So you're okay if we just…cuddle?"

"Are you kidding?" I said. "Maybe we can just round a few bases but no home plates."

"Baseball metaphors, eh?" she said, getting closer to me.

"Hey, you were rounding second base pretty hard when you were *washing* me," I said.

"It was pretty hard," she said with a wink, playing along. "You're right, we can do plenty of other stuff."

I pulled her close to me, wanting to feel her bare chest against mine, and kissed her again. She kissed me and worked at my shorts again, pulling the button free. Her hand slid once again into my shorts but this time she gripped it and tugged.

"I want to make you feel good. What do you want me to do to you?" Benji whispered in my ear.

I took a few steps up the beach, so my waist was above the water. She rotated with me, looking up at me with those blue eyes and a bright smile. She kissed my chest, working down until she was on her knees. She slid my shorts down just enough that I was out, dangling against her face. She cupped one of her breasts, feeling it and touching her nipple. With a few gentle kisses, she handled me with some smooth hand movements before letting it glide over her tongue and into her mouth.

A groan escaped me, and I felt as if I wasn't going to last more than a few seconds. Benji had me so close, her mouth moving and sucking while her hand touched and rubbed. Her hair fell forward, blocking my view, and she pulled it back and looked up at me with a smile that reached those sparkling eyes.

After a minute, I'd reached a point where I needed to give her a warning.

"Benji, I'm about to…"

Benji didn't slow down or stop but sped up and used her hand in hard motions while tightening the grip on her lips. She moaned against me. I tried to pull back, but she had a grip on me, and I had no choice; I had gone too far off the edge to have any chance of stopping what was coming.

Gripping her head with both hands, I tensed and released. The feeling flooded over me while Benji moaned louder. I melted, slipping out of her grip and down to my knees. I panted and held onto her, feeling as if I might fall right through the earth.

I went to her, kissing her neck and working my way to her breasts that were just under the water. Reaching behind her, I took her and lifted her up out of the water, carrying her to the beach. I wanted to make her feel as good as she made me feel. With her out of the water, while I was still partially submerged, I went between her legs and up to her stomach. I kissed her and licked her, sliding my tongue under her yellow bikini. Her hands were going through my hair, and I felt her tense as I went lower.

The cartoon character on her bikini bottom did little to deter me from sliding the fabric to the side. I kissed and then licked. It didn't take long to find her swollen button, and I went exploring with my tongue. She was just as ready to burst as I was.

"Don't stop, Jack. I'm going to…"

She groaned loudly, grabbing my head tightly. She wasn't going to last a moment longer, and as I pushed and moved, her thighs went tight against my head, gripping me so hard it almost hurt. She wailed and gyrated against my face in her completion.

After a few beats, I rose up and she sat up with me, hugging me and kissing me on the corner of my mouth.

"Oh my God," Benji said. "Thank you."

I laughed and said, "You're welcome."

After, we washed our bodies off in the steaming water, laughing and splashing each other on an after-sex high. While we didn't have intercourse, I was just going to call what we did sex. It left me wanting more, and I suppose that was a good thing. Playing in the water with her, I wanted her again. I didn't think I'd ever tire of Benji.

I wasn't sure how long we'd been gone, but when we got back to camp, the girls went silent, looking between Benji and me with faces full of pent-up laughter.

"What?" Benji said.

"Don't stop, Jack!" Aubrey said, screaming and breathing hard. "I'm going to…"

"Oh, screw you," Benji said. "You try being quiet with his face between your legs. He's like a freaking…*magician* down there."

Eliza sat next to Aubrey, a shocked look on her face, and she leaned over, whispering something to Aubrey. Aubrey smiled and nodded. Eliza just stared at me, mouth open, and I felt naked even though I had my clothes on.

"So, Kara," I said, trying to steer the conversation away from my sexual talents. "We found some clay down by the stream. There isn't a bunch of it, but I bet we can make some stuff."

Kara stared at me as well but didn't say anything. She looked me over as if I was a steak.

Sherri burst out laughing. "Did you hear him, Kara? He's found clay."

Kara blinked. "Yeah, I heard, sorry. Just lost in thought."

"Oh my, Jack. I think you are in for a long night," Aubrey said.

I looked at the sky. We still had plenty of daylight left in the day.

"We should get to work, ladies," I said. "I'd like to concentrate on the shelter first. If we can get the new platform built today, I think we can erect a few walls tomorrow."

The girls laughed, except Eliza, who glanced around in confusion.

"What are you bitches laughing at?" Cass said, sitting up from the platform, holding her hand over her head.

CHAPTER 31

Cass sat on the edge of the platform, looking as if she was suffering from the world's worst hangover.

"I need a shot," Cass said. "My head's splitting."

"Cass, oh my God," Sherri said, rushing to her side.

"What the hell did we do last night?" Cass said, blinking and looking around to us, the forest, the beach and ocean.

"You don't remember anything?" Sherri asked.

"Please, don't tell me I made a fool of myself," Cass said, keeping her eyes closed and rubbing her head. "If you bitches posted pics, I'm kicking asses."

"Cass," Aubrey said, moving to the other side of Cass. "We're on an island."

"Yeah, no shit. We're supposed to be on an island."

"Not that island. We ran into a bad storm, and we ended up…on this one," Aubrey said.

Cass opened her eyes, looking around at everything again as if for the first time. "What are you talking about?"

I stepped back and let the familiar faces of Kara,

Sherri, Aubrey, and Benji talk with their friend. Cass and I had a few pleasant words on the deck of the boat, but I doubted she knew who I was. I didn't want to confuse her any further.

It was endearing as they coaxed her to the realization that this wasn't a joke. There was love in their tenderness as guided their friend to a harsh reality. There wasn't some five-star resort just beyond the trees with a swim-up bar and poolside service. We were indeed stranded, and we had been on these islands for a week.

She seemed to take the idea of being stranded better than the fact we rescued her from snakes. That part sent her face sheet white. She got off the platform and rushed to throw up in the water. The girls stood by her, holding her hair and patting her back.

I kept an eye on the waters.

"You think she's going to be okay?" Eliza asked, standing next to me.

"She doesn't really have a choice," I said.

We watched the girls as they held Cass. She looked pale, and I didn't like seeing her get sick. She needed to keep fluids down if she wanted to survive out here. Sherri offered up a bag of water, which Cass drank down.

"Hey, at least I'm not the new girl anymore," Eliza said with a smile.

"Yeah," I said. "I hope she comes around quickly. We really need to get started on the shelter today."

"Hey, if they're busy getting Cass all set up here, we could go get some water at the pond. You know, fill up the stocks."

"The bags are full," I said, motioning to the bags near

the platform. "I assumed you guys filled up while we were at Food Island."

"Yeah, we did," Eliza said with a sigh, lowering her head.

Cass pushed Sherri back and then shoved Aubrey. She screamed and held her hands over her head.

"This isn't real. Stop messing with me!" Cass snarled.

I rushed toward them but Benji had a hand on me.

"Let them deal with her. She's about there," Benji whispered.

I took a step back. "If she attacks any of you, I will deal with her."

"It won't come to that," Benji said.

Suddenly I felt as if something was staring at me. It gave me chills on the back of my neck, and I whipped around to face the ocean. In the shallows was what looked like grey fish, floating on the surface. It was watching us. It was alone, and it didn't like us—it might have even hated us—but there was always that curiosity, as if the watcher was waiting to see what happened.

I stared at the thing and a wave washed over it, lowering the water level, and I saw the things face. It had to be a face. I looked into its dark eyes and saw its nose and mouth. It wasn't a human face because it had grey skin, with stringy, black hair and a pointy face.

It glared at me, and I glared back. I was sick of these coastal observers, spying on us and probably causing many of the problems we faced. Ignoring the girls still discussing the situation with an angry Cass, I moved toward the ocean, keeping my eyes on this face in the waters. It had smooth, wet skin over its face, giving it a more aquatic appearance, but I felt the complex emotions coming from it. I think it wanted to fight me, or perhaps it wanted to punish me, as if I had done something terrible.

A wave washed over the sand and around my feet. We weren't more than thirty feet apart now. Anger built up in me, and I closed my eyes, reaching out for the thing. I didn't know how far or how strong my ability would work, but it seemed to be getting more powerful each day. I connected with it in some way and I screamed in my head at it: *Leave us alone!*

Fear and shock filled the watcher. It dipped under the water, and I knew from how fast it faded away that it moved as quickly as a shark. Its fear of me hung in the air like the smell of sour milk.

Hopefully, the watchers would leave us alone now. I had enough to think about without some fish-head-person thing watching us from the shores. If it returned, I wouldn't be so kind as to send it away unscathed. I had a feeling I could hurt it by just thinking about it.

A hand touched mine, and I jerked back from it.

"Oh, sorry," Eliza said, looking embarrassed. "You were just looking into the ocean, and I kept saying your name."

"Did you see it?" I asked.

"See what?"

She hadn't, but that was okay. On some level, I knew the watchers were there for me.

"Sorry," I said, shaking my head and giving Eliza my attention. "What's up?"

"I think the girls are about to fight," Eliza said, nodding toward the girls around Cass.

Cass had her hands out like a Greco-Roman wrestler. She was taller than all of them, with broad shoulders and large arms and legs. She was fit, but not as toned as Sherri and Aubrey. She staggered as she took steps back from the advancing girls.

I rushed in, getting past Kara and Benji.

"Who are you, and please tell me these bitches are lying?" Cass asked.

"Everyone, back up," I said, facing the girls.

Their faces were red, and Aubrey looked as if she might stab Cass. I wasn't sure what had been shared in the exchange I missed, but it hadn't been pleasant. I took a step forward, with hands out to my side, in my best crowd-control stance. The girls backed up from Cass, giving her space.

I turned and focused on Cass. Her brown hair had matted to her face from the sweat.

"Cass, my name is Jack Sawyer. I was on the boat with you, and I know this is confusing, but we are here with you. We are in this together, and you have no idea how much these ladies did to get you to where you are right now." I laughed. "We have so many stories to tell you."

"Benji said it was Weekend At Cass's. That you were dragging my body all around these islands. That is crazy."

"It seems crazy; believe me, we've all had to struggle with the realization that this is real, but we've been here for a week."

She lowered her hands and grabbed her head. "Worst day ever to have a hangover," Cass said. "I don't believe a word any of you are saying. You're just fucking with me, and I want it to end!"

"Cass?" Eliza said softly as she stood next to me.

"Who's this?" Cass asked with a pained expression as Eliza stepped closer to her.

"Eliza," I said with a warning tone, but she didn't listen and walked up to Cass.

"Here, this helped me, and I think it helped you. You dropped it, but I picked it up, thinking you might need it again."

Eliza extended her hand and opened it, showing her the round rock sitting in her palm. Cass stared at the rock, confused.

"Take it," Eliza said.

It was like watching a giant and a dwarf with Eliza and Cass. She had to be a foot taller and half again wider, but Eliza seemed to have a spell over Cass. She stared at the stone sitting on Eliza's palm.

"Mrs. Granite," Cass said and took the rock in her hand.

She clasped the stone and closed her eyes.

"She's helped us, Cass."

Cass opened her eyes, hands shaking and tears filling her eyes.

"It wasn't a dream, was it?"

"No," Eliza said.

"I felt her with me, and I heard you," Cass said. "I think I heard all of you. You carried me when I couldn't move, didn't you?"

"Yes," Eliza said.

Cass broke down in a sob and lowered down to hug Eliza, while keeping the stone in her hand.

Benji, Sherri, Aubrey, and Kara went to Cass and

hugged her as well. Cass welcomed them. Benji started crying with Cass. In their group, they shared whispers that I couldn't hear. I waited for the group to break up, and after a minute, it did.

Cass pressed the stone against her head and the pained look returned.

"Can we give her more willow bark?" I asked.

"Yeah, we have some here," Sherri said, grabbing the bag Aubrey had made earlier.

She handed the bag to Cass.

Cass drank it and made a face at the taste.

"It's medicine, Cass. It will help with the headache," Sherri said.

"Thanks," Cass said. "You guys have really been here for a week?"

"About," Benji said.

"This camp is shit," Cass said, laughed a little and took another swig.

"We've been busy rescuing you and others," Benji said.

"And fighting crocs, hogs, sharks, whales, a freaking squid octopus thing and a psycho from a boat," Aubrey said.

"Plus earthquakes," Benji added. "The geyser destroyed that platform. Threw a rock right on it."

"What the…," Cass said.

"But it's not all bad," Benji said, looking to me and turning a light shade of red.

Cass frowned and looked to me and then back to Benji.

"Yeah, there are some fringe benefits to being out here," Aubrey said slyly.

"I love it out here," Sherri said, taking in a deep breath. "I've never felt so alive, and this place is an adventure a minute. Even thinking about rebuilding the camp is getting me excited. Oh my God, I love this shit, and as Aubrey said, there's certain benefits as well." Sherri looked to me and winked.

"I wasn't a happy person back home," Kara said. "I've never really been happy, actually. Most of these tattoos are just symbols of me fighting that crushing feeling that I'm nothing. That I'm not worth it and have no real future. When I got here, an island tried to crush me to dust, and if it weren't for these people around me, I wouldn't be here right now. But they found me, and in turn, I found myself. For the first time in my existence, I feel like my life has meaning. I can feel these islands, and this island is the best place in the world. I know it to my core, and I don't care if a rescue ever comes, as long as I have my girls and I have Jack—at least once a week." Kara gave me a sideways smile.

"Wait, are you all fucking him?" Cass said.

"No," Eliza answered.

Aubrey rolled her eyes, and Cass looked confused.

"Let's not overwhelm her," I said. "Benji, can you think of a nice mango dish you can make for this situation?"

Benji lit up with a big smile and hopped up and down. "Yes, it's not the perfect dish for this but…just wait, let me make it real quick."

"I hate mangos," Cass said.

"Get out of our camp," Benji said, pointing to the forest.

I wasn't sure if she was serious or not, and I waited to see. Benji raised her eyebrows, feigning anger for a moment longer until a smile crossed her face.

"I'm just kidding, Benji," Cass said. "I'm starving. I feel like I haven't eaten in a week."

"I know, give me five minutes," Benji said and went to the bag of food and the cutting rock she used.

"Holy shit, I just realized we're all stuck here in bikinis," Cass said, looking down at what she was wearing.

She wore a blue top that wasn't a bikini top but closer to a sports bra. It hugged her breasts tight against her body. Her bottoms were an orange color that had a small gator embroidered on the side. The bottoms were small—smaller than Sherri's red, white, and blue attire, and far smaller than the yellow bottoms Benji wore. Her muscular stomach had a V-line running down into the bikini, and if she didn't shave soon, I thought she might have a poof of hair showing above the orange. She had a pretty face, tan from the sun, as was the rest of her body. I suspected if she took that top off, she would have deep tan lines.

It didn't seem fair to have these many gorgeous women around me, but it was also a responsibility. I was the only man in the group of now six women. Four of these women, I had relations with, a fact that didn't escape notice from Cass. I could hardly believe it myself, but when I closed my eyes, I saw them in our moments.

I'd have to watch Cass, though. If she created trouble in the group, I'd have to be the one to deal with her. For now, though, she seemed confused but content, sipping on her bag of water. She didn't seem to even remember punching me in the face.

Benji outdid herself, mixing up some of the nuts we gathered from Eliza's island and creating an orange glaze over it all. It had a sour and sweet taste that you couldn't help but enjoy. It seemed to lift everyone's spirits up, and soon the encounter with Cass had smoothed out and we were laughing and joking as we ate. Once we were done, I started laying out tasks for the girls to do while we still had daylight.

Benji and Kara were back to making another ax and rock knife. Sherri, Aubrey, and Kara went to find long branches and cut some down that looked good enough to use. While I had been giving Benji swimming lessons, the girls had taken down much of the platform, but there was still the section that Cass had been laying on.

Eliza and I went took on the task of taking the rest of it down.

Eliza didn't speak much but was a hard worker and smart as anyone I'd met. She had great ideas about how to build the next shelter. There wasn't a perfect set of trees to hold the platform, but Eliza suggested we dig a post hole and create the fourth post. I loved the idea, and Cass, who had been watching most of the time. I had told her to take it easy and she heeded the advice.

Eliza and I started digging the hole.

I wondered if Benji could make a hole with just her mind. She had moved rocks in the geyser and rescued me from the birds in the cave. If we could start utilizing these skills we had, things could go much faster. Sherri might be able to pull the water out from our wood or even move ocean water to catch fish. It seemed ludicrous as I thought it, but there was something at work here, and I didn't think the girls wanted to talk about it. These extra skills were something they hadn't brought up to Cass yet. Tonight, around the fire, I planned on bringing it up. If we had these abilities, we needed to use them. And I think the more we used them, the stronger they got.

Cass had an ability as well, but she hadn't shared anything yet that would hint at what that would be. Of course, she could be the odd person out and not have an ability, but I doubted it. Nature would sometimes grant special abilities to a species in order for it to adapt and survive in a changing environment. These abilities were going to help us survive. Seeing what Sherri and Benji could do with theirs inspired me to work hard on developing mine.

Each woman we found would most likely have something in them special and I knew it would be imperative that we find them all.

As much as I wanted to go right then and search for another island, I was going to bring up the idea of staying on the island for a few days until we had a camp built. Aubrey was right; it was only a matter of time until we got hurt or killed by the environment surrounding us. It wouldn't make sense for us all to go on the raft each time, now that our group had grown to seven, plus one kitty. At least not with our current raft design. If I did leave someone behind on the island, I wasn't going to leave the girls without a solid cabin to protect them from birds, hogs, or crocs. Heck, I wanted to build it strong enough that those sea cats we saw on Food Island couldn't get in. Man, I hoped that croc took care of those cats. I didn't want to face them in the water or land.

I closed my eyes and reached my extra sense out to the ocean, feeling the static, but if I concentrated, I could single out a fish or a crab. I didn't feel the cats. Then I felt something larger out there. Maybe a shark, but I wasn't good enough to tell exactly what it was yet. If I kept practicing and working the muscle, I thought I could get to that point. Also, I seemed to be able to send that mental bullet to the watcher. Deep into my extra sense, I felt something that shot my eyes wide open.

I ran to the shore, Eliza following behind, alarmed, and Cass looking confused. Moshe ran alongside us just for the excitement.

I stared into the waters, knowing that we were about to be attacked. I felt it to my core.

The watcher had returned and brought an army with it. They were coming for blood.

The End

ABOUT THE AUTHOR

Author's Note:

Thanks for ready book 2 of the Island Jumper series. This is such a fun book to write. I hope you are enjoying the series as much as I am writing it. I am currently hard at work on book 3 and hope to have it out sometime in late March. I love how book 3 is turning out and the growth that Jack is going to have by the end of the book, is a series changer.

If you enjoyed this book, please leave a review on Amazon and don't forget to hit the follow button so you can be notified when the next book comes out.

If you want to reach out to me, I have a FB page under M.H. Ryan or you can email me at authorMHRyan@gmail.com.

M.H. Ryan

www.ingramcontent.com/pod-product-compliance
Lightning Source LLC
Chambersburg PA
CBHW071538030726
47598CB00001B/146